# BEHIND

# THE LIES

**Carol Gulliford**

Copyright © 2024 Carol Gulliford

All rights reserved

The characters and events portrayed in this book are fictitious. Any similarity to real persons, living or dead, is coincidental and not intended by the author.

No part of this book may be reproduced, or stored in a retrieval system, or transmitted in any form or by any means, electronic, mechanical, photocopying, recording, or otherwise, without express written permission of the publisher.

ISBN-9798328397162
Printed in the United Kingdom

For Joe

# ONE

## *Katie (1998)*

Throughout my life, whenever I was at my happiest, a small seed of doubt would inevitably creep into my mind and linger there. I'd force myself to ignore it and most of the time I would win the battle. I often wondered why it happened. Why would I want to sabotage my own happiness? I suppose I've always had an underlying fear that when things in my life are going well, something bad is bound to happen, something to bring me back down to earth.

Although since I met Lucas, just a little over two years ago, I've been happier than ever before, and finally I've been able to let myself truly relax.

Today it was Lucas's birthday, and after months of secret arrangements, he still didn't suspect a thing. How he hadn't picked up on my growing excitement, God only knows. It was fizzing away under the surface as I pretended everything was normal. So far, I had managed to pass off some of my good mood on the new job I would start after the summer. Don't get me wrong I was thrilled about that too, but that was months away, so I had pushed my joy and a large dose of trepidation aside until nearer the time. Finally, after finishing my six-year training, I would be stepping into the role of assistant vet at The Melandri Veterinary practice. A long-held dream coming to fruition.

But today was all about Lucas and him turning the big 30. I couldn't wait for the look on his face when he opened my present outlining our trip to Italy. It was something he had mentioned just over a year ago.

We had been in town late one evening, and we had passed a travel agents window showing the gorgeous Lake Orta. Lucas had been more than a little drunk that night. We had been out for a meal celebrating our first year's anniversary and he had stood staring at the poster for a few minutes before declaring his undying love for me and stating how one day we would go to beautiful places like this together. A lovely thought but what with neither of us earning much and after buying our first flat together only a year ago that pretty much put paid to those dreams for a while. Secretly though since that day I had been saving hard, each month putting aside a small amount of the meagre wage I earned while training. He would be gobsmacked that this time next week instead of doing DIY on our flat during our week off work, we would be jetting off and sitting in the sun, sipping cocktails alongside Lake Orta, eating as much pasta as we could manage.

That's why I couldn't sleep. Far too much excitement running through my veins. I lay as still as I could for another few minutes, and then gave up. A run might help, that would waste some time and calm me down. I'd leave Lucas in bed, softly snoring and go and get some fresh air. I loved to run and went out at least three times every week. It kept me sane, running through the lush greenery we were lucky enough to live nearby. Some days I would head towards the beach, but that was a much longer run and today I just wanted to burn off a little steam, so the meadows would do. By the time I would return, Lucas would be up, and I could present him with my gift, with a smug look on my face.

And then later he would still have an extra surprise when all our friends and family arrived to squeeze themselves in our tiny garden for a birthday BBQ.

I smiled to myself as I tucked a spare key in the little pocket of my gym shorts and picked up my CD Walkman, adjusting the headphones over my ears. I quietly pulled the door closed. It was cooler than I thought but the sun was beginning to rise. I walked for a while listening to my running compilation, letting the pumping music wash away all the thoughts coursing through my mind. That's what I loved about running, the way you can leave all your thoughts behind and concentrate solely on the physical exertion. Lucas hated it, he preferred team sports but for me I loved the tranquility and the rush I felt from it, long after I had returned home.

Turning the corner at Bourne Avenue, I continued along the tree-lined road which led to the park. There was nobody around, just a few parked cars dotted here and there. I jogged on harder now, sucking in the fresh air, feeling it fill my lungs. I completed the length of the road in no time and ran through the narrow alleyway before bursting onto the field. I pushed on towards the far corner, smiling to myself as I strode powerfully on. Just before I reached the last corner where I usually turned back, I saw him...

I felt his gaze on me even before I slowed down and pulled the headphones from my ears. The tunes that had been pounding moments before sounded tinny, and I could feel the vibration from the headphones as they lay discarded against my neck. I stared at him, completely thrown from my stride and not quite sure what to do. Although he was at least a few feet away from me, I knew instantly something was off and my skin began to crawl, as if we were touching. Slowly, he averted his eyes, but not before they moved from my face, downwards to my bare legs.

My eyes scanned the field beyond him and although it was vast, it was completely empty at this early hour. Only the two of us, as far as I could see.

Now that he knew I had spotted him, he stood rigid. I took in his black jeans and jacket, his face now turned away and unrecognizable under his hood. He wasn't a large man, but he was still much taller than I was, at 5ft 3. If he had been walking around the park maybe I wouldn't have found him so disconcerting. It was the way he just stood there, motionless. That would have made anyone stop and wonder, wouldn't it?

    I ran my gaze over him. His hands were pushed deeply into his pockets. The darkness of his clothing against the bright morning sun was what initially had caught my eye but the fact that he had the hood of his lightweight jacket pulled firmly up, hiding his face, made him seem even more threatening. There was something about his strong stance that made me feel vulnerable, like he could pounce at any moment. Would he be able to catch me if I ran? He remained still though; his trainers planted into the dewy grass that surrounded him. It wasn't how close he was that worried me, it was more that we were alone. Where was an early dog walker when you needed one?

    'Are you OK?' I ventured. My voice sounded thin and reedy, and I was momentarily mesmerized by the burst of breath which escaped with my words. Still no movement.

I made a conscious decision to move away but the last thing I wanted to do was to turn my back on him, so I started to inch sideways, keeping one eye pinned on his frame. The alleyway back to the road was about 20 meters away. Even though it wasn't a busy road, there was a chance someone would be there, and at least there were houses on the other side. As I moved away there was a small amount of doubt in my mind about his threat, after all, I had been known for my overactive imagination. Lucas had always ribbed me about it. He said I watched too many scary films, and it made me jumpy. The truth is, it did make me jumpy, but still I had a morbid fascination with the adrenaline that a horror film induced, and like lots of people, I enjoyed being scared. Not now though, this felt far too real.

A vision of Lucas asleep in bed filled my mind and I inwardly cursed. Of all days, why did I not take today off? If I was honest with myself, I knew the answer. It was because I was stupidly vain, and since I'd lost all that weight, I just couldn't chance the fact of putting another pound back on.

That was the crux of it. I had curbed my comfort eating and swapped it for another addiction. A healthier addiction it could be argued, but not when I couldn't manage to have one day exercise free.

By now I had made it to the edge of the field and my breath was coming in short little bursts; nothing to do with my fitness, but from the panic growing within. I fought to control myself, focusing hard on moving away without breaking into a sprint. I didn't want to start running like a frightened rabbit. I wasn't even sure why? Maybe it was because he hadn't threatened me as such, well, not directly anyway. It seemed embarrassing somehow to show him how much he had unnerved me, and I had never been one to make a scene. Keep everything calm even if you didn't feel it inside, that was my mantra. In any situation, you must always stay in control.

At the entrance to the alleyway, a thought occurred to me, and I faltered. *Wasn't that where most attacks happen? In a closed in space?* Not that I really had any other choice now I had come this far. I twisted my body around the metal bars that were there to deter bikes from using the narrow pathway, although it didn't stop many. Just last week, some snot nosed little kid navigated his way around the bars so fast he nearly ran me down.

I pushed on with a quick glance over my shoulder and my blood ran cold. He was moving towards me, not running but his strides were purposeful. I disappeared into the alleyway, out of his line of sight and sprinted. I was glad I had my favourite trainers on and within seconds I exploded out the other end of the alleyway, panting at the sudden exertion. I surveyed the empty road in despair, again cursing the early hour. I quickly considered my options. Could I outrun him up the hill?

I moved away from the alleyway, with another look behind me. I could see the sprawling grass beyond and the towering oak trees at the far end, but that was all. There wasn't a sinister figure bearing down on me. I began to feel more than a little ridiculous. I dragged a deep breath into my lungs and willed myself to calm down. It wasn't far home now, which made me feel better. I only needed to get to the top of the hill and around the corner and I would be able to see our apartment.

I started moving and despite the steep climb, I could feel my pulse slowing and returning to a relatively normal beat. By the time I was nearing the top, where only one more house stood before the corner, I could no longer ignore the screaming ache in my calves. I stopped for a second, leaning against a garden wall, giving them a satisfying stretch while keeping my eyes trained towards the bottom of the hill. A sudden movement caught my eye, and I stared in disbelief. How had he managed to get so far up the hill without me noticing?

He stood still but it was obvious that while my back had been turned, he had shortened the gap between us. He was on the same side of the street, only about 10 meters behind me.

I remained transfixed as he pushed his hood back a little, just enough so I could see his mouth and he smiled, ever so slightly. Such a small action but it left no doubt in my mind. He was after me, and he was enjoying the chase. Before I could reach the corner, I made a split-second decision. I darted sideways into the driveway of the last house and glad of my running experience, used my last spurt of energy to propel myself forward. Despite the long sweeping drive, I made it within seconds to the door and jabbed my finger desperately on the doorbell.

I kept looking behind me as I waited nervously for the owner of the house to appear. I began praying to a God that I didn't really believe in, that the house was occupied. The relief I felt as the woman opened the door was overwhelming. I realised I had been holding my breath and when I opened my mouth, my words came out in a rush.

'Sorry,' I blurted, 'I think someone is following me. Please can I come in and use your phone?'

The woman frowned and looked beyond me, as if she was half expecting some razor-toothed beast to launch itself at her. When she seemed to be satisfied that there was no such risk, she stepped aside.

'Yes, of course,' she said in a softly spoken voice. 'Come, quickly, come in.' She gestured with her hand, and I didn't hesitate. I stepped over the threshold, and she firmly shut the door behind me.

I stood gasping for breath in her immaculate hallway. Glancing around I couldn't help noticing the décor. It wasn't to my taste, but I had never been more pleased to see flowered wallpaper and oversized chintzy ornaments on every available surface. The house itself was impressive and on a normal day I'd have enjoyed looking around such a magnificently imposing property, but today was not a normal day. My heart was still racing, and I focused on slowing my breathing. The woman stood opposite me, still in her old-fashioned nightdress. It had bird feathers embroidered all over it and it reminded me of something my gran would have worn. At most she could have only been five or so years older than me, around Lucas's age. It seemed an odd choice of nightwear for someone so young, but she obviously had dubious taste.

I realised she was waiting for me to say something. She looked concerned by the state I was in. I took another couple of deep breaths and gathered my thoughts.

'I'm Katie,' I said. The woman smiled but didn't introduce herself. 'Thank you so much,' I stumbled on. 'I'm sorry to have disturbed you so early in the morning, but I was so frightened.'

The woman smiled kindly and with an effort to comfort me she reached for my hand. Her touch was warm, and her kindness made me feel like bursting into tears. I swallowed hard and tried to control my emotions. I was all over the place.

'It's really no bother,' she was saying. 'I was just about to get dressed when I heard the doorbell.' Her voice was soft and soothing, helping me to relax further. 'You're shaking, but you are perfectly safe now. She let go of my hand and moved away to peer out of a side window. 'Are you sure someone was following you?' She turned to look back at me. 'I can't see anyone there now.'

'I'm pretty sure,' I replied. I didn't want to admit that I was already beginning to doubt myself. 'I suppose it could have been my imagination, but I had the distinct feeling he was after me.'

Looking into the woman's sympathetic eyes I felt more than a little foolish. Now that I had pulled myself together it did seem like a major overreaction. *A man stood in a field and happened to have walked the same way home? Jesus, I really needed to take myself in check.* 'Would you mind if I use your telephone to call my boyfriend?' I asked. 'We only live a few streets away, so he wouldn't take long to come and pick me up.'

'Of course,' said the woman. 'No problem at all. While you do that, I'll go and get you a glass of water. The phone is over on the table.' She pointed to a small ornate glass table, and I watched her walk away.

I poked my head around a heavy velvet curtain for a quick look out of the window. To my relief all I could see was the pretty, blossoming garden, and an empty path. *Lucas and I will laugh about this one day* I thought, again feeling a little ridiculous.

I approached the table and took the cordless telephone from its cradle. I pushed the green button and put it to my ear to hear the dialling tone. Silence. The only noise was the woman's faint footsteps coming back from the kitchen.

'Your phone doesn't seem to be working?' I said, as I turned. A shocked gasp escaped my lips and the handset clattered to the wooden floor as every muscle in my body stiffened, frozen in horror. Standing there was the same man who had been following me, large as life.

I could hear the screams long before realising they were my own. My eyes widened as I gaped unbelievingly at him, willing myself to bolt. He didn't move towards me, but he stared, his gaze intense. My mouth dropped open in shock as I franticly tried to comprehend the meaning of his presence. The look on his face confused me, it was almost a look of regret. I watched his lips moving, but I couldn't hear what he was saying. Time slowed and blood was pounding hard and fast in my ears, making me deaf to his words.

I felt a scratchy piece of cloth being placed firmly over the bottom half of my face. Surprise overwhelmed me. Despite the initial paralysing fear, I realised I was lashing out with a disjointed flaying of my arms. I tried to hit out with purpose. Already the room was spinning. The drug was entering my blood stream and a fuzzy numbness followed. My last thought as I collapsed to the ground, was of Lucas. Then all went dark.

## TWO

## *Tom (2022)*

Tom Beatty was running late. It was becoming a standing joke. He had been trying to improve his timekeeping, the way you do in a new relationship, but time still seemed to run away from him and for the third time this week he realised he wasn't going to get to the meeting place before her. He pushed forward, quickening his step as he passed the old cinema at the corner of the high street. It was where they had had their first date just over six months ago and the thought even now, made him grin from ear to ear. Sophie, his perfect girl.

They had been inseparable ever since. Any day they couldn't manage to get together they would chat on the phone late into the night, until one or other struggled to keep their eyes open. He was already considering asking Sophie to move in with him. Even though his flat was poky, as most reasonably priced places in London were, there was more than enough room for the two of them to cosy up. To some it may have seemed fast, but he'd never felt like this about anyone and the thought of keeping their relationship long distance just didn't appeal. And what with Sophie wanting to pursue her dream of acting in theatre, it made it even more logical.

His best friend Simon's reaction was just what Tom would have expected. Following his true bachelor lifestyle, Simon had warned of how his friend's life would never be the same. But Tom didn't want his life to stay the same, that was the whole point. He wanted someone to share every day with, someone to share all the little things. Simon had always shied away from any hint at the word commitment but then they had always been very different, despite their bond.

Simon had been his main and quite frankly, his only proper friend at school. Even when he had turned up that first day with his loud voice and even bigger personality – the exact opposite at the time to Tom's painful shyness – they had hit it off straight away. If they hadn't been placed together on a chemistry assignment, Tom would have never plucked up the courage to talk to someone so gregarious. As time went on though, Tom came out of his shell a little, and in turn his calm nature seemed to tone down some of Simon's raucous behaviour. To outsiders they may have looked like an unlikely pair, but the deep bond they shared in their childhood remained just as strong today.

The only thing Tom would choose to change about his friend would be his lack of tact when they were in the company of girls. Simon's bold antics would frequently make Tom cringe, and nine times out of ten cause complete embarrassment, scaring off the opposite sex within minutes. That was one small mercy of now having a girlfriend. Maybe he could finally put those uncomfortable nights behind him.

On the night he met Sophie, luck had seemed to be on Tom's side. He had decided to call it a night, but Simon had managed to talk him into staying for just one more pint. It had been near the end of the night when they had spotted Sophie and her friend Carrie in the far corner of the dimly lit bar and approached them.

'Ladies, how are you?' Simon had said as he slipped into the booth, hemming one of them in. 'You don't mind if we join you, do you?' Not that he had really given them a lot of choice, but Tom relaxed a little when he realised the girls didn't seem to mind their intrusion. Tom couldn't take his eyes off the girl trapped in the booth by Simon's bulky frame and he watched her every move. The way she lifted her glass to her ruby lips and took a sip of wine. The way she smoothed the dark curtain of glossy hair, tucking it behind her ears before glancing at her friend sitting opposite. She raised her perfect eyebrows, just ever so slightly.

Tom dragged his gaze away and forced himself to perch on the seat beside the girl's friend. She introduced herself as Carrie, although he was barely listening. He muttered his name and locked eyes across the table again. The girl now introduced as Sophie was listening politely to Simon's bragging about his high-flying job, but she kept her gaze fixed on Tom.

'Do you want to dance?' The girl next to him had slurred, breaking the moment. He tried not to let it show on his face how disinterested he was. She seemed like a nice girl, although he was put off by how drunk she was, and by her clammy hand which kept pawing at his arm.

'Actually, I don't dance,' he'd replied. He dragged his eyes away from the girl opposite but not before he noticed the corner of her lips twitch, suggesting her amusement. That was the truth at least, he didn't dance, and no amount of alcohol was ever going to be enough to change that. He glanced towards Carrie and watched as she tossed her pale blonde hair away from her shoulders. She squinted at him through the darkness, disappointment visible on her pixie like features.

'Not ever?' Her eyebrows crinkled together.

'No never, I'm a prop up the bar kind of guy,' he said.

'What about your mate?' Carrie shouted over an up-to-date dance track which had started to blast from the speakers. She had already made her judgement of him, dismissing him as a bore.

'Oh yeah, he loves to dance,' he replied. He grinned across the table at his unsuspecting friend. Tom moved aside so she could wriggle out of the seating area and moments later; after not taking a blind bit of notice at Simon's protests, she had dragged his friend away.

Tom took the opportunity to shuffle closer to Sophie and by the time Simon and Carrie had returned to the table, Tom had secured a date with her. He had felt a little guilty, but he had pushed the thought away. The instant attraction he had felt for Sophie was too much to pass up and for once he was going to make sure it was him who came out on top.

He couldn't help but notice a flash of annoyance pass across Simon's face, but before anything could be said, Carrie began drunkenly throwing herself at him and Simon had let it go. Tom was glad that it hadn't been brought up again as Simon had started seeing Carrie from that point, even though that had only lasted a few weeks. And in the months that followed, Tom had managed to convince himself that Sophie and Simon would never have been compatible anyway.

He was pleased to have reached Spear Street, inching closer to where they had arranged to meet. He crossed the road towards the entrance to the park and made his way through the wrought-iron gates. He could see her waiting. She was facing away from him, her back leaning against a tree, close to the ice-cream kiosk. She was watching a young mum and dad swing their little girl high off the ground between them.

For a moment he stood mesmerised, taking in her delicate sandals, her bronzed slender legs and her pretty summer dress dotted with small red flowers against the cream background. The extra allure for him was that she had no idea how beautiful she was, which was a very rare trait to find. She continued to watch as her the father scooped up his daughter and spun her around. The little girl's laughter ringing out loudly before the inevitable "again daddy, again."

Sophie was smiling but he guessed she was thinking of her own father who she had lost to Cancer only a couple of years before. Tom moved a little closer, keeping his eyes fixed on her face and watched as she lifted her sunglasses and used her finger to wipe away a tear. He had such an overwhelming need to protect her, and he hoped she would confide in him more as time passed, but the subject was still obviously very painful for her, and he didn't want to push her to talk.

He was just behind her now and he softly called her name, causing her to swing around startled. He was pleased when her face lit up and she threw her arms around him. He nuzzled into her neck taking in the coconut sweetness of her hair that was now so familiar.

'Miss me?' she asked as she pulled away from him.

'Not much,' he teased. 'Had nothing better to do.'

She playfully slapped his arm and they fell comfortably into step alongside each other.

'I'm quite nervous. What if your parents don't like me?' she said.

'You are totally adorable, of course they will like you,' he replied. He stopped to pull her towards him and kissed her. 'Come on, let's get this out of the way and then I can take you back to my flat,' he said playfully, slapping her bottom.

'Behave yourself,' she chided but her eyes crinkled with amusement. 'You can't anyway, you'll have to go back to work.'

As they approached the restaurant an older couple were waiting outside, looking from one end of the road towards the other. The woman had the same blonde hair as Tom and looked elegant in a pale green knee length dress. Her husband was around the same height with a slight dappling of grey visible through his darker hair and he wore a perfectly fitted dove grey suit. As if knowing she was being watched the woman turned and broke into a big smile.

'You must be Sophie, we've heard of nothing else,' said Tom's mother. 'I'm Fiona. It's so lovely to meet you.' She bent down to kiss Sophie on the cheek.

'And you,' said Sophie. 'Both of you,' she added, turning towards Tom's father.

'David,' he introduced himself. 'Tom said you were a stunner, and he wasn't wrong.' He shook her hand firmly and beamed at her.

'Come on, let's go and eat,' he said. 'I'm famished.' He held open the door and let the others pass through. 'Good to see you son,' he added to Tom with a slap on his back as they all moved inside.

The restaurant was very posh. Tom knew it was the kind of place that made Sophie a little uncomfortable. The waiters were attentive and hovered near the tables to be of immediate service. It all felt a bit starchy to Tom, but this was the type of classy place his parents frequented, and he was quite used to their tastes. He found Sophie's hand under the table and gave it a squeeze and was glad to receive a confident smile in return.

'It's lovely to all get together, we would have come sooner if Tom had let us. He obviously wanted you all to himself for a while,' said David smiling knowingly at his wife.

'I think six months is early enough to meet the parents,' said Tom laughing.

'Well, we will try not to bombard you with questions my dear,' said Fiona. She passed a menu to Sophie, and they began to settle into their surroundings.

'Is Serena joining us?' asked Tom.

His younger sister had been away travelling the past year and was due back any day now. They were extremely close, and he had missed her dreadfully. Although they had been in touch at various intervals, having her back to spend some quality time with was something Tom couldn't wait for.

'I think her flight gets in too late,' said his mum. 'She said she would get a taxi home and that you could catch up with her tomorrow.'

'I thought she would stay travelling for longer,' mused Tom's dad. 'Mind you it'll be lovely to have us all together again for the summer.'

'We never would have booked our trip if we had known she would be flying home so soon,' his mum added. His parents were getting ready to embark on a holiday to Sri Lanka and his mum was already beginning to worry about Serena being left alone in their empty house. Serena wasn't the type to worry about such things, she was the most independent person Tom knew.

'Well, I did think I could invite her to stay with me in the flat for the first weekend you are away?' said Tom, hoping that this may set his mums mind at rest. 'I can't see her wanting to hang around in your house all the time on her own if she can help it. No offence Mum but you know what she like.'

Serena had always been the adventurous one and staying with her brother in the bright lights of London was much more her style. He could imagine her wandering aimlessly around their parents' large home moaning that there was "absolutely nothing going on and she was living in the back of beyond". His idea seemed to be welcomed by his mother though and he saw her visibly relax.

Conversation for the rest of the meal was mainly about his parents' trip and Tom was pleased to see their excitement. While growing up he couldn't remember a time when they both looked so animated, and it warmed his heart. They had provided the best childhood for Tom and Serena, and it was now time for them to enjoy some quality time together.

Sophie was deep in conversation with his dad, recounting her own favourite family holiday in Jamaica many years before. He was happy they were all getting on so well and it was a shame when Tom glanced at this watch and saw that they had to go.

'We had better get going,' he said. 'I've got a client at 3.15pm. So that just gives me time to walk Sophie to the station and get back to the office.'

He had only just started a new job in an international marketing company and his boss was a stickler for punctuality. It was only a couple of blocks away and he wanted to get to the meeting room in time to set up his pitch and catch his breath before the others arrived. Tom's dad lifted his hand to call the waiter and after a bit of playful arguing over it, his dad settled the bill. Tom insisted on leaving a sizeable tip and they all got to their feet.

When they stepped outside, the glare of the afternoon sun had them shielding their eyes. It felt warm and sticky after the coolness of the air-conditioned restaurant and Tom waited while Sophie rummaged in her bag for her sunglasses, before turning to his parents.

'I'll drive down tomorrow and see Serena and if she's happy to, she can come back with me,' said Tom. He embraced his parents in turn and waited while Sophie did the same.

'It's been lovely to see you Tom, and to meet you Sophie,' said David. 'We look forward to seeing you after our trip.'

'I'm glad to have met you both, thank you for lunch and enjoy your time away,' said Sophie.

Tom was happy the lunch had gone well, although he wasn't surprised his parents had loved Sophie. He couldn't wait for Serena to meet her too.

'Well, that was the easiest first meeting I think I have ever had,' said Sophie, as the couple walked away. Her smile showed how relaxed his parents had made her feel. 'Honestly, your parents are lovely. I suppose I shouldn't be surprised though, after all their son is so perfect,' she teased, poking him in his ribs.

They walked slowly to the station savouring their last few minutes together and then snuggled close at the far end of the platform as they waited. As Sophie's train drew into the station, they kissed, and she promised to send him a message when she got home.

'I'll call you over the weekend and let you know when I'm back. I may stay a couple of days and then drive Serena back with me.' With a last peck, she scanned her ticket and disappeared through the turnstile. Tom watched until she was out of sight before starting his walk back to his office.

# THREE

His journey the next day took four hours instead of the normal two and a half and Tom found himself cursing for most of the last hour. *Damn holidaymakers,* he thought to himself. *As soon as the sun shows its face, they all rush to the beach. And then they park their cars anywhere and everywhere just so they don't have to walk more than a few steps, before lying bunched up like sardines as close to the refreshment stands as they can.* He just couldn't understand the mentality.

He couldn't really blame them for coming to Lyhampton though. It was, in his opinion one of the most beautiful villages on the South Coast, all rolling hills and fabulous sandy beaches. It was hot and sticky in the car and the air-conditioning was struggling to make much of an impact. He made a mental note to get it checked when he got back to London.

Finally, he pulled into the drive of his childhood home and parked alongside his dad's Maserati. Smiling to himself, he checked to make sure he was parallel. He could imagine his dad peering out of the window checking everything was lined up properly, he was so pedantic about symmetry. Tom couldn't see what difference it made but there was no point in winding his dad up. In his early years it used to amuse Tom to move things around at home; like making the books in the bookcase out of line, that sort of thing. He had known it annoyed his father and that it would only be mere minutes before he would have to go and correct the disruption. These days though, Tom went out of his way to keep his dad happy. A sign maybe that moving out and standing on his own feet had made him grow up a bit.

As he switched off the ignition, he sat forward peeling his t-shirt from the seat. Out of the corner of his eye he saw the front door being flung open and Serena rushing to meet him. Laughing, he scrambled out of the car and scooped her up, planting a kiss on her temple.

'Urgh put me down!' She wriggled free. 'You're all sticky. Gross!'

'Lovely to see you too, little sister.' He grinned and they stood taking each other in.

'You've lost weight,' he said to Serena 'Didn't they feed you in Asia?'

She smiled. 'Must be all the sightseeing. I've eaten everything I could get my hands on so I should be as big as you,' she teased.

'I'll have you know, I go to the gym now,' replied Tom with a mock hurt expression, his hand moving instinctively towards his toned stomach.

'So, I've heard. All for your lady friend no doubt,' said Serena.

The reference to Sophie made Tom's face light up and Serena exaggerated an eye roll. In all honesty though, she was so happy for her brother, it was heart-warming to see him beaming.

'I'm glad you've met someone nice. She's a lucky girl,' she finished more seriously this time.

'Are you two coming in?' shouted Fiona from just inside the front door. They laughed in unison and made their way indoors.

Later as the sun went down, they enjoyed a barbecue in the back garden, basking in the warmth of the newly installed fire pit. Tom sat back listening to the tinkling sound of the fountain. It was set in the centre of the garden and surrounded by an array of blooms. His mother was a keen gardener and he'd never seen the colourful flowers looking anything other than perfect.

As he watched Serena, he couldn't help but notice a sadness in her eyes, making him wonder if there was another reason she had flown back from her trip so soon. He decided he would question her about it when they were in the car together on the drive back to London. If she would open up to him that is, because normally drawing Serena's feelings out of her, was like getting blood out of a stone. It had always struck him how brave his baby sister was and how fiercely independent. She usually travelled alone as this was apparently how "you get the most out of seeing the world." Though for him it was the opposite. He wasn't really interested in travelling unless he had someone special to share it with.

He knew without even checking that Serena would want to come and stay with him. She would of course want to meet Sophie, and he could guess that she would want to get away for a few days at least from the sleepy suburb where his parents lived.

His guess proved correct, and on Sunday afternoon they waved goodbye to their parents and set off through the winding roads towards the motorway. Serena looked sleepy. She leaned forward and switched on the radio, settling on a station playing soft, melodic sounds. She let out a considerable sigh as she leaned back into her seat.

'Everything OK?' said Tom as he turned off the roundabout onto the slip road.

'I'm fine, just a little sleepy,' she replied. She hesitated as if taking a moment to make up her mind before continuing. 'Look, don't get all freaked out but I've been feeling tired a lot of the time recently, and as you said before I seem to be losing weight for no reason.'

Tom thought of the amount of Sunday roast Serena had managed to consume only an hour before and the two helpings of Lemon meringue pie. He frowned. She had always had a good appetite.

'Do you think you should have a check-up at the doctors?' he asked, spotting the worried look on her face and suddenly feeling concerned. Now when he looked closer, he noticed she was a little pale for someone who had just returned from holiday.

'Maybe,' she sighed, 'but it will have to wait until I'm back at Mum and Dad's. I'm sure it's nothing.' She waved her hand as if swiping the worry away.

'Promise me you'll make an appointment for when you get back though. Don't just leave it,' said Tom. He couldn't bear the thought of anything to be wrong with his beloved sister.

'I promise,' she said. She leaned her head against the window and looked out at the grass verge as they travelled along.

Daylight was fading and Tom shifted his attention back to keeping them safe on the road ahead. The heavens opened and a substantial amount of rain spilled from the dark clouds above. Serena gave in to her exhaustion and slept the rest of the way.

The following few days in London with Serena and Sophie were the most fun Tom had experienced for a while. He had managed to get a few days off work and Sophie was free too, so she could join them. They went to all the favourite haunts and acted like tourists which gave Tom a fresh view of the capital.

They had lunch in an amazing restaurant high up in The Shard, even though eating that high up made Sophie's stomach churn. She sat with her back to the window once they were seated. It made her uncomfortable that the floor sloped towards the windows, no doubt to make the most of the fantastic views. A few cocktails later and she could no longer remember her fear of heights. Instead, she happily pointed out at the sights below, while Tom and Serena grinned at her transformation. They walked along the Embankment and went on the London Eye just as the sun was setting, enjoying the sights towards Tower Bridge.

By Friday Tom was exhausted. They had walked everywhere, and his feet needed a well-earned break. He took Serena in a taxi to Waterloo and waited until she boarded her train back to their parents' house.

'I approve of your taste in women,' she said. 'Sophie is an absolute gem. I hope you realise how lucky you are?'

'Agreed Sis, don't forget how lucky she is to have found a catch like me.'

She hugged him tightly.

'You are a complete weirdo,' she said. 'Although I see why she loves you.' She pulled away. 'I better get on the train before it leaves.' She started to walk away.

'Don't forget to call the doctor and let me know what he says,' he called after her. She nodded her head at him and with a last wave, she boarded the train. They had plans to meet up again in a couple of weeks and after a long sleep, he would begin to look forward to it.

He had a busy time at work and time moved on quickly. He'd only managed to see Sophie twice in the last week as she was helping a close friend to prepare for her forthcoming wedding. So, before he knew it, Serena was back on his doorstep.

She came bearing a Chinese takeaway she had picked up a few streets away from his flat.

'I was going to take you out,' he said when he met her at the door. 'It will just be you and me tonight, though Sophie may join us tomorrow.'

Serena handed over the bag of food while she hung her jacket over the balustrade, and they moved into the kitchen.

'We can all go out tomorrow then,' she said. 'I wanted to say a quick thank you for having me to stay again.' She pulled a bottle of red wine from her bag and placed it on the kitchen worktop.

'Ooh fancy,' said Tom looking at the label.

'Show's what you know,' said Serena, crinkling her nose. 'It was £6.99 but I did choose the one with the classiest label. When I get a job, I'll buy you a fancier one'.

'I'm not sure I would know the difference. I'm hardly a connoisseur,' replied Tom. 'Thank you, Sis, you didn't need to bring all this.'

Within ten minutes, the empty cartons were disposed of. The wine was going down well and with his stomach full, Tom felt happy and contented. Although that was all about to change. As they sat on the comfy sofa Serena curled her legs up beneath her and began to look serious.

'What's wrong?' Tom asked. He could instantly feel how anxious she was. She looked like she was about to cry, but she didn't speak. 'Come on Serena, you're scaring me now,' he pushed.

'Alright.' she said taking a deep breath. 'I don't really know how to say this, but I went to the doctors, and he ran some tests. I got the results back a couple of days ago.'

He kept his eyes on hers, feeling his heart starting to race. She was having trouble holding his gaze.

'It turns out that I have got an immune disorder. That's why I've been losing weight and feeling so tired all the time,' she finished. She sat miserably, waiting for his response.

'And what does that mean? It's treatable, right?' he blurted out. He could feel the blood draining from his cheeks.

'The doctor said that my immune system is attacking the stem cells in my bone marrow and that I will need a stem cell transplant,' she said. Her eyes had welled up, and a solitary tear escaped onto her cheek.

'Oh Serena, Jesus…I'm so sorry. Have you told Mum and Dad?'

She shook her head as he put his arms around her, noticing her fragile frame more now than when she had arrived. He realised her choice of clothes were to hide the fact. The thought of anything happening to her was more than he could bear, and his mind explored what to say next.

'How do we find you a donor?' He asked. He was completely bewildered. 'Would I be a likely match? You know I'd do anything to help, Serena.' He had no idea what that entailed or if it was a possibility, but Serena looked grateful.

'The doctor said a sibling is usually the best match so I was hoping you would get a test at least.' She visibly relaxed. 'Tom, you are the loveliest brother. I'm so grateful you would even consider it. I don't want to worry Mum and Dad yet, especially with them going away. Let's get some facts first.'

They stayed up late into the night discussing a plan of action. Together they searched the internet for more information about stem cell transplants and Tom agreed to go and be tested as soon as he could. Once Serena had fallen asleep on the sofa bed that Tom had set up for her, he kissed her gently and went off to bed himself although he wasn't surprised to find he couldn't sleep.

He was sure of one thing though. He would do everything he could to make sure his sister would be cared for.

# FOUR

Tom rested his arm on the soft leather chair so the doctor could take his blood sample. He closed his eyes in silent prayer and hoped they would get the result they needed. At least the doctor had managed to fit him in so quickly. The worst thing would have been waiting weeks to get the test when all he wanted was to help Serena get better.

'The results will be back within one to two weeks,' the doctor was saying. 'Make an appointment to come in then and bring Serena with you if you wish.' He showed Tom out to the reception area. Tom left the building and walked slowly to a bench in the park opposite and called Serena.

'Hi Tom,' she answered, in a voice that sounded like she was forcing herself to sound bubbly. She had been staying the past few days with him and he could see how tired she was feeling. This morning he had left before she had woken.

'Hi Sis, how are you feeling today?' he asked.

'I'm fine,' she replied. 'I'm feeling a bit frustrated. It just feels as if my life is on hold, that's all. I need to get back to Mum and Dad's and start looking for a job but with all this hanging over me it's hard to plan anything.' She let out a deep sigh.

'There's no immediate rush. You can stay with me for however long you want to.'

She sighed again.

'Thanks, you are lovely. I don't want to get in the way of your love affair though.'

'Of course you aren't Sis, you know you're welcome anytime. Anyway, the reason I called was to let you know I've just had my blood test so hopefully things will get moving along now,' he replied.

'Thanks for organising it all so quickly. You know how much I appreciate you doing that for me.'

'You know I would do anything to help. Wild horses couldn't stop me. Look, I'll see you at home later. Sophie is due over for dinner, so we can all catch up properly then.'

Tom could hear the relief in her voice and was glad he could do something to make her feel a little happier.

'I'm lucky to have a brother like you. I'll give you a big hug when you get back. See you later,' she said. He was smiling as he hung up and then glancing at the time, quickly got to his feet. He would have to hurry to get back to the office before his lunch hour had finished and his stomach growled reminding him that he hadn't had any lunch. As he made his way into the tube station to head back into the city, he was pleased to see there was only a short queue at his favourite pasty stand.

At 8pm Sophie arrived with a bottle of Tom's favourite wine, and they all sat down to dinner. Tom had spent the last hour preparing a curry with Serena's help, as sous chef. With music blaring, they had danced around the kitchen while they cooked. Serena seemed more relaxed now that she knew the blood test had been done. Although Tom hoped she wasn't pinning all her hopes on it being a match. He prayed it would be, because he knew they were both clinging to the fact that there was a fifty percent chance of a sibling being a perfect match. For tonight though they were going to put it all aside and have a lovely evening together.

The following Wednesday, Tom and Serena nervously climbed the front steps up to the doctor's surgery. Tom pushed the heavy glass door open and moved aside to let Serena enter before him. As she passed, she gave him an apprehensive smile. Together they approached the desk and the young receptionist looked up and smiled.

'Hello Mr Beatty. Right on time. You can go straight in. Doctor Waite is ready to see you both.' Tom searched her face for any clues but of course there were none. He thanked her, before gently knocking and ushering Serena through the consulting room door. They both greeted Dr Waite before settling themselves in the chairs opposite him.

Dr Waite had been Tom's doctor for the past three years and although he was direct, he had a friendly demeanour. Tom had always liked him and on a day like today he was glad to be sitting here in front of someone he admired.

'Hello Tom.' He turned to Serena with a smile. 'Hello Serena, it is nice to meet you. How are you feeling?' Tom could see her body relax ever so slightly.

'I'm not too bad, thanks. A little tired that's all.'

'Good,' he replied. 'And Tom, are you happy to talk through your results with both of you present?' he asked.

'Yes, of course' said Tom. He looked over and smiled at Serena.

'OK, well, let's get on with it then,' said the doctor opening the file.

Tom found himself holding his breath and he glanced over again at Serena. She was shifting in her chair and anxiously wringing her hands in her lap.

'Look there's really no easy way to say this but I'm sorry you are not a match Tom,' said Dr Waite. He hesitated, giving Tom and Serena time to digest the news. Tom was crestfallen and he couldn't imagine how Serena must feel. As he struggled with his feelings, the words that followed made his mouth gape open wider still.

'Tom, did you hear what I said?'

Tom dragged his eyes away from the doctor and towards Serena. She looked stricken and tears were beginning to fall across her cheeks. Tom shook his head. He had heard, or at least he had thought he heard those ridiculous words. He shook his head again, more as a gesture to clear his head. He looked the doctor in the eye and braced himself for the words again.

'I said, from the results I would be very surprised if you are actually blood related.'

# FIVE

## *Katie (1998)*

I opened my eyes and for a split second I thought I was waking up next to Lucas. It wasn't just the chill in the air but also a strong musty smell that brought me jolting back to the present. Suddenly alert, I flattened my hands out on to the floor and searched my muddled memory. My heart began to race as I tried in vain to peer through the darkness to see my surroundings but there was not even the slightest glimmer of light. I began to feel around the cold, ground that I was laying on. It felt like concrete. My body was stiff and every joint ached. As I sat upright, I felt a sharp, stabbing pain in my left ankle when I tried to move it.

Tentatively I reached forward, a millimetre at a time, scared of what I may find. It wasn't long until my fingertips brushed against a wall. Following it to the next corner I slowly crawled on my hands and knees until I had completed a circuit. From running my hands along each wall, I could tell it was a garage or basement of some sort. The smell of damp assaulted my nostrils. I traced my fingers around the uneven breeze blocks along each wall. As it dawned on me how small an area I was trapped in, my heart began to beat faster, and it was hard not to hyperventilate. It took every ounce of willpower to resist the panicky feelings invading my body.

I forced myself to concentrate on another search of the walls, going slowly and methodically over every inch. On one side there was a slim gap surrounding a doorway but however hard I searched there was no handle. Near the bottom of the door there was a small opening that my hand fit through but all that could be reached, a few inches inside, was a cold metal plate. I explored further and at the top of the metal plate was a hinge of some sort.

As I moved away from the walls pushing my hands out cautiously in front of me, I found the one and only piece of furniture in the centre of the room. A metal framed single bed with a flimsy mattress and a thin duvet tucked neatly at the end of the bed. I climbed up onto the bed and pulled the duvet over me.

The lightweight cover didn't warm me but still it made me feel slightly better. I curled up protectively and tried to cast my mind back, recalling what I could. I remembered coming into the house and the relief I had felt when the nice lady was going to help me. But then the man who had followed me appeared and I could only remember that I had been drugged. I still felt woozy, aware the drug must still be coursing through my veins. What if he had hurt the woman? She could also be being held somewhere else in the house. The guilt of my bringing the man to her house weighed heavily on my shoulders.

I could hear a noise. It was constant. A whining noise. It took a moment to realise it was the sound of my own whimpering. I focused on my breathing, counting in my head. In for three breaths, hold, out for five breaths. In for three breaths, hold, out for five. After a few minutes the shaking began to slow, and I could feel my breathing returning to a more natural rhythm. I lay still in the darkness with my thoughts whirring around my mind. What was going to happen to me and how was I going to escape?

I heard a door opening before a sharp burst of light dragged me from sleep. I must have dropped off and I struggled now to wake up. I must still be feeling groggy from whatever drug the man had administered. The fear of seeing him again made me back away as far as possible, pulling at the covers as if they would act as a shield.

He moved into the room, leaving the door slightly ajar so that a little light streamed in. For the first time it gave me a chance to examine my prison and it was pretty much how I had envisaged it. The only thing I couldn't have known was that there was a small window at the top of one wall. It was too high for me to reach or even see out of it, but there was some relief in knowing I may get some light in the daylight hours. I couldn't bear to be to be stuck in the pitch black I had experienced until now.

His voice was deep. Deeper than you would think to look at him.

'How are you feeling?' he asked. He made it sound like his question was aimed at a friend whose health he was casually asking after. I could feel the anger bubbling up inside of me, but I didn't reply. Instead, I kept my eyes trained on him and followed his movements as he shuffled over and sat on the end of the bed. I tried to push myself further away, but my back was already against the cold metal bars of the bed. I had not really had time to see his face before but now I couldn't drag my eyes away.

He could only be a few years older than me, and his face was long and thin. He had a slight curl in his mousey brown hair, and it looked like it needed a wash. His deep brown eyes were watching me too and a small smile came to his lips.

'There, there,' he said. 'Don't be worried, I will only keep you here as long as I need to and then I promise I'll let you go.'

He reached out his hand to touch my ankle and I jerked it away. Pain seared through it once more, but I didn't let it show on my face.

'Why are you doing this?' I heard herself ask, but it felt like the words were coming from elsewhere. He smiled again but didn't answer the question.

'I'll be back later,' he said as he got to his feet. 'I'll bring you some food, we need to keep your strength up.'

The thought of food made me want to gag but I knew I would have to try to eat whatever he gave me if I was to stay strong. I wrestled with my feelings; part of me desperate to get him away from me and then another part, now that he was here, didn't want him to leave. What I really wanted was answers, but I didn't believe he would tell me anything. I could feel a surge of distress building at the thought of being locked in again, alone.

'Please, let me go. I won't tell anyone. Please, my boyfriend will already be looking for me.'

I moved forward trying to reach him but found as my legs had been curled up underneath me for so long, they couldn't take my weight. He watched emotionless as I stumbled off the bed onto the hard floor and then he pulled his gaze away and stepped through the doorway, closing the door behind him. A multitude of bolts could be heard sliding across, and I shrunk back into the darkness which now engulfed me.

I sat still for a few moments trying to force my body to move. It was as if he had taken my last bit of energy with him, and it took every ounce of determination to drag my aching body back to the bed. Sobs wracked my whole body as I thought of Lucas and the unbearable realisation that I may never see him again.

Would he already be looking for me? I couldn't tell how much time had passed but while the door was open, I had seen darkness outside from the small window high above. It must at least be night-time and so Lucas would be worried by now knowing I should have been home a couple of hours after I had left. He would come for me. I was sure of that.

A new sense of dread came over me. How could he when nobody knew where I was or even the normal route of my run? The only chance I had was that the lady upstairs had managed to escape and would go for help. But surely, she would have found help by now?

I was finding it impossible to concentrate and my arms and legs felt heavy. Until the drugs were fully out of my system there wasn't anything I could do but lay back on the bed and rest. Within minutes I drifted into a deep sleep, my dreams of escaping a distant memory.

# SIX

Serena gasped and Tom was overcome with the same shock and confusion that was visible on her face. Their eyes were fixed on Doctor Waite.

'I don't understand?' he stuttered. Serena seemed incapable of words. The doctor looked back at them with his usual ultra-calm expression, but Tom focused on the slightest hint of a frown, a sign that he was finding this difficult too.

'Well,' said the doctor gently. 'Usually from a sibling we would expect would around a fifty percent match.' He paused and Tom willed him to get on with it. 'But you and Serena aren't matched at all.'

The words sent a chill down Tom's back. He took hold of Serena's shaking hand. As they left the consulting room Tom uttered a stilted goodbye to the receptionist. Serena lowered her head as she walked past the desk, her hair falling across her face, hiding her tear-stained cheeks. Tom pushed the door open, and once outside they both stood in silence, watching people going about their daily business. They made their way slowly down the grey concrete steps, Tom holding Serena's arm tightly to make sure she didn't fall. She was so pale, and he could envisage her falling into a heap at the bottom.

He kept his arm through hers once they had reached the pavement and they moved to one side so that they weren't blocking the entrance. Neither could bring themselves to move any further. They both stared out across the road and felt completely bewildered. A few long minutes went by where nobody spoke and then Serena turned sharply towards him.

'How can this be possible?' she said. Her voice was croaky with emotion, her eyes desperate and wide. Her troubled expression matched his own.

'I can't understand it either, why would Mum or Dad not tell us? Surely, they would think we have a right to know if either or both of us are adopted?' replied Tom. Absentmindedly he ran his hands through his thick hair as if to stimulate the thoughts shooting through his mind. He was trying his best to stay strong for his sister but underneath, he shaken to the core. *How could the person he felt closest to in the world, the sister he grew up with, not be related to him? They were so alike.*

'We need to find out, we must speak to them. Shall we try to get in contact with them on their trip?' said Serena. She started to rummage through her pockets, hunting for another tissue. The one the doctor had given her was now wet through. Unable to find one, she lifted her sleeve and wiped the dampness from her cheeks with the soft edge of her cardigan.

'Can we really have that conversation while they are so far away?' asked Tom. The idea of having such a personal conversation over the phone seemed wrong, however much they needed to know. He knew the only way was to deal with it face to face, to be able to calm the situation with hugs and reassurance. He could imagine his mum racing to get a flight home and what was the point? A few more weeks wasn't going to make much difference and maybe they both needed a little more time to make sense of it in their own minds before they confronted their parents.

'Yes, you are probably right. This isn't the type of conversation to be had over the phone,' Serena agreed, and they started the walk back to Tom's flat, lost in their own thoughts.

As they entered the flat, Sophie got up from the sofa to greet them. She had been waiting, hopeful of a good result but as soon as she saw the grim look on their faces, she knew the prospect of a match had been dashed.

'I'm so sorry guys,' she said, going in turn to hug each of them.

'You can explain,' said Serena tiredly, 'I'm going for a lay down and then we can all chat later.'

She moved towards the spare bedroom despondently and quietly shut the door behind her. Tom sat on the sofa next to Sophie and told her what the doctor had told them only an hour or so before. It was her turn to be shocked and she gripped his hand tightly as he explained. Her heart went out to them both.

A few hours later when Serena re-emerged, she found Tom and Sophie huddled over the computer screen whispering to one another. Tom looked up.

'How are you feeling?' He asked. He ran his eyes over her and took in the bit of colour that had come back in her cheeks, although her face was still very pale. At least she looked a little less exhausted.

'I'm OK,' she replied. She gave him a half-hearted smile. 'What are you two up to? Have you thought of a way to sort this mess? I honestly don't know if I'm more interested in finding out if we are related, or finding another donor,' she stated.

'Actually, Sophie did have an idea,' he started cautiously. He looked over at Sophie and she started to explain.

'Look, this may sound far-fetched, but it may help you at least know if you are related. My grandad has recently been looking into his genealogy and he sent off for a DNA test to see if he could find any other distant relatives. It can tell you of any cousins or relations that you may not know of, and it may shed some light on the identity of your birth parents.' She looked at Serena expectantly.

'Well, what do you think?' asked Tom. 'It could at least be something we can be getting on with while our parents are away?'

He waited for a reaction, but Serena just frowned. Tom felt increasingly uncomfortable. A few minutes ago, it had seemed like a lifeline, but it was probably just clutching at straws. All he knew for sure was that there was no way he could sit around and not do anything about the situation.

'Is it a mad idea?' he asked. 'Or shall we at least give it a try?'

Serena stood staring at him for what felt like the longest time.

'What have we got to lose?' She said with a shrug. 'I suppose if we can have the results back by the time our parents come home - or the parents we thought were ours - that would be useful,' she added thoughtfully. 'And maybe we will even find a relation that could be a possible donor match for me,' she added.

Sophie promised that over the next few days she would locate the website her grandad had used, and order two DNA testing kits. Tom walked over to his sister and took her in his arms for the umpteenth time that day.

'You'll always be my baby sister Serena, regardless of what any test says. We will get to the bottom of this and when Mum and Dad are back, we will confront them with whatever we find.'

## SEVEN

It was just under a week later when the DNA tests arrived. They took turns in carefully swabbing their cheeks and then packaged everything up and sent it back to the lab for analyses. The results would take a couple of weeks to arrive, so Tom tried his best to forget about it. Even so, it remained at the back of his mind each day. Somehow, he managed to go through the motions at work without causing any major disasters.

Each evening, he found Serena waiting at home and they kept their conversation strictly away from the test results. It may have gone unsaid, but Tom knew it was all she could think of too. At least

Serena's health seemed to be stable now and although she tired easily, she remained reasonably well. Her skin still looked translucent, and she struggled to put on any weight, however much food she consumed, but at least she was taking the time to rest when she needed to.

The following Friday, from the moment he walked into the flat after work, he could feel the tension before he even laid eyes on her. The kitchen and lounge area were open plan, and he could see her sitting motionless on the sofa as he threw his keys noisily into the ceramic bowl on the kitchen counter. She jumped slightly at the noise but didn't look up, instead she continued to fiddle with the letters in her hands.

'Why didn't you call?' he said. 'I would have come home early.' He moved to her side, and she turned to him slowly in a sort of daze.

'I didn't notice the time,' she said. 'When the post arrived on the mat, I knew what it was. I must have sat down here and not moved since. I must have been here for hours,' she realised.

As Serena got to her feet and stretched, she handed one of the envelopes to Tom.

'Are you ready?' she said. She didn't look ready. He could feel his heartbeat quicken.

He took off his jacket and walked back over to the breakfast bar, placing it on the back of one of the high stools. He took a deep breath before he turned.

'Ready as I'll ever be,' he said. As they ripped open the letters, they kept their eyes fixed on one another. Serena was the first to glance down and she let out a little gasp.

'Oh, thank God!' she said, holding her hand to her heart. 'Dad is my dad after all,' she said elated. She sank back onto the sofa with a sigh of relief at the first glimpse of her results. 'It doesn't have a match for my mother though but there are a few distant related cousins, so that's something.'

She was looking at Tom, but he was staring at the page, completely frozen. She immediately realised the implication of what she had just said and of the feeling of relief she had felt wash over her. If their dad was her flesh and blood, then most probably the news was different for Tom.

'Tom, what does it say?' Her heart went out to him. She waited. He looked up and the hurt was evident in his eyes. His chest felt constricted, like he couldn't breathe. He put out a hand and reached for the kitchen worktop to steady himself.

'Tom, please you are scaring me,' she pleaded. She got to her feet.

'There's no mothers' name on mine either,' he said. 'But there is a name that's showing as my father and it's a name I've never even heard of.'

'What?' Her voice came out high and screechy. 'Let me see,' she said. She scrambled over to him and snatched the paper from his hands. She looked at the name: John Hanson.

'Oh my God!' She took a few seconds to take it in. 'Who the hell is John Hanson?'

'I don't know,' said Tom. In contrast his voice was low and flat. He watched as Serena closed her eyes tightly and then opened them to look back at the letter for a second time, as if the result would be different if she willed it to be. A thought flicked into her mind.

'Do you think we have the same mum but different dad's?' her voice crept higher and higher with each word. 'You don't think mum had an affair, do you?' She looked aghast at this thought.

Tom leaned against the worktop steadying himself further. He felt lightheaded.

'I don't know what it means. Maybe I was adopted? What if I'm not related to any of you?' he said, the pain showing in his eyes. He put his head in his hands, his brain whirring. Serena rested her hand gently on his shoulder, dropping the letter on to the counter.

'I think we should ring Mum and Dad now and see what they say. Sod them being on a holiday of a lifetime. This is crazy.'

Tom placed his hand over hers.

'I don't want to have this conversation over the phone Serena. They will back in a few weeks, and I think for all our sakes we need to talk about this face to face.' His face was set, determined. 'In the meantime, maybe, we had better see if we can track down this Mr Hanson.'

# EIGHT

As the evening that Tom and Sophie had originally planned fluttered away like a strong breeze through an open window, Tom sat nibbling away at his fingernails. It was a habit he had kicked in his early teens but in times of stress he would revert to absentmindedly chewing the side of his forefinger. Sophie sat alongside him, busy at the computer. She glanced at him and gently pulled his hand away from his mouth so he wouldn't make his finger bleed. Keeping his hand in hers, she continued to manoeuvre the mouse around the screen with her right hand.

'Are you ready for this?' she said, searching his eyes for a sense of what he was thinking.

'I'm not really sure,' he answered honestly. 'There's no chance of going back now though. Both Serena and I need to find out some facts before we speak to our parents.'

It was strange to think of them blissfully unaware, sitting on a beautiful beach somewhere with no idea of the crisis building at home.

'It's not something we can just blurt out when they arrive back. I mean what am I accusing them of? It's a big deal to suddenly confront your mum about having an affair.'

Part of him wished they hadn't found out at all. Life had seemed so simple only a few weeks ago. He had heard of people finding out later in life that they were adopted but he had never considered he could be one of them. An internet search brought up eleven J. Hanson's' in the local area, which seemed like a reasonable place to begin.

They spent the evening checking the dates of birth of the eleven and by midnight had narrowed it down to six possibilities. Making calls to these random strangers filled Tom with a sense of dread and he was relieved when Sophie offered to call any that had a telephone number listed, the following morning.

They tried to get as much sleep as possible, but Tom was especially restless. At nine the next morning he was pacing back and forth as Sophie picked up her phone and started to dial the first number on the list. Standing next to her, Tom could hear the phone ringing and when he heard a faint click at the other end, he held his breath.

'Oh hi, I wonder if it's possible to speak to John Hanson?' she said, her eyes fixed on Tom.

He couldn't make out the voice on the other end of the phone, but when Sophie continued, he quickly realised it was a no go. She tapped her phone to finish the call.

'He was Jack," she said. "Let's try the next one.'

She crossed the number from the top of the list before dialling the next.

Tom ambled over to the breakfast bar and poured himself a coffee. He gestured to Sophie, but she shook her head.

'No answer,' she said. 'Tom why don't you go out into the garden and relax. I'll come and tell you if I get anywhere.'

He smiled and walked over to plant a kiss on her forehead. She was so thoughtful. He couldn't wait to get out of there to be honest. His stress levels were going through the roof.

'Thanks, I am a bit tense,' he said to her. That was a bit of an understatement. 'I expect you'll be able to concentrate better if I leave you to it.'

There was no sign of Serena, and Tom guessed she had probably had a bad night as well. Sophie promised to alert him if Serena surfaced, so he strolled outside and sat on the new oak bench he had bought recently for the patio in his small but perfectly formed garden.

Just a few weeks ago his life had been so easy. Having such a supportive, loving family and fond memories of growing up, it seemed as if someone had violently snatched the rug out from underneath him, leaving him confused and betrayed. He continuously replayed everything he could remember from his childhood, trying to pick up on any abnormalities but there just wasn't anything that would have made him doubt his parents weren't his biological parents.

Tom had mulled it all over in his mind so many times in the last few days. Could his mother have had an affair, and his dad didn't know? If this was the case, then it was no wonder there had never been any discussion about it. He picked up his coffee cup and found it had gone cold. He must have been sitting there daydreaming for longer than he realised.

A noise caught his attention, and he looked up to see Sophie emerging from the patio doors, with Serena following.

'I think I may have found him,' said Sophie tentatively placing an address in front of Tom. 'It's only around twenty miles from your parents' place. Surely that can't be a coincidence?'

Tom's heart began to beat faster as he looked at the piece of paper. He struggled to find the words to reply and instead he tried hard to concentrate on what Sophie was saying.

'I told him we found his name after looking into your genealogy and would he be prepared to meet up and try to work out if you may be related? I couldn't really tell him over the phone that he may be your dad, so I said it was possible he could be a distant relative,' she continued. She came around behind the bench and put her arms around Tom's neck.

'He was nice. It sounded as if he hadn't got any family around him, so he was happy to meet and see what we had found. It made me quite sad, the fact that he hasn't got much family left. He said we can go by on Monday. What do you think?'

Tom looked up at Serena who had moved nearer and was now standing in front of him, a concerned look across her face.

'I think we better go and see what we can find out,' he said slowly. 'I certainly need some answers.'

The rest of the weekend went by in a blur and first thing Monday morning Tom and Serena climbed into his car and started their journey. Sophie had to work but she had given strict instructions to call her as soon as they knew anything. Tom was grateful for all she had done and the support she gave him. He was glad she was in his life, and vowed to take her somewhere special, just the two of them as soon as this was all over.

Serena wasn't very talkative, and neither was Tom. They followed the route towards the coast in silence, each contemplating what today would bring. By late morning they arrived at a house set back from the main road. As Sophie had said, it was not too far from their parents' house. It was in contrast though, not a grand house with a sweeping driveway but a small, slightly dilapidated cottage in need of some tender loving care. An old Vauxhall Vectra which had seen better days was parked in front of the cottage and there were a few other old bangers dotted around the garden as if the occupant fixed up cars in their spare time. Tom parked behind the Vectra and looked over at Serena.

'Are you ready for this?' he asked. 'I feel a bit sick,' he admitted.

'I do too,' agreed Serena. She let out a deep sigh. 'Come on, we need to see what he knows. He may not even be our guy.' She pulled the door handle and opened it wide, stepping out onto the gravel driveway.

Reluctantly he climbed out to join her, listening to the crunch underfoot as he followed her towards the tatty painted front door. Large red shards had peeled off revealing a sandy tinted wood underneath and were now collecting on top of a threadbare welcome mat. It didn't look like anybody had used this door for years and it was certainly not overly welcoming. Tom reached past Serena, tentatively pushing the faded brass doorbell.

# NINE

A few long minutes past and they glanced nervously at each other. Just as Tom thought the door would go unanswered, they heard a male voice call out.

'Come round the back, the side gate is open.'

They followed the voice around to the back of the cottage and found a man in the garden beyond.

'I was just putting the washing on the line,' he said. 'It's such a lovely day. You must be Tom and Serena,' he said.

John Hanson was a tall, broad-shouldered man with a shaved head and warm sparkling eyes. His face was the same oval shape as Tom's and for a second this similarity took Tom's breath away. He felt uncomfortable looking for signs from this stranger that they may be related, but also found himself compelled to do so.

He listened to Serena talking, telling the man how long the trip had taken, but Tom could only stand silently and stare. It took him a moment to realise that they had stopped talking and were both looking at him. It appeared that a question had been asked and John was waiting for a response. By the time Tom had engaged his brain and opened his mouth, Serena had answered for him.

'We would love a drink, thank you. Something cold would be lovely.'

She lifted her eyebrows questionably at Tom as they followed John into the property. He made a face and shrugged his shoulders.

*'Flipping hell Tom, get your act together!'* he silently chided himself.

As they entered a spacious living room John gestured for them to take a seat and they positioned themselves on the largest of the two sofas while John disappeared into the kitchen to prepare the drinks.

'What are you doing?' Serena was whispering, so Tom could barely hear her. He shrugged again.

'It took me by surprise,' he whispered back, glancing at the doorway. 'He looks like me, doesn't he?' he asked. Serena didn't have time to answer as John appeared in the doorway with a tray of lemonade. He put a glass for each of them on the large oak coffee table in front of them and took the seat nearest Serena, which was a slightly battered but well-loved old armchair.

'I don't have many visitors,' he said. He smiled openly at them both. 'So, this is quite exciting. You said on the phone that I may be a long lost relative? So go ahead, tell me what you've found.' He picked up his glass and sat back waiting.

Tom was still a little shell shocked, so he left it to Serena to explain how they had done a DNA test in hope of finding a donor for herself, and how unwittingly they had found that they weren't related.

'And so,' she paused, and Tom could see signs of her nervousness, 'you didn't actually come up as a distant relative as was suggested on the phone, but in Tom's results it was revealed that you may be his father.'

The man spurted his drink out mid mouthful and looked from Serena to Tom.

'Goodness, you don't really believe that do you?' He looked again from one to the other. 'But that's impossible, I've never been in the position to have children.'

He frowned and slowly shook his head, trying to make sense of what they were telling him. He leaned forward and placed his glass back onto the table before looking Tom in the eye.

'What I mean to say is, I can't believe I could have a child and not know. I've kept myself to myself all these years and well, I suppose a better word for it is that I've been a bit of a recluse. So, it just doesn't make any sense.'

He took a deep breath. They stayed silent and watched as the man in front of them wrestle with his emotions.

'I mean of course I've had a couple of girlfriends, but I don't think either of them could be your mother.' His eyes were wide, and it was obvious he was beginning to get quite agitated. Tom stood up and paced towards the window, and back again.

'Did you ever meet my mother? Her name is Fiona Beatty, or her maiden name was Hunter?'

'I've not heard that name before, I'm sorry,' said John. It was plain to see on his face the regret he felt. 'I wish I did have more family. It's been quite lonely over the years.' His eyes travelled over Tom's face. It was his turn now to search for any likeness and from the look on his face it seemed he found some similarity. He stopped abruptly and turned his head away.

'How old are you?' he asked Tom.

'I'm 24.'

Tom could almost see the cogs turning in the older man's mind, going through the mental arithmetic to give him the timeline in his own life.

'I've only had a couple of girlfriends since then, and I'm sure it couldn't have been either of them.'

'What makes you so sure?' asked Serena. She felt awkward questioning a stranger, but this could be their only chance to get the facts and luckily John didn't seem to mind.

'Well, my last girlfriend and I parted on bad terms really, but I'm sure she would have told me something like this. She moved away but I've heard news of her life through friends, and I know she hasn't got any children. Anyway, I'm sure the timing doesn't add up.' He frowned.

'And the other girlfriend?' probed Tom.

Something about the reaction on John's face made Serena on edge. She worried that he was about to say she had died. But instead, his eyes flickered closed for just a second as if steeling himself to reply, then he looked straight at her.

'Actually, the girlfriend I had around that time disappeared,' he said.

Serena took a sharp intake of breath. The pain she saw in his eyes was all too evident.

'And she was never heard of again.'

A little later, Tom and Serena were sat close together on the sofa drinking freshly brewed coffee. John had left the room to find an old newspaper report of the disappearance. After what seemed like an eternity, he came back into the room and handed a yellowed newspaper cutting to Tom.

The report was dated the spring of 1998 and told of a young girl who had mysteriously disappeared. She had left her house early in the morning and never came home.

'But it says here, her boyfriend Lucas?' said Serena looking up from where she was reading alongside Tom.

'Oh, yes that's my middle name but Katie used to call me Lucas, she always said John seemed too old for me.' He smiled at the memory. 'Nobody has called me that for a very long time.'

Serena sat forward a little and softly she asked, 'So you've not heard from Katie after that day?'

'No,' he replied sadly. 'I helped in the searches but part of me died that day. There were never any sightings, it was just like she vanished into thin air.' His voice caught and Serena reached across to touch his hand. 'As the years went by, I just resigned myself to the fact that I would never find out what happened to her.'

Tears formed in Serena eyes.

'I am so sorry, I really cannot imagine what that must have been like,' she said. She looked over at Tom who had got up again and was now standing by the window, lost in thought.

'And you don't think it is possible that Katie could have been my mum?' Tom said. The scenario had been turning over in his mind since he had read the story.

'I can't see how,' replied John rubbing the side of his head. A headache was threatening, and he wished he had not agreed to meeting the young pair.

'What if our mum is Katie and she changed her name?' piped up Serena. John rose to his feet and moved to a tall cabinet in the corner of the room. He opened a small door at the side of the cabinet and withdrew an old photograph album. It was well worn, and it was obvious that he had looked at it frequently. He opened the book and placed it onto Serena's lap.

'Is this your mum?' John asked and he braced himself for the answer.

# TEN

## *Katie (1998)*

There was a small opening at the bottom of the door where twice a day; once in the morning early, and again just before the light faded from the tiny window in the evening, a tray of food would arrive. The creak of the metal flap being opened would startle me and although it was the slightest of sounds, it cut harshly through the unbearable silence.

For the first few days I had stubbornly pushed away any food that the man had left. It felt like the only control I had left of my own. But as the days wore on, I began to feel weak and dizzy and even thinking became a struggle. Part of me wanted to curl up in the corner, to give in to my fate, but there was another part of me that was stronger willed, pushing me to fight until the bitter end, whatever that may be. So, I forced those thoughts aside. Instead, I decided to eat every morsel and to keep up my strength, at least giving me a possibility of escape if the opportunity ever came.

When he had entered the room the first time, I had been too bewildered to notice any details, but the longer I remained here, a small seed of hope emerged that I may find a way. I daydreamed of finding a way to overpower him and of bludgeoning him with something to make my escape. I hunted for anything I could use as a weapon, but he seemed to have covered all his bases.

A close inspection of the bed frame left me disappointed. Even the smallest piece of metal couldn't be detached and however desperately my fingers searched each join, it was soon obvious that every part had been welded together.

The disappointment hit me hard and angry tears escaped the corners of my eyes. The rest of the day I lay on the bed, lethargic and depressed. I flitted in and out of sleep and dreamt of Lucas. It was the day of his birthday - the party I never got to see - but in my dream it was vivid and fun. Everyone was there, all our friends and family. There was laughter and the drinks were flowing. The love between Lucas and I was strong, and I soaked up every image.

It was freezing when I woke up and I wrapped myself tightly in the thin duvet, my mind replaying the dream over and over until I started to slowly forget some of the finer details. Gradually my memory faded and was replaced by other random thoughts, of a documentary I had seen many years before.

It had been one of those shows where the army cadets were learning self-defence, and I squeezed my eyes shut trying to cast my mind back to their suggestions. There was something about a palm of your hand to his nose and how to get out of a hold from behind, but the details were sketchy. The only thing I could recall clearly was the simulation of a young female cadet planting a hard knee blow between the instructor's legs.

I kept this at the forefront of my mind in case there was ever the chance to use this tactic. But what then? I asked myself. What would I find if I managed to get past him? Would I just discover another door outside to get through?

The next time the man made an appearance it felt as if a week had gone by. I listening to the numerous clunks of the bolts being removed from the outside of the door, and then there he was. He was dressed in pale blue jeans and a canary yellow T-shirt, and he looked like any twenty something, no different from most young men you would find wandering down any street. He entered the room cautiously as if walking into a wild animals' cage, scared that the animal within would pounce on him and claw him to death.

I sat in my usual place at the top of the bed, wide eyed, watching his every move. He moved closer and lowered himself onto the far end of the thin mattress, just as he had the time before. There was something different in his eyes today, something that sent shivers down my spine. I got the impression he was there to tell me something but was reluctant to begin and it filled me with an unimaginable dread.

'Please, let me go' I whispered. My voice sounded weak and reedy.

He frowned. He took a deep breath.

'I'm sorry, there's no way I can do that yet,' he said keeping his voice low. His head had dropped so he was staring into his lap. He took another long-drawn-out breath and then in what seemed like slow motion, he lifted his head and looked me straight in the eye. A hardness had replaced the soft colour of his brown eyes and even before he spoke, I knew I was in danger.

'There's something I must do first.'

His eyes began to travel from my face, down my body, and in that instant, I knew what was about to happen. A small gasp escaped my lips and I pushed myself up from the bed and stumbled towards the corner of the room. I forced my body against the wall, as far away from him as possible. I squeezed my eyes tightly shut, like you do in a nightmare with the hope that you will wake. I could hear the creak of the bed as he got to his feet and a rush of adrenaline shot through my veins.

My mind screamed at me, fight Katie fight. I could feel him close by. As panic flooded my body, my arms began to flay wildly in front of me, hitting out at his chest. My head shook from side to side. A squealing noise came involuntarily from my mouth.

He wasn't the most well-built man but as he grabbed hold of my arms and pinned them to my sides, his strength was overwhelming. My eyes shot open to find that he was keeping his gaze away from my face. His face was hard, determined, his jaw tense as he dragged me across the floor towards the bed.

Once there he pushed me down with one hand against my shoulder, almost a gentle motion which took me by surprise. It was almost in the same way as a couple about to have consensual sex would move to the bed. But this wasn't consensual and as I felt my back hit the mattress, I tried hard to twist my other arm from his vice like grip. With every fibre of my being, I tried to break free.

He adjusted his stance so he could hold both of my arms above my head with one of his and it shocked me how little I could do to stop him. The tightness of his grasp was excruciating. I was screaming now, as loud as I could, but in the back of my mind I knew there was no-one there to help.

With one hand he unzipped his trousers, and I squeezed my eyes closed, trying to blot out any sounds and feelings. I continued to kick out with my legs, trying desperately to make contact, but I was growing weaker with every second. He held on to me and waited until I was exhausted, until there was no fight left and as I quietened down, only able to emit a faint whimper, he pushed his way into me.

My mind shut down. My only thoughts now were about how many times I would have to endure this torture and then the cold realisation hit. He was unlikely to ever let me go. How could he? Not now, after the crime he was committing.

He stopped moving and I felt the weight of his body roll away from me. I opened my eyes just the tiniest amount. His face showed little emotion but just before he turned away, I was sure I caught a glimpse of shame in his eyes. He shuffled through the doorway and as I heard the bolts being drawn into place, I curled up with my knees close to my chest and wept.

# ELEVEN

The main investigator on the disappearance of Katie Reed back in 1998 was Detective Alan Fairbrother. He was a meticulous man who had found it hard to come to terms with an unsolved case and it still rattled him. People didn't usually leave their house one morning and disappear without a trace. Usually someone saw something or would come forward at a later date. Over time he had moved on to other despicable crimes and he hadn't thought of her in years.

He was wading through a seemingly never-ending pile of paperwork when the call came, that a young man was down in reception asking to see him. When the Reed case was mentioned, it sparked his attention and he put the papers aside, glad for anything to get him out of finishing his mundane task.

As soon as he saw Tom Beatty, something registered. A passing resemblance to someone he had seen before maybe? He couldn't quite place it. He listened as the young man sitting on the other side of the desk in the interview room told him why he was there. He seemed to be implying that the missing girl could be his mother. It was too far back in his memory to recall if the man before him looked like the missing girl, but he could remedy that with another look at the file photo they were given at the time she disappeared. Later he would have a look but for now he listened to the story he was being told.

'So, let me get this straight,' he interrupted, holding up his hand. 'You believe that this missing girl from 1998 could be your mother on the grounds that a man you don't know, says you are around the right age to be her child?' He sighed, starting to wish he'd stayed upstairs with his paperwork.

'Not exactly,' said Tom. 'I have the DNA test which proves my father is John Hanson or Lucas as he was known to her. He was her boyfriend at the time. Who knows? Maybe she just went off to have a child without telling him?'

'So where do you think she is now, then?' asked Detective Fairbrother.

'I don't know,' replied Tom. He knew it sounded far-fetched, but now he'd managed to track down the man in charge all those years ago he didn't want to leave without some clarity of how the case was handled.

He watched as the detective raised his eyebrows, just ever so slightly and it annoyed him that he was being dismissed.

'Well, I can't see how I can help you. We never found out what happened that day and no one has come forward since,' said Detective Fairbrother. 'Look son,' he continued. 'I wasn't convinced by the boyfriend's story at the time. It was only his word that she had gone off for a run, never to return. There were no sightings of her leaving the house or on her run. We searched the house of course but there was no evidence of any foul play. Now, if you had a DNA match to the missing girl that would be something else. I'm sorry, but it's a dead end.'

The detective watched as the young man's shoulders slumped. He tried to think of something else to say. 'Look, like you said she may have left him and had a baby without him knowing but to stay away this long and to give up the baby shows us that if she is out there somewhere she probably wants to stay hidden.'

'Yes, you are probably right,' conceded Tom. 'I just wanted to cover all the bases and speaking to you made sense. I'm sorry if I've wasted your time.' He felt a little daft to have even come. Just because John hadn't recognised Fiona it didn't mean this mysterious woman was his mother instead. He was letting this all get to him.

Tom got to his feet and hesitated at the door as if he was going to say more but realised there was little more to say. Detective Fairbrother sat back in his chair lost in thought.

# TWELVE

Tom fidgeted as he waited, shifting his weight from one foot to the other. He leaned his head to one side, pressing his ear towards his shoulder, feeling a satisfying crack as the tension was temporarily relieved.

His parents were due in on the next flight and a stubborn knot of worry sat deep in his stomach. However much he had mulled everything over, he still couldn't decide how to broach the subject of his DNA results but more importantly at this moment he had the unenviable task of telling them about Serena's illness. There was no doubt in his mind that his mum would have questions as soon as she saw that only Tom had arrived to collect them from the airport. Her sixth sense would tell her instantly that something was up.

He moved to a plastic seat and sat down only to rise again a few seconds later and start pacing back and forth impatiently, keeping an eye on the gate that they would be coming through at any minute. He caught sight of his dad first. With a flick of his hand in a short wave, his dad let him know he had spotted him and moments later his parents and a trolley full of luggage stood before him. They looked tanned and rested and happier than he had seen them in years.

His mother pulled him in for a lengthy, tight hug, followed by a shorter one and slap on the back from his old man.

'No Serena?' his mum asked, as he knew she would. She was glancing over his shoulder in case she was on her way back from the toilet or from one of the kiosks serving drinks.

'She wasn't feeling all that well,' he said. He quickly fended off any other questions with 'she's at your house waiting so you will see her in no time.' He took hold of the trolley and moved off using the tactic as a distraction method. He called back to them over his shoulder. 'The car parking runs out in five minutes so we better get going.'

For now, his mum seemed happy enough with his answer and Tom kept slightly ahead of them as they made their way out of the terminal building towards the carpark. As Tom lifted the luggage into the boot, Fiona settled herself in the passenger seat with David sitting directly behind her. Once they had clicked in their seat belts, Tom checked his mirrors, and they began their journey home.

The excitement of their trip was evident as Fiona relayed stories of all the far-flung places they had visited and the many colourful characters they had met. David only spoke to fill in extra details or in answer to one of his wife's questions.

Tom was happy to listen, although he remained distracted, pondering how to break the news. With only a few miles left to travel Tom knew it was time to speak up. He couldn't turn up at the house without warning them how ill Serena was.

Her appearance would speak volumes and they would immediately see her loss of weight as well as the darkness under her eyes, even more prominent now that her face was so pale. When his mum finally stopped for breath and before she got going with another story of their adventures, he rather clumsily blurted the words out so that he had no more excuses to put it off any longer.

'Look Mum, Dad, I don't want to worry you, but the fact is, Serena's been feeling unwell a lot lately.'

An immediate look of concern filled his mother's face. Tom took one hand off the wheel and gently squeezed her hand.

'You're going to see a change in her, so I needed to warn you before we get home.'

He glanced sideways at his mum. Tears were already beginning to form in her eyes and his dad kept eye contact with Tom in the mirror.

'What's wrong with her?' his dad asked.

'The doctor says she has an immune disorder.' His mum let out an involuntary groan.

'She has had blood tests and a bone marrow biopsy. There are drugs to manage any infections but ultimately, she needs to find a stem cell match,' Tom continued.

The tension in the car became overwhelming. Tom spotted a lay-by up ahead and he pulled the car over to the side of the road, so he could give them both time to take it all in. The last thing Serena needed was his mum's distraught tears and being bombarded with questions the minute they saw her.

'Why didn't you call us?' his mum was asking. She had an edge to her voice, part panic and part anger. 'We would have come straight home.'

The anguish in her eyes made Tom feel dreadful.

'There was nothing you could do,' he said gently, 'and Serena made me promise not to. She didn't want you to cut your trip short and she is adamant that she will be OK. Although we need to find her a stem cell donor as soon as we can.'

Tom couldn't help but watch for a reaction from either parent. His mum was still crying, so it was hard spot any reaction from her. His dad was facing forward staring intently at the back of his wife's headrest.

'Of course, we will get a test as soon as we can. I will call our doctor in the morning,' he said. His eyes connected with Tom's again in the windscreen mirror and Tom held his gaze for a moment.

'I had a check but unfortunately I wasn't a match,' said Tom and this time he was sure there was a small flicker in his dad's eyes. He longed to bring up the facts of his paternity, but he knew now wasn't the time, so he pushed those thoughts firmly to one-side. They had more than enough to be dealing with for tonight. His main priority at this moment was Serena, and he knew that they must put all their efforts into making her well again.

Tom watched as his mum wiped her eyes with tissues she had found at the bottom of her handbag and began to calm a little. His dad looked tense and deep in thought.

'Are you ready to head off and see Serena now?' asked Tom.

'Yes,' said his dad. 'Come on, let's go and speak to her and tell her that we will of course be tested to see if either of us are a match.'

Fiona had shifted around in her seat so she could look directly at her husband and their eyes stayed locked for a few moments before she turned back around and leaned her head against the window.

As the car entered the driveway, the outside light was automatically triggered, bathing them in crisp white light. The front door of the house opened as they were getting out of the car, and there stood Serena. She looked better than when Tom had left. She had obviously tried to put a face on, and with the subtle make up she had succeeded in it at least giving her cheeks some colour. It was easy to see the weight loss though and he heard a soft intake of breath from his mum as she laid eyes on her youngest child.

'Hi guys,' Serena said brightly as she reached them. 'You look wonderful. I've put the kettle on,' she added with a smile.

'That's my girl,' said David putting his arms around her. 'Let's get inside. It's cold out here.' Tom followed the others in. He decided to bring their bags in later when everyone had settled down.

Once inside the large hallway, Tom watched as his mum and Serena embraced. He could see that his mum was trying hard not to show any reaction of how fragile Serena seemed. Serena was so upbeat that he imagined his mum wanted to keep the mood as light as possible and he was glad when she smiled as brightly as she could at her only daughter.

Watching her closely though he could see a sadness behind her eyes, and he knew it was taking all her strength not to burst in tears again. She busied herself by hanging up their coats on the cloakroom hooks and Tom ushered the others into the kitchen to make some tea, giving her a few extra moments to collect herself. Tom was proud of how well Serena kept it together as she explained her illness to their parents. She kept her emotions under control and answered their questions directly and calmly. It appeared that in the last few days she had come to terms with at least some of what was ahead of her and was determined to use all her energy to fight against it.

Tom carefully studied his parents as Serena explained that with a stem cell transplant, she would be able to have a full and active life. The distress was still visible on their faces, but they were beginning to understand what was ahead for the whole family. It would be later that evening when David and Fiona were alone in their bedroom, that the worry would hit them, and they would hold and comfort each other after the day's events.

As Tom prepared for bed, he felt relieved that they had promised once again that they would be tested as soon as they could. Serena had seemed grateful for this and if it turned out there was no forthcoming match, there was still some vague hope of finding a long-lost relative who could help her.

Of course, when the time came to talk about their parentage, Tom knew he would feel upset at being lied to all this time, but he also knew deep down that his feelings for his mother wouldn't change. She had always been a perfect mum and he was sure nothing could make him feel any differently and that Serena would feel the same. As for his dad, David would always feel like his real dad. He was the one who had been there throughout his life and even though Tom now knew that he wasn't his flesh and blood, his feelings wouldn't change towards him. All he could hope for was that David was already aware of the fact because if not a whole can of worms could be opened.

As he laid his head on the soft pillow in his old childhood bed, he wished they hadn't started all this now and that they were still in the dark. At least Serena could be certain after the DNA test that David was her father, and they would all have to pray he would be the match they were hoping for.

# THIRTEEN

The next morning after a hearty breakfast, Tom drove back to London. His parents proved true to their word and before he had left, he had heard his dad making an appointment with his doctor.

Serena was happy that progress was being made and she promised him she would spend most of her days watching old movies and resting. For her, the garden was a godsend, big enough for her to get some gentle exercise but closed off enough not to have to socialise with others. Tom understood that she wasn't keen on the looks people would give her, instant judgments on why she was so thin. He knew it made her feel uncomfortable, but he wished she would venture a bit further afield. She had already confided in him that she was looking forward to a time when she would be able to join him in London. In the big city she would be one of many and to be honest no-one took much notice of anyone else, so it wasn't the same as the small village of their childhood.

Tom knew the wait for the result would feel as excruciating slow as last time and he found it hard to think of anything else. He called Serena each evening after he returned home from work, smiling to himself as she complained of being 'thoroughly smothered,' and how their mums continual feeding her up was driving her mad.

'It's just like she can't have any other conversation with me except something to do with food. All she ever says is "Are you hungry? What will you manage to eat?" Blah blah. I know she means well but I wish she would give it a rest.' She moaned.

Tom could imagine his sister pumping her arms against the soft duvet in frustration as she spoke.

'You'll just have to think up another conversation to draw her into,' he said. 'Anyway, it's only for a few more days and it's how she copes with the worry. Don't you remember when either of us were off sick from school? She would bring us that awful soup until we got better.'

'Blimey, yes, I'd forgotten about that stuff. Maybe you can't buy that vile stuff anymore otherwise I would be full of it now. OK maybe I'll stop moaning now. At least the food I've been getting is edible.'

Tom was just grateful there with someone on hand in case she took a turn for the worst.

'Well, good luck for tomorrow,' he said as they ended their call. Serena was due at the hospital the following day to start what was likely to be numerous blood transfusions, while they waited for a match. Tom knew she was nervous, and they had already chatted longer than usual, and it was way past the time she should have gotten to sleep. He hoped she could put her head on the pillow and drift off straight away. They were both trying not to pin their hopes too firmly on David being a suitable donor.

Sophie stayed at Tom's flat now, more often than she was at hers. She had been propped up alongside him in bed, reading her book while he was talking to Serena. She had been a godsend, and he didn't know how he would have coped without her.

'Is she nervous?' she asked, placing her book on the dressing table.

'A bit, but I think she's ready to start treatment.'

'I'm sure she is. Hospitals just make me nervous. We can check on her tomorrow evening and give her some moral support,' she said. He leaned over and kissed her on the forehead.

'Definitely,' he replied. 'So, tell me more about your news' he said changing the subject. Sophie had turned up earlier, excited that she had got a small ensemble part in a West End show and was due to start rehearsals in a couple of weeks. He thought back to earlier when he had asked her to move in full time and the squeal of delight she had given as she leapt into his arms. He was delighted that she wanted to, and they talked excitedly about spending their evenings together curled up together on the sofa or taking long walks in the leafy park at the end of the road. By the time they drifted off to sleep it was decided. This weekend they would pick up her belongings and move them into his flat.

The call came a few days later just as he was putting his key in the door after a long tiring day at work. It was his mum, and she relayed the news that David had been confirmed as a match. Her voice cracked a few times with emotion and Tom could only just hold back the tears himself. There was no mention of her test results, but Tom couldn't have cared less. This was the breakthrough they had all been hoping for.

She explained that they would have a few more appointments to get through and an array of blood tests to endure before the transplant could take place, but the relief was enormous. Tom was determined to be around when Serena went into hospital and promised to drive down every weekend to see her, as she would be in hospital for at least a month.

When Sophie arrived home, he picked her up and twirled her around, so she knew it was good news even before he could explain. She was as happy as he was. She had become extremely close to Serena in the past few weeks. They opened a good bottle of bubbly that night over dinner and toasted to a life that would hopefully get back to normal in the not-too-distant future. As the weekend approached Tom and Sophie packed a small bag of clothes and necessities ready for their trip to Lyhampton to visit Serena. They were looking forward to the chance of spending some time with Serena and from what they had heard from Fiona, although she still needed a lot of rest, she was in good spirits.

Traffic was light and they sang along with the tunes on the local radio station. As they turned into the driveway, they found Serena perched on the front porch waiting for them. Tom hugged her tightly before Sophie took her turn to wrap her arms around her. They then made their way through the side gate to the back garden. The sun was shining brightly, and the beautiful surroundings lifted their spirits further, as they greeted Tom's parents'.

David finished pruning the last of the roses before he came over to join them. Fiona went into the house to collect a large jug of iced tea. She appeared minutes later with a tray holding some beautiful cut glasses along with a matching jug and place it onto the wrought iron table. She poured the cool liquid into the glasses and then passed a glass to each of them.

'Wow, it's getting hot,' David said before downing the contents in one go.

'We couldn't have picked a more beautiful day,' agreed Fiona, 'and even better to have us all together.' She was absolutely beaming and looked more relaxed than she had since finding out the news on the way back from the airport. It was lovely to see that part of the weight had been lifted off her now that treatment was on the horizon.

Tom felt her squeeze his shoulder as she sat down next to him. He thought she looked lovely in a long flowing flowery dress with a soft pink cardigan. It looked perfect for the weather and her elegance made David look hot, sweaty, and quite scruffy in comparison.

'I think I will have a quick shower,' David said as if hearing Tom's thoughts. He absently rubbed his left arm, drawing Tom's attention to a large purple bruise which looked like it was beginning to fade.

'That looks sore,' said Sophie, following Tom's gaze.

'No, it's nothing. Always happens with blood tests, I must be oversensitive to the needle,' he said. 'I won't be long, just a quick freshen up.'

'Glad I don't bruise like that,' piped up Serena 'I'm beginning to feel like a human pin cushion.' But this was said with a glint in her eye, and she was coping well with the treatment so far.

'We are just glad your father can help you with his stem cells,' said Fiona. She smiled at Serena. 'I wish I had been a match but at least one of us was,' she finished thoughtfully. Tom could feel himself stiffen slightly, but he kept his facial features relaxed, not wanting to give away any reaction. He wondered how she had explained not being a match to David or if he had known beforehand that all hopes relied on him?

Later Tom lay in bed trying to sleep, listening to Sophie's laboured breathing. *What if his mum hadn't even bothered to get the test?* He thought. *If she wasn't Serena's biological mother, a test would be useless. But surely that would have been hard to keep from his dad? Maybe she just went through with the test and knew it would come back with the result she expected?*

Tom made a mental note to do his best to find out any other information from David tomorrow. He would have the opportunity as Sophie and Fiona were going to have lunch and do a bit of shopping together. He was pleased that his mum was trying to get to know Sophie and as Serena was likely to have a rest at some point, he was sure he could get his dad alone for a while. *Yes, I'll do that* he thought, feeling slightly better and with a plan in mind, he managed to drift off to sleep.

The following day while Fiona and Sophie were in town, the others relaxed in the spacious garden. David was surprisingly talented in the kitchen, and he had whipped up some omelettes that were delicious. Serena was pushing hers around her plate and only managing to eat small amounts.

They were talking about the games they used to play in the garden and how Serena would always go to the same hiding place when playing hide and seek. It was always a source of amusement to David, although Tom in his younger years would become totally frustrated. Serena was just over two years younger and, while Tom had mastered the idea of hiding in new and exciting places – and the garden was full of wonderful places to hide – Serena seemed to think the idea was to always hide behind the wooden shed. After a few games, Tom would get angry and shout at her and the whole thing would end in tears.

They all found it funny now and it was lovely to see Serena laugh. She was laughing so much she made a loud snorting noise, which set them all off again. Tom stopped abruptly when he saw the blood starting to trickle from her nose. A steady stream started, and he rushed inside to grab some tissues.

'Don't panic,' said Serena, her voice muffled through the tissue, when he had returned. 'It happens quite a lot recently. It's only a nosebleed. I'll go and lie down for a bit. You two have fun and leave me some cake for later.' She carried on eyeing the lemon drizzle cake until she disappeared inside.

'I could show you my new vegetable patch?' said his dad. He laughed as Tom rolled his eyes.

'Go on then,' said Tom with an exaggerated yawn. 'It's probably the best offer I'll have today.' David chuckled. He waited for Tom to get to his feet and then led the way towards the end of the garden.

# FOURTEEN

'Things seem to be going well with you and Sophie,' said his dad as they approached his prized vegetable patch.

'She's great. Honestly dad, I never thought I'd meet someone so perfect for me,' said Tom. A happy grin followed his words, totally lighting up his face. 'She's agreed to move in with me. I can't believe my luck.'

'That's fantastic son, I'm really pleased for you both.' He gave his son a pat on the back.

'I hope we will be as happy as you and mum,' said Tom and was surprised to see a slight flicker of doubt in his dad's eyes. It was so quick that he wasn't sure if he had imagined it. 'You and Mum are happy, aren't you?' he asked, watching his dad's reaction closely.

'Of course,' his dad reassured him. 'It's just that relationships can be complicated, and you should always go with your gut feelings. But you and Sophie seem good together.' They sat down on the small wooden bench that Tom and Serena had bought for their parents' last wedding anniversary. Both stayed silent for a moment, staring ahead at the array of vegetables his dad had managed to grow. Then Tom turned back to his dad.

'Do you regret something Dad?' he asked.

'No, I don't believe in hanging on to regrets and we probably all have a few. Your mother is a wonderful woman, she would do anything for you kids. You do know that don't you?' said his dad. Tom nodded and waited for his dad to go on. He could feel an underlying melancholy in the way his father spoke. He watched as his father rubbed the side of his head. *Was he about to come clean and tell Tom that he wasn't his real father?* Tom steeled himself for what was to come. His dad took a deep breath and then the moment seemed to pass.

'I'm becoming a sentimental old fool,' he said. 'Take no notice of me. I'm just glad I can help Serena in her time of need.'

'We are all glad but Dad, if there's something else you are trying to tell me, I'd like to hear it,' Tom pushed. His heart began to quicken in anticipation. His dad frowned once more and paused as if considering how to start. After a few of the longest seconds imaginable he opened his mouth to speak.

'Look Tom, the thing is…' Just at that moment Tom heard voices and David heard them too. He stopped mid-sentence and when they looked towards the house Tom could see that his mother and Sophie had arrived back.

'Dad?' he said again. His eyes pleaded with him to at least spill some of what he was about to say. Out of the corner of his eye Tom watched as Sophie plonked herself into one of the garden chairs, taking off her shoes and leaning back to take in the sunshine. His mother stood behind Sophie's chair staring towards Tom and David. Her eyes locked with his for a second before settling on David. She started walking up the path towards them and Tom could feel his dad's body stiffen.

'Dad?' he said once more, but David was no longer listening. He was transfixed on his wife approaching, and she firmly held his gaze. Fiona's face changed from the grim expression she wore until she reached them, into a smile.

'What are you two up to then? Huddled up here on your own?' She kept her eyes on David.

'Nothing much,' replied his dad and he stood up. He took hold of his wife's arm, and they began to walk back towards the house, leaving Tom to follow.

Tom stayed for a moment where he was. *What was that about? It seemed as if his dad was about to spill the beans on his parentage and his mum was having none of it. If she hadn't returned home, would his dad have opened up?*

It made him more determined to corner his dad another time and get to the bottom of it. Next week Serena would be having her transplant and once she was recovering, he would try to get some answers. For now, he felt like his life was on hold. Yes, he had fabulous parents and he had never wanted for anything, but he needed to find out the truth.

That evening they had a barbecue in the garden and the mood was light. There were fairy lights dotted around the garden and as night-time descended on them, it felt like a wonderland. The melodic trickle of the water in the fountain brought a certain calm and Tom felt content as he sipped his glass of red wine. He was holding Sophie's hand under the table and there was laughter as his parents told her of his past adventures.

The time he fell out of the big apple tree and nearly landed on the dog. His beloved 'Sooty' who had survived that ordeal but passed the summer after at the ripe old age of sixteen. Sooty had been Tom and Serena's best friend and the passing had hit them hard but memories of him and the fun they had in this garden over the years still warmed Tom's heart. He had been lucky to have had the happiest of childhoods and he must always remember that his parents couldn't have done a better job. He beamed at them now as they sat side by side across the table from him and Sophie. They both looked relaxed, so whatever had happened earlier had been long forgotten.

Serena was curled up in her chair with a warm blanket wrapped around her. It was obvious that she was enjoying the conversation and she piped up with a story of her own.

'Do you remember when I wouldn't leave Tom's room that time?' she asked, looking over at Fiona and David. 'I think I was bored, and he really wanted some privacy, so he picked me up and threw me out, not realising that I still had my fingers in the door when he slammed it!'

Tom rolled his eyes upwards and squeezed Sophie's hand tightly.

'She screamed the entire house down. It sounded like I was murdering her!' said Tom wincing at the memory. 'Doors had to remain open after that day if I remember correctly. Although I think you learnt your lesson Sis and didn't keep coming in to pester me after that.'

'Well, I realised I needed those fingers for my piano lessons,' said Serena, laughing at the memory.

'And on that note, I think we will go up to bed,' Tom said, getting up from the table, 'We need to head back after breakfast, but we will see you all in the morning.'

Sophie stood up to join him and hand in hand they made their way upstairs. Once encased in their room Sophie threw her arms around him.

'I love learning more about you,' she said as her lips nuzzled into his neck. 'Now I might do some exploring of my own,' she continued and started to unbutton his shirt. Tom let himself be pushed gently onto the bed and closed his eyes. He was worn out but as she nuzzled into his neck, he felt his body react. All thoughts were pushed aside as he happily succumbed to Sophie's touch.

The next morning after a quick breakfast, Tom and Sophie hugged the others and for about the third time in the last hour, wished Serena luck for the day of her transplant that coming week. Tom held on to her longer than usual and she gave him a big smile as they parted.

'I will be just fine,' she reassured him. 'Before you know it, I'll be back to my annoying self.' She laughed at him as he made a face.

'Let's make you better, but not well enough for that!' he teased.

Once in the car, Sophie put the radio on, and they travelled back to London. They listened to the tunes, engrossed in their own thoughts, without hardly a word uttered.

Back at the house Serena had gone back upstairs to get dressed and Fiona and David busied themselves clearing the table.

'You weren't going to tell him, were you?' Fiona asked under her breath, looking cautiously towards the door in case Serena reappeared.

'Of course not,' replied David. He kept his eyes averted from her, instead concentrating on collecting up the dirty plates.

'You know we can't speak about this to them, don't you?' she pushed. He could feel anger radiating from her, although the only tell-tale sign of this was in her tone of voice. On the outside she looked as calm as could be as she folded the tablecloth and placed it in a nearby drawer.

'Fiona, I know this. How many years has it been? Have I ever given you cause to doubt me?'

The plates he held made a faint clinking sound and he realised his hands were shaking. Fiona noticed too and made her way towards him.

'Come here, you are an old fool,' she said and took the plates from him, setting them down on to the sideboard before putting her arms around him. 'I'm sorry, I just panicked.'

'We are a team, you and I,' he replied holding her tight.

'Like I said, I panicked,' she said again, the anger beginning to subside. A small sob escaped, and he held her against his shoulder, until he felt the tension leaving her body. He slowly lifted her away so that he could look at her face.

'OK?' he said, running his finger down her cheek and collecting a tear. She nodded.

'I just couldn't bear to have the children look at me in a different way,' she began. 'I am their mother. I was the one who brought them up. I may not be their flesh and blood, but I did everything for them. I'm so happy that you can do the right thing for Serena and make her life better. But David, you must promise me they will never find out that I didn't give birth to them.' He could feel her desperation.

'I wasn't going to tell Tom anything. Come on love, I know how much you love the children. As far as I am concerned, they are our children through and through.'

She smiled at him.

'You mustn't torment yourself so. There is no need for either of them to ever find out. We covered the blood test, didn't we? Thank goodness I was a match. That at least made us have no reason to worry. Now go and get dressed and we will speak no more of it.'

Fiona looked deeply into his eyes and was reassured. He was her one and only love and she believed him when he said they were a team.

'Thank you, my darling,' she said and turned to leave the room.

David stood for a long time, staring into space. It took a massive amount of energy to push the thoughts of the children from his mind. He felt an enormous guilt that they didn't know the truth, but what good would it be now to bring it up? He consoled himself that he was able to make some amends. Helping Serena become healthy again was something he could do and maybe that would help remove some of the regrets of the past.

# FIFTEEN

## *Katie (1998)*

Mornings were the worst. As soon as I opened my eyes, the dread of another long day in captivity would hit me, hard. It had been weeks since he had stepped foot into the room, and slowly over time I had begun to relax. Maybe he wouldn't come back and violate me again. I prayed each night for this to be true.

The opening of the hatch and the delivery of food still made me jump each day though. My whole body would instantly tense as I listened for the bolts on the door being opened in case he would reappear. But so far, I had been left to my own devices.

The food was always good quality and very balanced. It was as if someone had taken great thought over my nutrition and what my body needed to remain healthy. I started doing exercise in the afternoons, mainly to while away some of the time. Physically I was probably as fit as I had always been despite the lack of space. I would pace up and down and do press ups against the wall, lunges, and squats. But regardless of my efforts, my mental health was suffering badly.

I would wake up throughout the night, sometimes with nightmares – or something I found even more distressing – I would have a lovely dream. I was in a park with Lucas, and we were holding hands. I basked in the love and happiness of this dream and then I would be hit by the harsh reality as I awoke, and I was still locked away. The feelings of joy at seeing Lucas would stay with me for hours afterwards and I began to daydream as often as I could. It felt like I was losing my grip on reality. And maybe that was a good thing.

By now I had lost all track of time and of how long I had been here. I just couldn't understand why he would keep me here. For sexual gratification? That seemed unlikely as he had not been near me since. After the day he had forced himself on me, I thought that was the explanation. That he would turn up whenever he felt the need and would force himself on me time and again. My relief that this hadn't happened was immense, but it also made me worry about what else he may have in store for me. I just couldn't shake the feeling that one day he would just stop bringing me food or that he would come in to kill me.

These thoughts would play over and over in my mind, and I could almost feel my sanity fading away, day by day. I would spend a lot of time thinking about Lucas and the turmoil he must be going through. Surely, he would be out looking for me, never giving up on the chance that I would be found. I had to hold on to hope in my heart, that he would never give up on me.

At the beginning, I had counted the days by watching the daylight turn to night in the window above. But as time went on, I tired of it and quickly lost track. Once I had missed a day, it just didn't seem to matter anymore. There was no purpose to my day, except for staying alive and some days I longed to just curl up and die. Not knowing when or if I would ever be free filled me with the most despair. It must have been around a week later when the conundrum of why I was taken was solved.

I had just finished my breakfast and as requested placed the tray back at the hatch as I did every day. I listened to the familiar scrape of the metal flap opening on the opposite side of the door and the tray being removed. I waited, breath held, straining to hear the departing footsteps. For almost a minute there was no noise at all. I took a slow breath and then held it again so I could focus on any sounds. Then, through the silence came the unmistakable clonk of the bolts and the threat of the heavy door being opened. In an instant, adrenalin coursed through my veins, and I had to force myself to breathe. He was back…

I braced myself for his entrance, planting my feet solidly on the concrete. A strong stance, ready to fight. My skin began to crawl at the thought of him touching me again and I knew I was going to fight hard and at least bring some pain to him for what he was about to do.

When the figure moved into view, I was shocked. My first thought was that he was bringing the woman into captivity with me, and I looked beyond her, waiting for him to appear behind. But the doorway remained empty, and I soon realised he wasn't coming. I stood completely still as the woman moved further into the room. The same woman that I had asked for help all those weeks before, but she looked different somehow.

It was like a new person altogether. Her whole demeanour was different. Gone was the meekness she had shown the day I had arrived at her door and what replaced it was a cold, hard stare, a steeliness not obvious at our last meeting.

It wasn't just the dark blue power suit she was wearing, which was a total contrast to the old dowdy nightdress she had been wearing before. This was a woman in complete control. She looked at me now, a smile playing with her lips as she registered the confusion on my face. Automatically I backed away.

'Surprised to see me?' She stopped just short of the bed. 'I expect you are. I've brought something for you,' she said. Even her voice was sharper and the whole scene threw me completely. I could feel the energy draining from my limbs and I had to hold onto the head end of the bed to stop myself from collapsing.

'Why are you here? I don't understand,' I managed to blurt out, eyes wide.

A cruel smirk remained on the woman's lips as she stood in front of me. She was holding something in her hand.

'No dear, you probably wouldn't understand, and I really don't have time for a big explanation.' She moved closer to the bed, and I watched her tossed an item on top of the bedclothes.

'Go and pee on this and then I can get back to my day.' The woman spat the words at me with such venom it took my breath away. I drew my eyes away from her spiteful face and looked towards the stick like item she had thrown. I moved closer and slowly picked it up. I knew from the shape of it what it was without studying it closely, but still I turned it over and over in my hands. It was a pregnancy test.

Vomit rose sharply in my throat, and I couldn't hold it down. The meal I had recently eaten came up violently and half-digested pieces of toast shot across the floor.

'Christ!' shrieked the woman as she moved back sharply, but not before a few flecks of my sick landed on her polished shoes. Her eyes narrowed on the scene before her. 'Maybe that gives us a clue,' she added, and a sadistic glint of hope appeared in her eyes.

I felt dizzy and weak, so I lowered myself gingerly onto the edge of the bed.

'Great, now I'm going to have to clean up before work. You can get on with that.' She gestured to the test I was still holding in my hand. 'I will send him down in about an hour for it and to clean up this mess.' She didn't try to hide the distaste across her features as she glared at me. 'You had better hope that one time got you pregnant, or you'll be expecting another visit.'

And with that she swept out of the room. The door slammed shut and I could hear the bolts being viciously forced into place.

I stared blankly at the test in my hand. My whole body was shaking with the stark realisation of why I had been taken. They were keeping me here to have a baby. This also told me that I was not going to get out of here for months. The thought made my head spin and I swallowed hard, fighting to keep the sickness from reappearing. *And what happens then? When I have had the baby, and am no longer needed? What will they do to me then?*

# SIXTEEN

Detective Alan Fairbrother was on the last day of a week's holiday in the beautiful coastal resort of Bigbury-on-sea. He was sitting on a soft tartan rug on the beach with his wife of 25 years, Pam.

She was a petite woman with hair the colour of milk chocolate. She looked much younger than her age but there were a few tell-tale grey hairs creeping along her hairline. She had an attractive oval shaped face, and she was a happy soul. It was probably what Alan had been drawn to, her positive attitude to life, along with her good looks of course. He was more than aware that he was no oil painting, and numerous times he had had to endure someone telling him what a lucky man he was, complete with a condescending raise of their eyebrows. But luckily Pam loved him with all her heart and had done since the day they had met. He was a lucky man indeed. He often thanked his lucky stars, that after a day of dealing with violent and often heart-breaking crimes, he could at least come home to Pam, and this balanced things out a bit.

Alan stared at the foam along the shoreline as the gentle waves lolled inwards. Pam was oblivious to her surroundings as she rooted around in the ice box trying to find the butter knife that had inevitably travelled to the bottom of the box. Eventually she managed to hook her finger round it and then proceeded to lather a thick layer of butter over the soft baguette they had picked up from a bakery earlier that day.

'Where did you fancy eating later?' She asked her husband. There was not even a flicker of attention on her husband's face.

'Alan! Are you listening to me?'

He was lost in thought. Gazing further out now at the vast body of water in front of him. He brought his mind back to the present.

'Sorry honey, my mind was elsewhere.'

'That was obvious,' she said. She smiled. 'I was just wondering if you fancy the pub we passed on the way down the hill. We could go there for dinner, or shall we eat back at the cottage?'

'Let's go to the pub as it's our last night,' Alan replied, before his attention returned to the sea.

The subject on Alan's mind was Katie Reed. Something had been troubling him since he had met the young man claiming to be her son a few weeks before. He couldn't put his finger on it, but the case remained at the back of his mind, gnawing away at him. *Maybe when I get back, I'll pull the file and just read it over* he thought. *It was a curious one.*

After they ate the crusty bread and various cheesy delights they had picked up at the morning market, he lay back and closed his eyes, putting all thoughts out of his head for an afternoon snooze.

Back at the station a few days later as lunchtime approached Alan Fairbrother was reading through the file. There was something about the photograph of the young girl that haunted him. Maybe it was because she was roughly the same age – when she went missing – as his daughter Sarah and he couldn't imagine how her parents had coped. He also remembered how distraught her boyfriend had been, even though there had been doubts about him at the time. Not that there was any evidence that the boyfriend had hurt her but most times he had seen this type of disappearance, the ones closest knew more than they let on.

  Due to the lack of sightings on that day, the only explanation they could eventually come up with was that the girl had just gone off on her own free will. Sometimes it really was as simple as that, with some poor soul being left by their partner with no word. Maybe they had a secret they felt they couldn't share, or they had just plain had enough of the life they had been living.

  No one had seen the girl leave in the morning. The only comments from the neighbours were that the couple who lived in the flat didn't socialise much. It seemed like they were too engrossed in each other to let anyone else in. The boyfriend had told the police that his girlfriend had only started running a few months before. She had mentioned to him that she usually did a circuit of Bay Tree Meadows, but nobody knew which route she took to get there and there were several. Police officers were sent door to door in the area surrounding the meadows and covered the vast area with a fine-toothed comb, but nothing had come to light.

After a lunch of a pre-prepared salad, Alan wandered down to the tiny kitchen at the end of the corridor. As he put two heaped spoons of strong coffee into a mug, he took a couple of chocolate covered biscuits from the communal tin, which held all sorts of naughty treats. *So much for sticking to the salad* he thought but he found the temptation too much.

By the time he had stirred the boiling water into his coffee, he had demolished the biscuits, so he picked out another couple before making his way back to his office. As he stood looking out of the window, watching the bustle of cars and people down below, he made his mind up to look up the boyfriend. There was no harm in seeing what he was up to these days.

On his next free day, he found himself sitting outside Katie's boyfriends' house, wondering why he was dragging all this up. When he had phoned ahead, he had to admit the reception had been a little frosty, but he couldn't really blame the guy for that. Part of him felt like he should have just left it alone but now he was here, parked up outside, he couldn't just change his mind. He could imagine the complaint to the station of him calling out of the blue and then not following through.

The house wasn't the same one Alan had visited all those years before, but it wasn't that far away. Alan sat for a moment thinking to himself. *If it was Pam that had gone missing, wouldn't he want to get further away than here? Start his life again, without the constant reminders?*

He considered this for a moment and then, tried to imagine himself in the boyfriends' shoes. Would he make the decision to stay close by in case she ever returned? Focusing on what it would be like if Pam disappeared, he could understand how hard it would be to leave the area when there had been no closure and there was still the faintest hope. The curtain twitched and he realised he had been spotted, so somewhat reluctantly he got out of his car and sauntered up to the front door.

'Detective,' John said, as he swung the door open.

'Mr Hanson,' said Alan. 'I'm sure you remember me.'

'Of course.' He stood aside so the detective could enter. 'Don't worry, I don't believe in holding grudges. I may have blamed your department at the time for not doing enough, but it wasn't personal. Just despair, I suppose. I just couldn't believe she was gone.'

He directed the detective into the kitchen and offered him a drink.

'A coffee would be great please. Black, no sugar,' said Alan. They remained silent while John prepared the drinks, and once he had handed one to Alan, they moved towards the sitting room next door.

'I assume you are contacting me after all this time because of Tom?' began John once they were seated. 'He came to see me, to tell me he thinks I am his dad, but honestly, I don't believe it. How can I get my head around that? I don't think I want to consider that Katie went off while pregnant to have a child on her own, or worse she ran off with someone else. She would have told me. I know she would have.' He trailed off, as if not knowing what else to say.

'Dragging all this back up must be hard on you,' said the detective. 'Tom came to see me too, but I had no other information for him. Since that day I've been mulling the case over again and even though no other evidence has come to light I've found myself not being able to move on without at least checking in with anyone involved. In case we can find any answers to his claim.'

Alan sat forward in his chair.

'Look, I know it isn't something you want to think about, but could that have been what happened? Is it possible that Katie left deliberately that morning to have the child alone, or to leave you for someone else?'

John frowned. The poor man looked defeated.

'Who knows?' he replied, 'At the time I would definitely have said that there was no way. But now? I've never had any luck with love, so I suppose I can see it could have been possible.'

'Why do you say that?' asked Detective Fairbrother.

'I had a relationship after Katie went missing, a year or so after, with a friend of both of ours. It was with a girl who used to be in our group of friends. To start with she was a shoulder to cry on and she missed Katie too. Then, many months later it just sort of morphed into us being together. It was another six months after that when I found out she was sleeping with one of my best friends Matty, and I was left crushed. Since then, I've been pretty much alone.'

Alan felt sorry for the man in front of him and the cards he had been dealt. He could imagine a younger John, the one before his girlfriend had gone missing, had probably been a happy go lucky type, without a care in the world. But even now, after all the years that had past, it was obvious that the man before him was still feeling the effects of the trauma he had endured.

'To be fair to her now,' John was saying. 'I think she had always wanted to be with Matty, but she had felt sorry for me, I guess. And once we had crossed that friendship line, she saw no way of going back to being just friends. Basically, it was one big mess, and it ruined a lot of relationships.'

Alan couldn't tell if John seemed more distraught about the girl he had a relationship with, or that a best friend had done the dirty on him. Both would be hard to deal with.

'But looking back on it now,' continued John, 'if I am truthful, she never filled the void that was Katie.'

'So, you don't think you always know what is going on in your partners head?' said the detective. 'Is that what you mean?'

'Yeah, that's about right,' said John sadly. His thoughts were, as Alan had guessed, more on his broken friendship with Matty but he just couldn't bring himself to forgive him for the betrayal, even after all this time.

'I hear through the grapevine that they are still together but no kids. Matty never wanted any as far as I can remember.'

Detective Fairbrother took the last sip of coffee and placed his empty mug on the side table before he stood.

'I'm sorry to have brought all this up again,' he said. 'I'll try and talk to a few of the people interviewed at that time and if I find out anything else I'll be in touch.'

They reached the front door and John opened it. The detective turned to him as he passed though the doorway.

'So, are you going to have a relationship with this guy who thinks he's your son?'

This fascinated Alan. He felt sorry for what John had gone through in the past but maybe this was something positive that could come out of it all. He could see that John was considering the question.

'I've spoken to him on the phone a couple of times, and he has suggested that I get a paternity test. Which I suppose will confirm it. When I'm ready, I will do. I suppose it would be better to know one way or the other. But I enjoy having him to talk to regardless, so yes, I think we will stay in touch.' He smiled now and thanked the detective for coming and for caring enough to look once more into Katie's disappearance.

As Detective Fairbrother returned to his car he felt determined to find some sort of closure for the man he had just met again, whose life had not seemed to move on since that day so long ago.

# SEVENTEEN

Tom answered the phone on the second ring. He had kept his mobile phone close to his bed and had been awake for the last two hours, facing towards the bedside cabinet, willing it to ring. The clock showed 7.30am. It felt like he had not had a wink of sleep.

'She's fine.' The relief in his mum's voice was apparent. 'And your dad's fine too. Obviously, it will be a while before Serena feels better, but the doctor is happy with how it all went.'

Tom wished he was there with her and able to give her a hug.

'Thank goodness!' said Tom, sitting up. Sophie stirred next to him and looked up at him with a smile on her lips.

'I'll give you a call later,' said Tom to his mother. 'We will come down and visit her in the hospital this weekend.'

He put the phone down and wriggled back down under the duvet. Sophie snuggled up to him and as she held him, she could feel his tension receding. With her head on his shoulder, they drifted back into a peaceful sleep.

It was just over a month before Serena came home. It was a miserable Thursday afternoon, but they were all hoping to have better weather when Tom and Sophie drove down to see her at the weekend. Until then Serena was going to rest as much as she could.

Saturday morning rolled around before they knew it and by 9am, Tom and Sophie had packed the car with some essentials and a few presents for Serena and they headed excitedly off towards the South Coast. It was going to be a flying visit as Tom had an important meeting at his office on Monday and he needed to prepare for it.

This time the atmosphere for the journey was relaxed and they sang along to some old 80's hits on the radio. It was just coming into September and the weather was changeable. The morning had started off with light rain, but that had quickly dispersed and now they were swathed in beautiful sunshine.

As they pulled into the driveway, they couldn't be happier. Sophie was first out of the car and set about getting the presents out of the boot. They had brought a large bouquet of flowers to cheer Serena up and Tom had picked up some books written by Serena's favourite author and some Belgian chocolates for her to enjoy.

The house felt different as soon as they entered. It was lighter somehow.

'Hi, you two,' said his mum coming into the hallway, as they let themselves in. 'Help yourself to a drink. I'm just taking this up to Serena and then you can go up and see her. She's finding it hard to stay in bed, so she will be pleased to have some visitors,' she added. She made her way past them and up the stairs.

Tom and Sophie walked through to the kitchen and Tom opened the fridge. He pointed out to Sophie which cupboard the glasses were in and she retrieved two tall tumblers. She placed them on the worktop, and he wandered over and filled them with ice cold orange juice, before returning the carton to the fridge door. They wandered through to the lounge and found David asleep in one of the armchairs, his newspaper still across his lap. He stirred as they entered and gave a little jump.

'Oh hello, I must have just rested my eyes for a moment,' he said pulling himself back upright. Sophie grinned at Tom.

'How are you feeling?' asked Tom. He bent down to pick up the newspaper that had slipped to the floor in his father's haste to appear awake. He placed it neatly on the side table.

'I'm great,' replied his dad. 'It's nice to see you both. Serena will be glad to see you.'

'She's just eating the food I took up and then you can go and see her,' said Fiona, reappearing at the door. She walked over to the chair next to her husband and waved her hand at Tom and Sophie, indicating for them to sit on the leather sofa opposite them.

'So, how are things in London?' She asked.

'Work is fine thanks. Same old thing,' said Tom 'but Sophie has some news.' He turned to Sophie with a proud look on his face.

'I've just auditioned for a new play,' said Sophie beaming 'and I heard a few days ago that they want me for one of the roles.'

'Wow, that's fantastic,' said David. 'Congratulations!'

Fiona got to her feet and leaned down to give Sophie a hug.

'That's wonderful news. We will definitely come and see you on opening night,' she promised.

'We have a few months rehearsals but that would be lovely,' said Sophie pleased with their support. Tom was grinning from ear to ear.

'I am so proud of her,' he said. 'We have a star in our midst.'

'OK, steady on,' said Sophie, but it was obvious she was happy with his praise.

When they had finished their drinks, Tom left Sophie downstairs while he went up to see Serena, and she said she would follow in a little while. As he walked up the stairs, he thought of all those times when he used to sneak into Serena's room for a midnight feast and chat while their parents were sleeping. It made him smile remembering that they had only been caught once in all the times they had done it.

He tapped gently on the door and a soft voice could be heard on the other side. He pushed open the door slowly and as soon as Serena saw it was him, her face lit up.

'Oh, I'm glad it's you! Mum's fussing is getting a bit much,' she said rolling her eyes.

'At least you won't starve,' said Tom looking at the half-eaten tray full of food on the nightstand beside Serena's bed. She was propped up with at least three enormous plumped up pillows.

'Yes, you are right,' she said with a small laugh. 'There was enough food for at least three patients. It is nice to be looked after though,' she conceded.

'So, how are you feeling?' he asked. He took her hand and gave it a squeeze.

'I'm not too bad. The doctor said I will probably feel like getting up in a few days' time. You have no idea how much I want to do as soon as I have the energy.'

'I'm happy for you Sis, but make sure you don't overdo it,' said Tom. He knew her too well and she had always been a nightmare when she was ill. Never able to sit still for more than five minutes. No wonder she was finding it hard.

'Don't you start,' she replied but there was a smile on her face.

'Are you going to get your better half to come up and see me?' she asked.

'I'll go and get her,' he said amused. He was happy with the instant bond his sister and girlfriend had. Serena didn't have many female friends, she had always felt more comfortable with men, but Sophie seemed to be the exception.

'Oh, and bring some playing cards or something back with you. I am so bored and that'll keep us entertained for a while.'

Once they had caught up on their various news, they played Gin Rummy for an hour or so. When Serena began to yawn, Tom signalled to Sophie that it was time for her to have a nap. Serena smiled tiredly at them.

'I'm so happy for you, Sophie. Congratulations again for getting the part,' she said. 'As soon as I can, I'll come up and stay with you for a few days in London if that's OK?'

'Of course. We'll look forward to it,' said Tom. 'Now get some rest and save that energy.'

With those last words Tom and Sophie backed out of the room and Serena sank back under the heavy duvet and was asleep before they had reached the bottom step.

'Don't worry too much about her,' said his mum when they were back in the lounge. 'We will take good care of her until she has recovered.'

'I know Mum. You really are doing a great job,' said Tom pulling her towards him for a hug. 'Sorry we can't stay longer but as soon as we have more time we'll come back down.'

Once in the car Tom and Sophie talked of how well Serena looked considering all she had been through.

'When she is better and comes up to visit, I'll have the chat with her about the results and we can finally decide whether to bring it up with Mum and Dad or to do some more digging,' said Tom.

'Yes,' agreed Sophie. 'I know you've been dying to find out more, and that time is coming.'

'After what we've been through recently, I'm not sure it's as important as I once thought,' he added. 'Serena needs to concentrate on getting better and we can go from there.'

# EIGHTEEN

## *Katie (1999)*

The sickness had stopped, and I had lost count of how much time had passed, but from the size of my belly I could guess there wasn't long to go. I no longer had to fear the man's visits. Since becoming pregnant he had been courteous and even kind to me. He never came any closer than he needed to, and I had slowly relaxed into our new routine.

The day he had come to collect the pregnancy test, he had looked almost as relieved as I felt, and I remember finding this odd. It was as if the act of forcing himself on me wasn't something he wanted, only something he was prepared to do to father a child. I had watched him slowly turning the test over in his hands as he read the result. His body visibly relaxing in front of my eyes as he stared at the two lines on the display indicating a positive result. He kept his eyes diverted away from me as he shoved the test into his jean pocket and abruptly left the room.

Time moved on as slowly as ever. I read and re-read the magazines he had brought for me over and over until I could recite them word for word. The magazines were old, from at least a year before I was taken, and I guess this was to disguise how much time had passed.

    The thoughts of escaping no longer went through my mind. I had resigned myself to my fate and tried to keep as calm as I could, eating all the nutritious food that was delivered. Regardless of what would happen to me, I wanted the baby growing inside of me to be healthy. I had a lot of time to sit on the bed and think. Feeling the changes going on in my body, I would one minute feel elated that I would become a mother, and then in the next moment, a crippling dread would take over. I knew deep down that they couldn't let me go, and I also knew that it was likely when the time came that they would take my precious baby. For now, all I could do was to put my worries aside and do whatever was necessary to keep this baby alive.

I would sit for hours with a protective hand across my swollen belly, feeling a closeness to my unborn child, daydreaming constantly and shocked by the fierce love I already had for the little miracle growing inside. I would imagine that he or she was Lucas's, and I held this dream tight, playing it over and over. I conjured up a scene in my mind of the two of us pushing a pram through the park, delighted to be new parents. With my eyes closed I could bring such belief to these visualisations, enough even to cause physical reactions. A comforting warmth laced with excitement, my heart beating faster, followed by a prickle of goosebumps spreading across my skin. In my mind I found I could escape, and I held on to these sensations for as long as I possibly could.

The contractions started in the middle of the night, and I was jolted out of my slumber by the sharpness of the pain. I sat up in bed, wide eyed, scared by the sudden intensity. Within minutes the pain had gone again, and I tried to focus. Unsure of what time of night it was it dawned on me that it may be hours before someone brought my breakfast, and I knew however much I screamed no one would hear me. I had never been around anyone with a baby so didn't know the first thing about labour, although somewhere in the back of my mind was a fact that firstborns normally took a while to get going. Squeezing my eyes tightly shut I prayed for this kind of luck to be on my side.

I sat as still as possible, conserving my energy, propped up against the bed frame, panting my way through the pain when it came. In between the pain I whispered softly to my unborn child to hold on.

By the time the breakfast tray was shoved through the gap in the door I was beside myself with worry. I pushed up from the bed and staggered over as quickly as I could, the heaviness of my bump pressing down. Normally it would have hurt to bang my fists against the sturdy door but the sharp pain across my stomach was all I could feel.

'Help me please! The baby is coming,' I shouted as loudly as I could. I strained to hear any noise on the opposite side but there was only silence. 'PLEASE, HELP ME!' I screamed and then a guttural sound came from somewhere deep inside. It was a sound I hadn't realised I possessed. Seconds passed as I slowly slid down the wall until my bottom met the floor, my legs stretched out in front of me. Then I heard the heavy bolts being pushed aside and the relief was so great that I thought I must have wet myself, before realising it was my waters breaking. I held my breath as the door opened and prayed it would not be the woman who was about to walk into the room.

I must have beamed at him as he walked in, the relief at not being faced with that vicious woman evident across my face. His surprise to find me virtually behind the door, half crying, half smiling, in an ungainly heap was overtaken by a natural concern. Although he looked petrified, he came towards me and gently helped me to my feet. The contractions had stopped for a minute or two and he managed to position me back on the bed before I felt the next sharp pain.

'I need to call her to help me,' he said.

'No, no please, I beg you,' I pleaded. 'We must do this. Just you and me. Please do this for me.' No doubt he could hear the rising pitch of my voice, and the fear on my face must have also been plain to see.

'But I should…She won't be…,' he started. I could hear notes of panic within his own words but then he stopped abruptly and looked deep into my eyes. He had made his decision.

'OK, we can do this,' he said. 'I am going to be here with you throughout. I will help you any way I can.'

I wanted to respond but the sharpest pain hit suddenly and all I could do was pant, pushing short, strong breaths from my lungs. Without the luxury of pre-natal classes I was glad that breathing through the contractions seemed to come naturally although it didn't help massively with the pain. It did at least give me something to concentrate on.

'I'm going to have to take a look,' he said, almost apologetically. I immediately stiffened. The thought of him anywhere 'down there' filled me with disgust, but the contractions were coming faster and stronger now and I knew I really had no choice.

I was making a conscious effort not to make too much noise in case the woman heard any screaming and turned up to get involved. The man stood waiting for an answer, and I managed a slight nod of my head, giving him the green light to move to the end of the bed. Gently I felt him lift the hem of the soft, jersey maternity dress that they had given me to wear. I screwed my eyes tight as he removed my underwear.

I couldn't control the jerking of my body from the pain searing through it and he shouted to me that he could already see the crown of the baby's head.

'It's coming,' he said nervously peering at me over the bump. Tears were now streaming from my eyes, and I could only just make out the shape of him though the haze. My face felt flushed and momentarily I wished for a fan or just a cold cloth to cool it down. How different this could have been if this was Lucas's child, and we were safe in a hospital right now. I still wasn't sure I could do this, but I had to. It was time. Somehow my captor and I were going to have to get through this.

'Please, make sure my baby is safe,' I begged.

'I think it's time to push,' came his reply and I bore down with all the strength I had. It seemed to go on forever, the break in contractions and then the pain and the overwhelming urge to push. The man stayed in his position by my feet and muttered over and over that the baby would be here soon. His voice was surprisingly soothing, and I was grateful that he was there.

'One more big push,' I heard him say. I gritted my teeth and pushed as hard as I could. Suddenly there was a 'whoosh' from between my legs. I heard him gasp and the next moment he held up a tiny body. A small cry escaped the tiny infant, and the man walked a couple of steps before placing it carefully onto my stomach. I could feel the stickiness against my sweaty skin as I put my arms around the child and brought it towards me.

The man looked almost as exhausted as I did as he stood, stamping his feet so the blood would return to his legs. Our eyes locked and he smiled. 'That was the most amazing thing I have ever seen,' he said. It was obvious from the relief on his face that he couldn't believe we had safely delivered a baby.

'I need to go and get some scissors to cut the cord,' he said. 'I won't be long'.

He left, taking the time to lock the door behind him, which was almost laughable. *Where did he think, I was going to go at this present moment?*

But I was relieved to have this time. As I lifted the child up, I could see it was a little boy and the instant love I felt for it took me completely by surprise. For the first time since being held in captivity I remembered what it was like to feel blissfully happy. He was so beautiful, so perfect, so tiny.

I shifted myself, slowly re-positioning until I was sitting up against the head of the bed. It made it possible to pull the top part of my stretchy dress down, giving him access to my breast. It took a few tries but then he greedily latched on and started to guzzle. It wasn't long before we were interrupted again. The man returned with a pair of large shiny scissors. He looked at the bed beneath me and realised it was coated in blood.

'I need to make sure the placenta is out within around half an hour,' he said looking concerned. He put the scissors down. 'I've been reading up about it the last few weeks.'

I held tight to the baby while he looked, and he asked me to push which produced the placenta.

He looked relieved. He placed the placenta in a plastic bag.

'Am I OK? I asked. Will the bleeding stop.'

'It's already slowing,' he said. 'I'll bring you some new bedding.'

He picked up the scissors and I watched as he cut through the umbilical cord and tied it as best, he could. He had brought a bucket of water and a sponge back with him to clean up and he placed a soft cream towel on the end of the bed before reaching for the baby. I clung to my son, my eyes pleading with him not to take the child away. He shook his head.

'I just want to clean him up and put a nappy on him,' he said. I let him gently take the child from my arms, but my eyes didn't leave him for a second. I observed as firstly he bathed the boy and then laid him on the towel. He fumbled around with a nappy that he had brought with him and once he had secured it tightly, he gave the baby back to me.

'I'll leave you now,' he said. He picked up the bag and bucket and moved towards the door. 'I'll bring you some more nappies later.' He unlocked the door and opened it. 'He's beautiful,' he said, a wistful look upon his face. Then he turned, disappearing through the door frame, leaving me alone with my child.

In the days that followed he brought a small cardboard box into the room and that became a makeshift cot. The woman had thankfully not shown herself and I spent every waking moment of the day tending to my little boys every whim. Feeding, changing, staring at him while he slept. He was happy and contented. He would fix his soft eyes on me as he guzzled vast amounts of milk.

I let my imagination go and would pretend that he was Lucas's and mine and that Lucas was in the next room making us lunch. I found myself spending more and more time daydreaming and less in the reality of my situation. I was determined to relish every second I had with my baby and for most of the day I could, at least for now, push any intrusive thoughts to the back of my mind.

But as I lay at night trying to sleep, I couldn't help but acknowledge that one day someone would come and take away my last reason to live.

# NINETEEN

For the next few weeks Sophie kept herself busy learning lines or singing through her songs and she found herself too tired for much else. Tom was busy at work too, so the time they had together late in the evening would result in one or both falling asleep on the sofa.

They pencilled in a date night for the next Saturday so that they would make the effort to go out, and Tom booked some tickets for a play Sophie had wanted to see for some time. It was an adaptation of Twelve Angry Men. Sophie had seen the movie years before and as they watched the live performance she grinned from ear to ear. It just made her more excited to be on the stage herself.

    She couldn't help but feel the nerves as her own opening night got closer. Her fellow actors were a friendly bunch, and the buzz of excitement grew with each passing day, as the countdown began. Some of them had been in other West End shows and Sophie looked to them for advice. The director could be relentless, making the cast go over and over a song and dance number to get it spot on. It was exhausting but Sophie wanted it all to be perfect, so she didn't really mind, and she was glad Tom was being so understanding.

    By midday on most of the rehearsal days, Sophie would be longing to replenish the energy she had burnt off and today was no exception. She purchased a protein filled wrap and an energy boosting smoothie from the cafeteria and made her way outside to where she knew some of the cast congregated. She had instantly been drawn to a few of them; a petite blonde girl called Jane, whose vivacity was infectious and Lana, who was gorgeous, with a model type stature and a long, glossy mane of deep red hair. Both girls were around the same age as Sophie and the three of them had become friendly from the first day.

Two of the male actors often joined their little lunch group and when Sophie stepped into the sunshine, she could see that Harry was already sitting with the two girls. They were in a little huddle, cross legged on a small square of grass in the courtyard behind the rehearsal studio. Harry was pale skinned and gangly and on stage he towered above the others. He was sat to one side of the others with his back against a brick wall and his long legs jutting out at awkward angles.

The other man who usually joined them was Trent, who was the good-looking male lead, but as far as she could see he wasn't with them. His good looks were the classic type of tall, dark, and handsome and when he turned on his megawatt smile you could almost hear the soft gasps of girls swooning. Sophie thought they all acted ridiculously around him but in the few weeks that she had known him she found him to be down to earth and quite good fun.

The group welcomed Sophie and carried on chatting about the other parts they had been auditioning for, and Sophie sat listening intently. It was heart-warming to realise they had all experienced good and bad auditions and she immediately felt like one of them; a proper jobbing actress, and this filled her with joy. A few minutes later Trent arrived to join the group and squeezed himself into the spot next to Sophie.

'Blimey, that was an intense morning,' he said, collapsing dramatically to the floor. Everything Trent did was dramatic. It was like he lived his entire life on stage. He smiled at her. 'He's in a proper picky mood today. How many times did you hear him shouting my name? "Trent, you need to turn quicker. Trent, slow this part down!" Jeez, I couldn't do anything right today.' He mimicked the directors voice perfectly and it made Sophie giggle.

'I know, my throat is sore from singing the harmony in the first number. We must have gone through it at least thirty times.' Sophie took a long gulp of her drink, which soothed her vocal cords slightly.

'Fancy a drink later?' said Trent, directing his question at Sophie before looking around the rest of the group.

'I'm free,' said Jane, and Harry agreed he too would be up for a quick one.

'I've got to get home early, it's my sister's birthday meal tonight. Another time though,' said Lena.

'Sophie?' said Trent again, his eyes lingering for longer than she felt was necessary. Sophie was flattered by his attention, but she had told him about Tom, so his obvious interest made her slightly uncomfortable. Maybe that was the way he acted with any new females that joined the cast. He probably saw her as an enigma because she hadn't automatically fallen at his feet. She brushed her worries aside.

'Not tonight,' she said. 'Tom and I are going out tonight' she added, pushing the emphasis on Tom's name, just to make sure Trent picked up on it.

'No worries,' said Trent smoothly. The slightest flicker of annoyance showed on his face, so quick that after a moment she wasn't sure she had seen it at all. Did she imagine it? Almost immediately he had slipped back into his usual friendly persona. No one else picked up on it and it wasn't long before they were called back to rehearsal. It played on Sophie's mind throughout the rest of the day. She couldn't help but feel a sense of unease when she was around him. He was so intense. As she said goodbye that evening, she watched him closely and he was all smiles. *Maybe I did imagine it,* she thought. *He does seem like a nice guy.*

She didn't want to make it into a big deal but something her late grandfather had told her years before popped into her head. Something about people not always being what they initially seemed and always to go with her gut. And if she was honest with herself, her instinct was telling her that Trent was not a man to be crossed. It was obvious that he was a man used to getting what he wanted, and she would have to stay firm and make sure he understood that she wasn't interested in that way. It was easy to guess that he wasn't the type to be turned down very often, but she was more than happy with Tom, and nothing would change that.

By the time she walked into the train station she had forgotten all about Trent and was looking forward to getting home to Tom. They had a lovely evening planned. She closed her eyes and rested her head against the train window as the train left the station.

# TWENTY

Christmas was fast approaching, and Tom had been searching for the perfect gift for Sophie. He spent hours traipsing the streets of London, until he found a beautiful little corner shop with delicate jewellery displayed in the windows. He pushed through the door and made his way towards the counter. The shop assistant looked up from her magazine and smiled. She was heavily made up and immaculately dressed in a dark red trouser suit.

'Can I help you find something, Sir?' she said as she stood.

'I'm trying to find a present for my girlfriend,' he replied. 'In her own words she's a bit fussy about what she likes, so any suggestions will be gratefully received.' He smiled. 'Nothing "too bling" apparently and it must be silver. I was thinking a necklace maybe?'

'OK Sir, let's see what we can find,' said the shop assistant, as she moved out from behind the counter. Half an hour later, Tom had the perfect gift in his pocket and was making his way back to the tube station. He was happy with his purchase and was sure Sophie would be delighted. It was a dainty silver chain with a heart shaped filigree pendant, and he could picture her wearing it. The jewellery wasn't her only present and he knew he was being extravagant, but it was their first Christmas together and he wanted to show her how much she meant to him.

He had also organised a couple of nights away in a beautiful old cottage. It was the same place she had visited with her family years before. Sophie had mentioned it on many occasions, and he wanted to surprise her with the two-night break he had arranged. He was hoping she would take him to some of the places that her dad had taken her before he passed away, and that together they could make some memories of their own. The cottage was near the city of Bath in Somerset and Tom had always fancied visiting the Roman Baths if they had time. He had planned it so that after their trip they would drive back towards his parents' house, arriving on Christmas Eve.

Tom's mum loved Christmas and each year the house would be covered with lights inside and out. He had fond memories of the festive season at his childhood home. The lights were always a classy off-white colour and would look tasteful but plentiful. They would lead visitors in from the road and down the driveway. As soon as the house came into view, your eyes would be drawn up to more lights which continued along the guttering, pretty and twinkling. A life-sized reindeer made from glittery wire stood to one side of the imposing front door and the large brass door knocker was surrounded by a crisp ring of holly and ivy.

Once inside the hallway, one of three lavish trees would be decorated in minimal white and silver. Another identical tree stood majestically on the upstairs landing and an even larger, fuller tree stood proudly in the front lounge. Tom and Serena used to enjoy wrapping the 'fake' presents as children. Empty boxes of all shapes and sizes covered in beautiful, shiny paper topped off with a large glittery bow. Tom would race around, placing the presents under the various trees and his mother would go around later and tidy up the display. It was an amazing sight and Tom couldn't wait to show Sophie how his folks celebrated Christmas. She was in for a treat.

Serena was now feeling better and had taken on a part-time job in a nearby cafe in town. She could walk to work most days along the beach if the weather permitted it. Tom was pleased at how happy she seemed when they chatted on the phone. For a girl who liked adventure in her life, she seemed to have settled down into a quieter existence.

She spoke happily of her love of being outdoors and the joy of not needing to use the car very often. It saved her the expense of running a car and she could borrow their mums car if she needed it. It was lovely to hear that she was enjoying life again. She had even hinted to Tom about a guy that she liked, who worked in an office a few doors down from the cafe. Even over the phone Tom could sense she was smiling as she told him how the man came in most days. She had laughed then and said, "*of course a man needs to eat*" but Tom could tell from the lilt in her voice that she believed there was a mutual attraction. It was just waiting for one of them to make the first move.

The trauma of going through her illness seemed to have made her more content with a slower pace of life, and Tom was delighted that she wasn't jetting off again around the world anytime soon. The closeness he had with Serena, she also now shared with Sophie, and it was a joy for him to see them getting on so well. A few times a week, after he and Serena had chatted, he would hand to phone over to Sophie and leave them to catch up.

Tom was on his way to work the next morning, and as the tube train swept through the underground he thought of John. He had been planning to call him and arrange a visit for a coffee over the Christmas period. He knew John only had a few friends and that his parents were sadly no longer around.

Even though Tom hadn't found any extra proof to show that John was the right John Hanson, he still wanted to keep in touch. If later it was uncovered that he wasn't his father, he had still been moved by the story of John's missing girlfriend and felt for the man.

The flat was empty when he arrived home. He put his things in the hall and went into the kitchen to make a cup of tea. Once he had made himself comfortable in an armchair, he decided there was no time like the present. He took a sip and picked up his mobile.

The phone rang for what seemed like an eternity and he was just about to ring off when a sharp voice answered.

'Yeah,'

'Hi John, it's Tom. How are you?' he asked.

John's voice immediately softened. He sounded pleased to hear from him.

'Oh, hi Tom. Sorry I must have dropped off to sleep on the sofa for a minute. Sign of old age,' he said and laughed gruffly. 'How are things with you?'

'All good, thanks. I just thought I'd call and see if you were around on Boxing Day? Sophie will be with me, but we thought we could pop by to see you?'

'Great,' said John and his voice sounded tight. 'That would be lovely.' He was a man who wouldn't want to admit to the loneliness, but Tom guessed the Christmas period could be a tough time for him.

'Fantastic, it will be nice to see you. We will bring some mince pies and some…'

'I sent the DNA test swab off,' interrupted John. Tom paused to digest this news.

'Wow, that's good.' He swallowed. 'I guess we will find out for definite then,' he pondered. He felt stumped as what to say next. It wasn't a conversation you would have every day.

'For what it's worth, I do hope you are my son,' said John. 'Although I don't really understand it all…that would be the outcome I would like.'

Tom smiled to himself. He felt an instant warmth towards the man at the other end of the phone. He realised the strength required for him to put himself out there and he hoped it would be the result John wished for.

'I would like that too,' he replied. 'When will you get the results?'

'About 2-3 weeks, so if we're lucky I might know by the time I see you,' said John.

He proceeded to tell Tom about the visit from Detective Fairbrother and why that had spurred him on to take the test.

'It would mean the world to me, even after all these years, to find out what happened to Katie,' finished John. 'Whatever the outcome, even if I have to come to terms with her leaving of her own free will.'

He sounded sad, and Tom could tell how much pain John still carried with him. He couldn't even begin to imagine how he would feel if Sophie had gone missing, especially if he had never been able to say goodbye. All those years wondering if it was something he had said or done? And the thought of her being hurt somewhere and not being able to help her. He couldn't bear to think about that.

'Well, let's hope we get the outcome we both want,' said Tom. 'But even if we don't, we will definitely stay in touch.' He hoped this reassured John that he wasn't about to sweep in with his theories and then just leave if he wasn't who Tom believed he was.

As Tom ended the call, he heard a key turn in the door, which announced Sophie's arrival home. As he made his way to greet her, it hit him that he was more hopeful than he realised too. He may already have one loving father but to have John as another male influence in his life was all good with him.

# TWENTY-ONE

Detective Alan Fairbrother looked at the list of names in front of him. They were the occupants of the houses in roads close to where Katie Reed had gone missing in the early spring of 1998. A section on each sheet had been left for notes, and alongside each name, officers had recorded any sightings of the girl in the weeks leading up to her disappearance or any other relevant information.

Alan sat with one hand under his chin, propping up his head. The other hand ran slowly down the list, his finger tracing along, and stopping at some of the entries. He used a red pen to highlight details he thought may hold any significance of what residents at the time had seen. There were only a few who believed that they had seen Katie in the weeks before she went missing, but nobody claimed to have seen her on the day.

In the week before her disappearance, a man had stated that he had seen a girl of Katie's description running in the park on a few occasions. The time noted also coincided with Katie's morning routine. Due to the early hour the man had only glimpses of the runner from his bedroom window just after his alarm went off. The house backed onto the sizeable field and as the man also had to look across his own garden the statement had been put down as a possible sighting. There was an extra note alongside stating that from the officer's opinion it would be difficult to identify someone due to the distance. The man himself though had been adamant it had been the same young blonde girl on each occasion but other than the stature and blonde ponytail he couldn't say it was the same girl they showed him in a photo.

Alan found a more credible witness further down the page, someone who was at least in the park itself. It was from a professional dog walker who walked the park most mornings and she would frequently pass a girl of the same description. She said that she would always have to keep an eye out for joggers, as one of the dogs she walked didn't like people running past, so she had to be aware in case he snapped. According to the note, she was quite annoyed that she had to change her habits in a field that was so large, and she couldn't understand why people couldn't keep away from her and her dogs. The officer who had filled in the entry had added a couple of exclamation marks at the end of the note, indicating their own thoughts of this woman's anger on the subject.

The main thing Alan could discern from the entries, was that Katie had used a tried and tested route each day around the same time. It was obvious to him that if someone had wanted to harm her, they wouldn't have had to watch her for long to know exactly where she would be.

Alan paused for a moment, letting these thoughts run through his mind. There were no obvious signs that anything untoward happened to her. Maybe it was as straight forward as her leaving her boyfriend once she had found out she was pregnant and not looking back. It always puzzled Alan that a person could just leave regardless of the consequences, with hardly a thought of who they left behind. It did happen though. He had been involved with a missing person case in the past, where ten or so years later the person had materialised. They found they couldn't cope with some of life's dramatic events and had just opted out. How they could do that to someone else was beyond him.

He rubbed his temples. His head was beginning to hurt. It had already been a long day, and this would have to wait until at least tomorrow. Alan was tempted to take the list home, but he had promised Pam he would spend the evening with her, and it wasn't going to go down well if he turned up at home with papers to go through.

He stood now, stretching as he took his coat from the hook on the back of the door and left his office. It was spitting with rain as he made his way through the double doors at the front of the station. He waved goodbye to the young constable on reception duty and headed out into the night.

It took at least thirty minutes to drive home. The traffic was slower than usual, although he didn't come across any reason why. He wasn't overly bothered by the length of the journey as it gave him more time to mull things over but by the time he arrived, he pushed any thoughts of work from his mind. He was looking forward to spending some quality time with his wife and his belly was already rumbling with the anticipation of whatever delicious food was on the menu tonight.

Pam was a fantastic cook and she loved to spend time in the kitchen preparing new recipes. As soon as he opened the front door, he could smell something magnificent. He took off his shoes and placed them to one side, before wandering into the kitchen. Pam was standing at the sink as she washed some broccoli florets. She gave them a brief shake and then turned towards him.

'Great timing, it will be ready in about ten minutes,' she said. She gave him a kiss on the cheek. 'We are having Salmon fishcakes with new potatoes and broccoli. Thought we both needed to eat a little healthier'. She added this with a little tap of her hand against her stomach.

'Sounds lovely. You're an angel, I'm ravenous as always.'

He wasn't sure he would feel full enough after dinner but understood her sentiments. He eyed a freshly baked loaf cooling on the worktop, so he had plenty to fill him up later if necessary.

'No change there then,' said Pam over her shoulder as she moved to the hob to stir the bubbling pot. 'You've got time to freshen up,' she added. 'And dry off a bit from the look of you. Goodness, it's been a lousy day today.'

Alan was already climbing the stairs and shedding his jacket as he went. He stopped at the bathroom and dried his hair off using one of the fluffy white towels and proceeded on to the bedroom.

Once he had changed into a more comfortable attire of jeans and a t-shirt, he padded barefoot back down the stairs. He placed his arms around Pam who was getting cutlery out of the drawer and nuzzled into her neck. She laughed and turned around to give him a big hug.

'Long day? Let's get you fed and then we can curl up on the sofa for a film,' she said. She could pick up on his mood within seconds without him uttering a word. He smiled back at her.

'Best thing I've heard all day,' he said letting her go. He opened one of the recently updated soft grey kitchen cabinets and reached inside for a couple of plates.

Later that night when Pam was sound asleep, Alan lay beside her trying his best not to fidget and wake her. It still amazed him how little time it took for her to nod off. She would place her head on the pillow and a few moments later she would be gently breathing. He had always been the one to lay awake for what seemed like hours, even before joining the police force. From an early age he had been told that he had always struggled to sleep through the night. Something his mother used to remind him of on countless occasions.

    He tried not to let it annoy him as he lay there. He knew from experience that it wouldn't help one bit, but that was easier said than done. Since becoming a policeman his sleeping pattern had taken a turn for the worst and he found it hard to switch off his thoughts. His brain would carry on dissecting whatever he had been working on that day and today it was the case of Katie Reed still playing on his mind.

    As he wasn't back on shift until Monday, he made a mental note to stay later that day and make a few calls to some of the people on the list. If that didn't bring anything up, maybe then he could put the case to bed. He could always give that guy Tom a call and see if he had spoken to his parents yet about being adopted. Maybe that was the way to go? He hadn't heard from John either to see if he had got that paternity test. It was possible that the boy had got that wrong. It could even be another John Hanson that was his father. *Christ,* he thought, *I'm never going to get to sleep at this rate.*

He rolled over onto his side and forced himself to think of the lovely evening he had spent with Pam. As usual he had eaten too much. He had given in and consumed two slices of delicious bread after his meal and then they had sat on the sofa with a bottle of wine watching an old classic movie. Those were the things his mind needed to hold on to. He looked over to his wife who was facing away from him and concentrated on the steady rise and fall of the duvet she was cocooned in. He snuggled closer and gently put his arm over her. She murmured slightly and sleepily linked her hand through his. They lay together until eventually Alan drifted off to sleep.

## TWENTY-TWO

Tom and Sophie were getting ready for their double dinner date with Tom's best friend Simon and his new girlfriend. They hadn't met her yet although Simon had filled Tom in with some details about her.

He certainly seemed smitten, and this was a new thing for his oldest friend. Tom hoped she could be that someone special for Simon and maybe the girl he would eventually settle down with. He felt bad that recently they hadn't had so many boy's nights out but since he had got together with Sophie and what with helping Serena through her illness it had been hard to schedule time.

He thought back to a night a few months ago when they had managed to meet up just the two of them and it had been nice to catch up, but the way Simon had seemed that night had worried Tom. Simon had got more than a little drunk and confided in Tom that his life seemed to have no meaning, just the treadmill of work and the gym and little else. Tom had been a little taken back as he always thought his friend had liked to play the field, enjoying his bachelor life but on this occasion, he seemed genuinely depressed. It was the first time Simon had confessed to how he longed for what Tom and Sophie had.

The problem was that he still compared every girl to his long-lost love. She had been a free spirit that he had met whilst travelling in his younger days and it seemed that no other girl could compete with the memory of her. It was rare for Simon to let his guard down and be honest about how he felt, but that night the drink and emotions had been free flowing. Still, they hadn't mentioned it since. Tom had called him a few days later and he seemed back to his old self, and then about a week after he was full of himself after meeting this girl. It was obviously early days, but Tom hoped something would come of it. It would be lovely to see his old pal happy.

He thought back to the night he met Sophie and how he had swooped in and stolen her from under his friend's nose. A small prickle of guilt passed through his mind, and it made him wonder if Simon still held a grudge against him. He couldn't count how many times Simon had mentioned how wonderful Sophie was on that night when he was baring his soul, and he hoped his friend had meant how wonderful she was for Tom. The next morning though as he re-played the conversation through his mind, he started to doubt his memory of it.

He couldn't deny the slight niggle in the back of his mind about the first time they had met the girls. Although Simon had moved his attentions onto Carrie and later taken her home, he had seemed a bit miffed about the way things had worked out. A few weeks on though and he began to declare his infatuation of Sophie's best friend and Tom began to feel less awkward that he had made a play for Sophie. Not that he regretted it, he'd do it again in a heartbeat. If you believe a certain person is for you, what else can you do but to go for it?

It was unfortunate that things hadn't worked out between Carrie and Simon but in the long term it was obvious, to Tom at least, that Simon and Sophie would never have got together. He had watched frequently as Sophie recoiled from Simon's overconfident manner and although she had always tolerated him for Tom's sake, in private, she had always referred to him as "a bit much". Although recently, she had mentioned the beginnings of a soft spot developing for him, once Tom had explained that although he could be loud and obnoxious, it was insecurity that made Simon quite so full on.

'Well, I'm sure he has a lot of qualities I haven't picked up on yet,' she would say. 'And as he is one of your longest friendships, I will bow to your experience.'

Secretly she was grateful to Simon for looking out for Tom. Just watching them together, it was easy to see that they would always watch each other's backs and that was the best quality you could find in a friend, as far as she could see. And Tom seemed glad that she was slowly warming to his friend. It made double dating a lot easier, and she could always hope that Simon's new lady might calm him down a little.

Tom watched as Sophie came out of the bathroom and set about the task of getting ready. She had found the lipstick she was looking for and had returned to her position at the dressing table. He stared at her reflection as she applied the cherry colour to her full lips, the final touch of her otherwise natural make up. Tom's breath was taken away at how beautiful she was.

The red dress she was wearing clung to her soft curves as it draped down to just past her knees. She reached down to put her high heels on, skilfully buckling the strap around each ankle with one hand. He wandered over to her, smiling at her reflection in the gilded mirror and planted a kiss gently on the bare skin of her neck.

'Your hair looks lovely pinned up like that,' he said. She turned towards him.

'Thank you,' she said, clearly pleased he had noticed the style that had taken her so long to perfect. Glancing at her watch she realised they would have to leave in the next five minutes to be on time to meet the others.

'Have you called for a taxi?' she asked.

'Not yet, but I'll do it now,' Tom said, and he grabbed his wallet and mobile from the bedside cabinet as they left the room.

When they entered the restaurant, Simon and his date were already seated at the table facing away from the door. They could see Simon's broad shoulders as he sat with his head bent affectionately towards his date. All they could see of her from this angle was that she had dark brown corkscrew curls that cascaded down past her shoulders.

'Hi guys, sorry we are a few minutes late,' said Tom as they approached the table.

Simon laughed loudly, turning to see his childhood friend.

'No problem, mate,' said Simon as he stood up. 'This is remarkably early for you! Sophie must be a good influence.' He patted his friend on the back before kissing Sophie on both cheeks. He turned back to his date and sat back in his chair.

'This is Jenna,' he said putting his arm across her shoulders. As they settled themselves in the vacant seats he added. 'Jenna, this is Sophie, and this big brute is Tom,' he continued, grinning at them both.

'Nice to meet you,' said Sophie, smiling at the other woman.

'We've heard nice things about you,' added Tom.

'Lovely to meet both of you too,' said Jenna. She looked confident and relaxed, and Tom decided he liked her immediately. Once the pleasantries were out of the way, the couples enjoyed some wine chosen by Simon, who fancied himself as a connoisseur in fine wine. There were a few jokes at his expense, but Tom had to give it to his friend once they had all had a sip, as it was the best wine he had ever tasted. It was a lovely full-bodied red that neither of them had tried before but would surely become a firm favourite.

They ordered their meal and then the conversation moved on to Sophie's new job in the West End.

'It's so exciting, to have finally landed a job doing what I love,' she said and from her beaming smile it wasn't hard to see how much it meant to her.

'I love a good musical,' said Jenna. "We will definitely be there on opening night supporting you.' She looked over at Simon, who made a face.

'Hold on there, don't start promising outings we may not be able to fulfil.' Jenna looked shocked for a second before he cracked a smile and she realised he was joking.

'I'm not so keen, as you know. All that bursting into song all over the place,' he teased. 'But seriously, yes of course we will come and cheer you on.' He squeezed Jenna's hand.

'Well, I appreciate that, especially as I know it will be torture for you Simon, sitting still through a whole show!' said Sophie with a playful roll of her eyes.

The four of them had a fantastic night, finished off with Expresso Martini's at a new cocktail bar which had just opened on the corner near the taxi rank. As Tom and Sophie got into a taxi late into the night, they snuggled up together on the back seat.

'She was lovely, wasn't she?' Sophie said, and Tom agreed wholeheartedly.

'Let's hope they make a good go of it, and we get to do some more double dating. It was a fun night.'

'I agree. After that little fling he had with Carrie, I worried he would always be on his own. I know he's a lovely friend to you but in a relationship, he seems a bit intense. I remember Carrie even thinking she kept seeing him after she ended things and thought he was stalking her! That all got a bit messy. But I am glad he's met someone that he seems so in tune with.'

They pulled up just outside the flat and Tom paid the driver before they got out onto the pavement.

'He seemed to be going through a little self-doubt back then and Carrie did end things very abruptly before starting up with that Jack fellow,' he reminded her, feeling the need to defend his friend.

'Yes, I know. There was blame on both sides, but she got herself into a right state at the time and I felt a little guilty since our relationship was going so well. Anyway, it won't be that long until I can see her too. She's due back from Australia just after Christmas.'

Tom turned the key and they stumbled into the hallway, suddenly realising how much drink they had consumed. Giggling like teenagers they made their way to the kitchen to get some strong coffee.

'Maybe we should have a party for New Year?' suggested Tom. 'What do you think? It would be nice to get some of our friends together.'

Sophie had pulled herself up on to the counter and was rummaging through the biscuit tin.

'Sophie, how can you still be hungry!' exclaimed Tom. Laughing she found what she was looking for, a lonely milk chocolate digestive nestling at the bottom of the tin.

'I didn't even have pudding,' she said. 'I was so full of that gorgeous meal but now I'm craving something sweet. Do you want some?'

Tom held up his hands.

'God no, I would never come between you and the last chocolate biscuit in the tin,' he said. He moved forward, placing his body between her legs and hugged her close.

'And yes, a party sounds lovely,' she said over his shoulder. 'But right now, I need to go to bed.'

The next two weeks flew by, with opening night approaching far too quickly. The day before Sophie would be making her stage debut, Tom was picking her up from rehearsal and taking her for a quiet dinner. The whole family had tickets for the show and would be arriving around 6pm the next day. Even Sophie's mum and her partner Leo were coming down from Wales and they would bring Sophie's grandad too. He relaxed against a wall outside the stage door, watching busy people pushing their way past each other to get wherever they needed to be. He loved the bustle of central London, but it was nice to stop, and people watch sometimes. A minute or two later he heard his name being called and turned to see Sophie and Jane approaching. They said a quick hello before Jane left to do some last-minute shopping and Tom and Sophie walked towards Leicester Square tube station hand in hand.

'How are you feeling about tomorrow?' he asked.

'Ok, I think. I'm sure I'll be nervous, but we have drilled it over and over so I should be able to perform it in my sleep.'

'Great. Well, we are looking forward to it. Serena is over-excited. I think she will become your biggest fan. I'll probably be as nervous as you from the stalls.' He laughed. Nothing would ever get him treading the boards. He couldn't imagine being up there in front of all those people and was amazed at how calm she seemed. Ten minutes later they were at the flat where they quickly popped in to freshen up, before making their way to a little Italian restaurant nearby. After a delicious meal of spaghetti and prawns with chilli and a glass of wine, they called it a night. Tom stayed up watching a wildlife documentary and a tired Sophie turned in early.

The following morning, they had a quick breakfast together. Then Tom wished her luck for later, planted a kiss on her lips and left her contemplating the day ahead. She had a long shower before getting her things together and leaving for the last dress rehearsal. When she walked into the theatre, she could feel her excitement bubbling up. This would be her first proper performance on a stage. They had had a couple of dress rehearsals and a pre-opening show a couple of days ago but this time there would be paying public and people she knew in the audience. Lana came in behind her and they walked to the dressing rooms together.

'Thought I was late,' said Lana, catching her breath. She sounded a little stressed which Sophie hadn't seen before. Normally she was so calm and collected.

'You never get used to the feeling just before opening night,' she said, and Sophie realised it was excitement spurring her friend on. 'God, I love the buzz!' Her enthusiasm was infectious and made Sophie smile.

'As long as I can eat lunch later and hold it down, I'll be fine,' said Sophie.

'You'll be fine once we warm up and get into it. Come on let's go and find the others.

And Lana was right. As the curtain came down following an evening of energetic songs and dance routines, Sophie was ecstatic with how it had gone. She knew Tom and his family, her family and even Simon and Jenna were all there, and she couldn't wait to get changed and meet them in the bar area. Jane went with her to the bar while the others were still getting out of their various costumes, and they entered to sounds of loud whoops.

'You were so good,' said Tom. He directed this at both girls although he saved a little wink for Sophie. He had been blown away by the talent of all the cast. There were hugs all round and Sophie was especially touched by her grandad's reaction. He hugged her tightly from his wheelchair and there were tears in his eyes. 'Let me stand' he said. 'I needed the wheelchair because it was a long way from the carpark, but I want to hug you my girl, you were amazing.' She helped him to his feet, and he hugged her again. Sophie's mum got him to sit back down before he fell and then she gave her daughter a congratulatory hug too.

After a quick drink all Sophie could think of was how much her feet were beginning to hurt, and she could barely manage to stifle her yawns. Once the adrenaline had left her body, she descended quickly into sleep mode and couldn't wait to get home to bed. She thanked everyone for coming and let Tom steer her away towards a well-earned rest.

## TWENTY-THREE

Sophie was quite excitable, and it was sweet to see. As it would be their first Christmas together, they planned to do the rounds of Sophie's relatives before leaving for their break. Tom had told her that they were going away for a couple of nights, but she had no idea where and as she packed a bag, she was asking a continuous string of questions.

'Will I need any posh outfits? What about a swimsuit? Walking boots? Heels?'

'Blimey, girls sure need to know a lot for a two-day break!' he said, rolling his eyes with mock exaggeration.

'We just like to be organised for any eventuality,' she replied, giving him a playful punch to his shoulder.

About twenty minutes later she was satisfied with what she had packed, and she wandered into the lounge where Tom sat, nursing a coffee.

'Ok, I'm all done. Let's go to my grandad's now and on the way back I want to take that plant into Aunt Claudia's.' She gestured to the pretty pot plant on the table.

Sophie had told him on many occasions how she held such a special place in her heart for her grandad and Tom was glad. He liked the old man. Although Sophie saw her mum now and again, she had relocated after Sophie's dad died and had moved in with a new man. Of course, Sophie loved her mum, but she had always been a daddy's girl and it was hard to deal with him being gone. That made seeing her grandad, her dad's dad, so much more poignant. Tom wished he had met her dad too and if he had been anything like his father, he would have been a great man to know.

He looked at her now, stood with hands on her hips, waiting.

'I'm not sure I'm ready now,' he teased, 'I might just need to go and do some organising.' She laughed and picked up the pot plant.

'Come on, or I'll have to throw this at you!'

By the time they arrived home, it was late. They had stopped off at a local takeaway to pick up dinner. Chinese was Sophie's favourite. Tom busied himself in the kitchen, transferring the chicken in black bean sauce and Singapore noodles onto warm plates. He couldn't believe how hungry he was after all the tea and cake they had consumed on their visits.

It had been lovely to see Sophie's grandad. He was such a jolly soul, and the others in the nursing home where he lived were a lively bunch too. The home had provided some musical entertainment and the oldies – well the ones that still could – got up to have a jig about with the staff and their families.

Sophie's grandad had dragged her around the floor a couple of times, and she looked like she enjoyed it as much as he did. It was easy to get caught up in the party atmosphere. The residents who couldn't get out of their chairs did a sort of chair dance that involved waving their arms around or shaking maracas that the staff had handed out. Tom had even danced awkwardly with a couple of the older ladies who seemed smitten to have a young man to fight over. He had tried to protest and sited his no dancing policy, but they were having none of it.

*It must be all that dancing* he decided now, watching Sophie dig into her food. She had an appetite too.

'So, when are you going to tell me where we are going?' she asked, looking over at him.

'In the morning when we set off,' he replied. 'I think I'm up for an early night. We've got a bit of a drive tomorrow,' he said and winked at her.

'I hope I can sleep,' she said, 'with all this anticipation!'

Once they finished their meal, they each carried a glass of wine into the lounge and cuddled up together on the sofa. Tom put on some chilled music, and they spent the rest of the evening reminiscing about past Christmases.

The next morning after a quick breakfast of toast and orange juice, they packed up the car. Just as they were about to lock up a delivery driver stopped just behind them.

'Sophie Willis?' he enquired as he opened his door. She nodded.

'Yes, that's me,' she said.

'I have a parcel for you.'

They waited while he opened the side door of the van and rummaged around before handing a small package to Sophie.

'Thank you,' she said. 'Have a good Christmas.' She watched as the delivery driver got back into his cab and drove away.

'I wonder what it is?' she said looking at Tom. 'Is it to do with my surprise?' she asked.

He held up his hands.

'Nothing to do with me,' he said. 'Open it and then we can put it inside before we go.'

Sophie ripped at the packaging and revealed a small box inside. Opening the box revealed an expensive looking, gem encrusted keyring in the shape of a flamingo.

'Who is it from?' asked Tom, peering over her shoulder.

'Oh, it must be from my aunt in Canada,' she said quickly scrunching up the wrapping and placing it in the wheelie bin next to her.

'Looks very expensive. That was nice of her,' said Tom. 'Actually, you've just reminded me, the bin collection day is while we are away,' he said, 'I better put it out.' He wheeled the bin into place. Sophie stayed routed to the spot staring at the gift.

When he returned to her side, he took the key ring from her to get a closer look. 'It's cute. Here, you take my key to lock up, and I'll put this on your set.'

'Great,' Sophie said swapping her keys for his. She moved towards the door. 'Actually, I'll just nip to the loo one last time,' she said over her shoulder and disappeared inside.

Once in the bathroom she looked at her reflection in the mirror and splashed some cold water on her face. She knew full well who the present was from, and it wasn't her aunt. Although she had kept her distance from Trent during the last few weeks of performances, she couldn't help but notice his intense gaze following her every move, and it worried her. He had begun to follow her around endlessly and taken none of her hints, always there, always watching her whenever she looked up.

Each morning before their singing warm up, the group would have an acting improvisation session to loosen them up for the day. The director insisted on everyone taking part, and woe betide anyone turning up late. It wasn't Sophie's favourite task. She always felt awkward and wished just occasionally that they would skip it.

She remembered a day a couple of weeks before when they were told to partner up and each think of an animal. Then in turn they had to portray traits and characteristics of this animal. It was laughable really watching adults jumping around pretending to be bunny rabbits or growling like bears. She had partnered up with Jane, who decided to transform into a mouse, while Sophie did her best bouncing around as a kangaroo. At the end of the session, which was mainly taken up with endless giggling, she bumped into Trent who had been on the opposite side of the room.

Trent had brushed past her and whispered that the animal she should have been was a flamingo. A flamingo was elegant, he had said, and with gorgeous long legs. She still remembered the way his gaze had strayed to her legs and slowly moved up her body. She had found herself laughing off the comment while she blushed uncomfortably.

Now, she looked at her reflexion as she wiped her hands on a towel. *The flamingo couldn't be just a coincidence. He was sending her a message.* Although there wasn't a card or message, she was sure this was Trent's way of telling her that he wasn't going to give up.

'Are you ready?' She heard Tom's voice through the door.

'Just coming,' she shouted. She wondered if she should tell Tom, and then almost instantly decided against it. It could ruin their break together. She would have to talk to Trent again and make sure he knew where he stood, once and for all.

A minute later she walked back outside, locking the front door behind her. She handed over Tom's keys and he gave hers back to her. She looked at them briefly, now sporting the flamingo keyring, before pushing any thoughts of Trent from her mind. They were driving down in Sophie's pale green Mini and so Tom waited until she was in position behind the wheel, before he handed her an envelope. She beamed at him and ripped it open, a gasp escaping her lips as the card inside revealed a picture of the familiar old cottage.

'Oh my! Oh Tom, I can't believe this is where we are going.' Her eyes filled with tears, and she reached over to kiss him. 'It is perfect. Thank you.'

'I'm so happy you love it,' said Tom holding her hand. 'Now you can show me the places you remember going with your family.'

She wiped the tears away with her hand. 'I wish my dad had met you,' she said, wistfully. 'He would have loved you too.' She was lost in thought for a moment and Tom squeezed her hand, bringing it to his lips for a gentle kiss.

'Right, let's get going,' she said pulling herself back to the present and starting the engine. As they pulled away, Tom relaxed back in the passenger seat. He was relieved and excited now that she knew the surprise.

Hours later, when they arrived at the old cottage, Tom could see why this place would be so special to Sophie. They had turned off the main road and travelled down a narrow dirt track, only accessible for one small car at a time. Someone had placed a hand painted sign announcing 'Farley

Cottage' just before it came into view, and as pretty as it was, it was the view behind that took Tom's breath away. He glanced at Sophie, and she was grinning from ear to ear. She slowed the car and came to a stop just in front of an old barn. As they clambered out, she rushed around to the passenger side of the car and gave Tom a great big hug.

'I can't believe I'm back here. There are so many memories. It looks exactly as I remember it the last time I came with Dad,' she said as she squeezed him tightly.

'The lady who owns it said we would find the keys in a locked box, just inside the old barn,' said Tom as they moved towards the doors.

Once inside, Tom got his phone out of his pocket, and they followed the instructions on the booking confirmation until they found a small metal box with a keypad. He scrolled further down the email looking for the code. He typed in the four digits and the small door pinged open, revealing a set of keys. Tom took them out and closed the panel before turning to face Sophie.

'Come on then,' he said, sweeping her off her feet. 'Let's get inside.'

Tom carried her out of the barn towards the house with Sophie holding tightly around his neck. Once through the front door, he spun her around before placing her feet firmly back on the stripped wooden floor.

'Now, you need to come and see this view,' said Sophie taking control. Tom followed her into a lounge area where a breath-taking sight of open fields could be seen from every angle. At the far end of the room there were bi-folding doors that ran almost across an entire wall. Some may have thought that wasn't in keeping within such an old house, but it certainly showed off the stunning vista. An array of different shades of green spread out as far as the eye could see, with a contrasting blast of yellow rapeseed in the furthest corner.

'It's amazing,' he said mesmerised.

'I'm glad I brought walking shoes,' said Sophie. She was still grinning from ear to ear. 'There is so much countryside to explore.'

He pulled her gently into his arms.

'A few quiet days just the two of us, before a Christmas with the family. I honestly can't think of anything better,' he said. He kissed her gently.

'Let's go and check out the other rooms and then once we've unpacked, we can go and explore.'

By the time they were ready to leave, Tom and Sophie were totally relaxed. It felt unusual to them as it wasn't a state either of them had experienced for a long time, but they were glad to have left any worries behind for the moment. The secluded walks and copious amounts of fresh country air had done them both the world of good. That added to the simple but delicious food they had both cooked, made it feel like they had been away for much longer than the couple of days they had been tucked away here. They had talked for hours, learning more about each other with each passing day but they had equally enjoyed comfortable silences, finding themselves totally at ease in each other's company.

'I'm looking forward to spending Christmas with your family,' said Sophie as they carried their bags out towards the car. 'They are so lovely and welcoming, and Serena is so funny. I'm excited.'

Tom was pleased. He couldn't wish for anything more than how well Sophie had fitted in to their family. He loved the way he could tell Sophie's innermost thoughts from her expressions. She was so easy to read. He hadn't had this kind of relationship before where they were so well suited, and everything seemed so easy. Thinking back to a couple of his ex-girlfriends, he remembered being totally confused about what they were thinking and how they were likely to react in any given situation. Sometimes even when he had dragged out of them exactly how they were feeling, he was still none the wiser.

It was refreshing that Sophie was so upfront and straight forward and he couldn't believe his luck. He was looking forward to spending time with her and his family and was dead set on it being the best Christmas ever.

# TWENTY-FOUR

## *Katie (1999)*

My precious boy was growing quickly and was the only light of my otherwise mundane existence. I would hold him close and sing old songs my mother had once sang to me. A song about little speckled frogs that at first, I had trouble remembering, but slowly the words or words similar enough came back to me. He would stare up at me as I sang the melody softly, his interest never wavering but I was yet to see him smile. His gorgeous blue eyes wouldn't leave my face, until the soothing tones would send him off to sleep.

He seemed a contented baby and our bond already felt unbreakable, even in the small amount of time that had passed. When it was dark outside, I would look up at the tiny window far above our heads and sometimes I could make out the tiny sparkle of a distant star. I would point it out and he would gurgle approval at whatever his mummy was so focused on. These tiny moments would be cherished, and I would concentrate hard on each, taking a mental picture, and storing them away as deeply as I could. The man came in every so often and checked on us. Food still arrived twice a day and the bucket of toilet waste was collected and replaced.

My fear of the man had dissipated over time, and I found I had even begun to look forward to seeing him as he was the only adult interaction I had. We wouldn't speak much but just the presence of him coming in and out was strangely calming. Partly I was annoyed at having to remind myself that he was the one keeping me hostage but deep down I could sense he may not have had as much choice as it first seemed. The woman was the one I feared. She seemed to be the one calling the shots.

Even just thinking about her sent shivers down my spine.

I could remember the day the woman had come in with the pregnancy test like it was yesterday. Still recalling the way her presence had filled the tiny room as she entered, almost adding an invisible heaviness to the air. Even now, I couldn't believe that I had worried about the woman at the beginning, worried for her being locked away too and then the shock of realising what was really happening. But it was more than that. If I believed in the supernatural, I would have said that a force of evil had entered the room. An invisible energy that made your hackles go up and it instantly harder to breath.

It was the look in the woman's eyes that scared me the most. The cold, hard stare. Devoid of empathy. Eye's that followed your every move, leaving you in no doubt of the malice behind them. The realisation that if you were to step out of line, even the tiniest amount, this woman would enjoy destroying you.

As the weeks past, I didn't think about Lucas as much as I had in the beginning. As time went on, I found it more and more difficult to imagine what he might be doing now. It almost felt like that part of my life had been a dream.

There were times while the baby was sleeping that I would sit on the hard floor just staring at the wall, my mind completely blank. I no longer had the energy to turn over old events and memories. It felt like a switch had been turned off and all that was left was me and my precious boy. I was solely alive for the purpose of keeping him happy and healthy and curiously I began to become comfortable with this task. Every second of my waking day was spent with him but I also noticed that recently I was sleeping more often.

Maybe the tiredness was from boredom. It had become increasingly hard to pace around the sides of the room or to do any of the exercise I had always loved.

*Or maybe I was in the grip of depression?* I had to fight hard to concentrate, trying to hold onto the thoughts wafting through my sluggish mind. *That would make sense. Not knowing how long they were going to keep me here.* I could feel how heavy my eyes felt even now. *Why do I feel so tired?*

A few minutes later I felt my eyes opening slowly. *What was happening? Did I fall asleep?*

I realised I was laying on the cold floor, my face pressing up against one of the legs of the metal bed. I tried to get up, but quickly realised it was impossible. I knew I was awake, but however hard I tried, I couldn't move a muscle. My heart began to race, and I could only move my eyes. I rolled them from side to side trying to see something, anything.

The faint sound of the baby cooing happily not far from where I lay focused my mind. Frustration was kicking in as I tried in vain to lift my head from the concrete. My brain registered that my mouth was open, so I tried to speak. A small grunt was emitted but as hard as I tried, I couldn't force out an intelligible word. I was paralysed. Completely devoid of any movement and petrified of what was happening.

I wasn't sure if I had drifted back to sleep or just closed my eyes again, but the next thing I was aware of, was a figure at my side. A burst of adrenaline kicked in. *Maybe I wasn't paralysed?* I could feel it pumping through my veins, but still all I could do was stare straight ahead.

Suddenly I felt hands clasping around my arms and another pair taking hold of my ankles. There was feeling in my limbs, so I wasn't paralysed. *What was happening?* I was being lifted from the floor and placed onto the bed. From this angle I could see the makeshift cot and my baby's arms and legs wriggling vigorously. The elation that he was safe spread through my entire body. I could hear voices and I strained to hear what they were saying.

'Take the boy upstairs,' came the female voice. She must have been stood near the end of the bed, near to where my feet had been placed. I couldn't see whose voice it was, but I didn't need to.

'Don't take my baby! Don't take my baby!'

It took a minute for me to realise the scream was only inside my head. There was no other noise in the room and all I could do was watch helplessly as the man appeared and reached down to pick up my son. The only sound now was of my own breathing, a pounding through my ears as I desperately tried to do something. The man glanced over quickly as he picked up the baby and then immediately away as if he couldn't bear to see my pain.

I focused my eyes on the back of his head willing him to look around again. If I could just look into his eyes, maybe he would stop.

'Go on.' I heard the voice again, harsher this time. 'I will stay for a moment and see that she is calm before I join you.'

The man shuffled towards the door with the child in his arms, not looking back. Once he was out of view, I found it harder to breath. I could hear the gasping sounds coming from my throat. It felt like the breath was sticking in my windpipe. A hand gently brushed my hair away from my face as if to sooth me. I briefly closed my eyes, flicking them open again as I felt my head being turned. Now I was looking upwards at the ceiling and all the while her hands carried on with the soft stroking motion.

A face came into view, and I tried to focus, blinking though the blurring of my tears. The woman lowered her voice, barely to more than a whisper. She bent her head close to my ear and I felt a wisp of her hair tickle my cheek.

'It's such a pity that things couldn't have been different,' I heard her say. 'I think we could have been friends under different circumstances,' she went on. 'We're so alike you and I, well physically at least. That was your downfall really, my dear. Parading around the park each day with your perfect body, fit and healthy. The child had to at least look like me, and you unknowingly presented yourself as a likely candidate. And you did your part well my dear but I don't need you anymore. It really is such a shame.'

The woman shifted her head position so that her emotionless eyes could stare down at me. I knew deep down that this time would come but still, I pleaded with my eyes for my child, I pleaded for myself, for the life I could have had.

For a minute or two, the woman continued to stroke my hair and then suddenly she stopped. She smiled. The smile was manic and didn't reach her eyes. It sent an ice-cold shiver through my motionless body.

There was nothing I could do to protect myself as the woman violently yanked the pillow from under my head and brought it down over my face. I saw the cheeky face of my beloved baby before me. And then darkness…

# TWENTY-FIVE

Christmas Day had always been a big deal in the Beatty household. The radio kicked in at 9am and Tom dragged himself from sleep. He could already hear activity downstairs. He reached out and hit the alarm button before draping his arm over Sophie and gently nudged her awake. She could sleep through any alarm.

'It's Christmas, sleepy head,' he said in a hushed tone, kissing her on her nose. She grinned as she prised her eyes open, wrapping her arms around his neck.

'Happy Christmas,' she said. She wriggled her body up into a sitting position and leant against the headboard. 'What's all the noise about?' An array of bangs and clatters could be heard from below.

'There will be a whole platter of breakfast items by the time we get down there,' said Tom, 'which is perfect as I'm ravenous,' he added.

'Come on then,' said Sophie, 'I'll have a quick shower and then we can get down there.' She pulled back the covers, swung her legs out from underneath and paced towards the ensuite bathroom. He watched her appreciatively until her naked body had disappeared through the doorway.

'On second thoughts, I think I may need a shower too,' he said hurrying to catch up with her.

The others were already seated around the kitchen table when Sophie and Tom entered. Fiona jumped up from her position before being waved back down.

'Don't interrupt your breakfast mum, I can sort us out with coffee' he said as Sophie took her place next to Serena. There were choruses of 'Happy Christmas' around the table and Tom placed a cup of tea in front of Sophie as he took a sip of his own extra strong coffee.

The spread was impressive. At one end of a large side table were cold hams and cheeses, a homemade loaf of seeded bread, a mixture of jams, hot sausage rolls, various cereals, and a selection of chopped fresh fruit. At the other end were a pile of blueberry muffins, a loaf of banana bread and freshly squeezed orange juice.

They made their way over to the table. Sophie hadn't realised how hungry she was until faced with the variety in front of her. Tom passed her a large plate and waited while she filled hers. He took no persuading to tuck in after she had finished, and he sat down at the table with his plate piled ridiculously high.

The mood around the table was relaxed and jubilant. Serena asked Tom and Sophie if they wanted to join her for a walk after breakfast as the sun was out, even though the air was cold and crisp. She began telling Sophie about a den the two of them had built in the forest behind the house many years ago.

'It was deep in the woods so I guess there could still be some remains of the structure,' she said.

'That sounds fun,' replied Sophie. 'I'd love to explore your old stomping ground.'

'I'd nearly forgotten about that,' piped up Tom. 'Why haven't we been back before?'

'Probably because we grew up,' Serena countered. 'Well, some of us did anyhow.'

'Very funny Serena,' said Tom. 'I'd like to see it too. Let's head out once all this food has settled.'

After helping to clear the table and wash up, the three of them put on their coats and boots and left the house. At the end of the drive, they met one of their parents' neighbours, who was off to have his own brisk walk, to build an appetite ready for his Christmas lunch. Tom and Serena hadn't seen Mr Trowbridge for many years, so they stopped and chatted for a while and introduced Sophie.

Stan Trowbridge had always been friendly with the family, being the only other to have lived in the road for almost as long as they had. Tom thought he was a nice old man. He had lived on his own for the past twenty or so years since his wife Margaret had died.

Serena had always been a little cautious of him. Of course, she would always be polite, but there had always been an underlying wariness that had been there since her early years. Although she couldn't quite put her finger on it, he had always made her slightly uncomfortable. When she was younger, she would only say a quick hello and then move away as quickly as she could. She almost felt guilty now, as he had never done anything to warrant her feelings about him, but she still couldn't shake the uneasiness.

She watched him now, while he greeted Sophie and there it was again, the slightest hint of inappropriate suggestion. It was as if he became too engrossed in what was being said when it was a young female who was doing the talking. She watched how his gaze never wavered from Sophie's face, as if memorising every feature. It seemed that no one else noticed. Sophie seemed comfortable and Tom was laughing and obviously totally unaware of her suspicions. Serena shook the thought away as they moved on.

'He seems nice,' said Sophie, making Serena feel even more guilty than she had a second ago.

'Yes, he is a nice chap,' said Tom as he grabbed her hand. 'It's sad that he lost his wife so long ago, not that we remember her as she died when we were young. I think his son lives in New Zealand now so he's mostly on his own.'

'That's sad,' said Sophie.

'Blimey, I'd forgotten about his son,' Serena interrupted. 'You used to play with him, didn't you?' She remembered a little blond boy who had come to play in their garden a few times.

'Yes, only a couple of times. I do remember him being a bit strange. He didn't speak very much and as far as I recall we didn't have much in common except living in the same street. Then later in his early teens, I think mum said he had got in with the wrong crowd and I didn't see him anymore except in passing. I'm sure Mr Trowbridge told mum he was a lawyer now, so he obviously did quite well for himself.'

As they crossed the field beyond, Serena forgot about their neighbour and his son and concentrated on her surroundings. She enjoyed the crunch of the leaves and twigs under foot as they headed towards the old den. It was a beautiful crisp day, and their breath could be seen bellowing out in front of them as they exhaled. They walked for a while in silence taking in the scenery.

'It's just over here,' said Serena eventually. She pointed to a spot a few yards away. Sophie followed, ducking down to avoid a low-slung branch. She smiled, taking in the child sized structure made of twisted branches and sturdy logs. It was quite a spectacular den. The branches had all been woven together, which was why she supposed, it had lasted so long.

'How sweet!' she exclaimed, and she crouched down to poke her head into the small opening.

'We spent many a fun hour out here building this,' said Tom with a satisfied glint in his eye. Sophie had now shifted her body to get inside the den and Serena was right behind her.

'Squeeze up,' said Serena pushing her way in. 'Blimey we must have been tiny to fit in here.' She sat crossed legged next to Sophie, with their knees at awkward angles as they tried to make themselves comfortable.

'There were four of us one time. There were these twins from across the street who wanted to see it once it was finished,' reminisced Tom, bending over to get a better look into the doorway.

Serena snorted.

'I'd completely forgotten about them coming over, that was hilarious,' she said. She grinned at the memory. 'That soppy Claire got scared when you kept telling scary ghost stories and she ran back home crying.'

'And her brother pushed me over,' said Tom. 'They never did play with us again.'

'Well, I think it's lovely,' piped up Sophie. 'I wonder if anyone else has come across it in the years after you left.'

'I doubt it,' said Serena. 'It's so far into the woods, that's why we chose to build it here. Our own secluded hideaway. Even our parents didn't know about it. Oh, actually I think we showed mum it once'

'There wasn't much to do around here when we were young, so it kept us occupied,' said Tom. 'We knew every part of these woods, and I don't think we ever saw anyone come this far.'

'There's an old road that runs not far away, over there,' said Serena pointing to the left through a heavy wooded area. 'Nobody uses that road now though as the farm, which is the only thing the road leads to, has been closed for at least ten years. There was a creepy old building down at the far end, but nobody ever went near it. I expect it's been knocked down by now. I don't think anyone would want to live this far out.' She looked at her watch. 'Blimey, we had better get going or we'll miss lunch.'

Tom reached down and pulled the girls up one by one from the floor. They ducked their heads low as they emerged from the den and then started making their way back through the dense forest towards the house.

The smell hit Tom as soon as they bundled into the hallway, and he realised how hungry he was. The sound of Christmas songs could be heard blaring from the kitchen, and he could just make out his mum softly singing along.

'You sound happy,' he said, putting his head around the door.

'I am happy,' replied his mum. She finished basting the turkey and leaned down to return it to the oven. 'I have my kids here for Christmas. What more could I want?' Moving towards him, she placed the oven glove down on the island in the centre of the kitchen.

'Give your old mum a hug,' she said, and Tom obliged.

'It's lovely to be home Mum,' he said squeezing her hard. There were tears in her eyes when she pulled back from him.

'Oh Mum, is everything OK?' he asked.

'Of course. I'm just being silly. Nothing like the holidays to bring out all sorts of emotion.' Tom watched as she wiped another small tear which had escaped from the corner of her eye. 'I'm fine,' she said again. 'I just miss having you all home, I guess. Now go and tell the others food will be ready in 15 minutes.'

He lent down and kissed her cheek and then turned to go and find the others.

# TWENTY-SIX

The next morning as they said their goodbyes, Tom hugged his mum for a little longer than normal. She seemed frailer than he remembered on his last visit. Although neither of his parents were old, each year there were subtle differences highlighting how fast the years were going by. He made a mental note to give them a call in the next few days, just to check in.

'It's a shame you can't stay longer,' his dad said giving him an affectionate slap on his back.

'That's my fault,' said Sophie, leaning in to kiss David on his cheek. 'We have arranged to pop in to see my aunt later today. But we will come and visit you both again after the New Year.'

'And I will see you on New Year's Eve,' added Serena. She was looking forward to the party they'd been planning and was going to stay with them for a few days. Once they were in the car and pulling out of the drive, Tom and Sophie looked at each other.

'I feel a bit guilty,' said Sophie. She screwed up her face.

'I know, so do I.' Tom agreed. 'It probably isn't the right time to explain now though, and I feel slightly better knowing how much John will be looking forward to our visit.'

'Yes, you're right, and it will be great to meet him,' said Sophie, relaxing a little. 'I suppose it wasn't a total lie, we will be seeing family tomorrow.'

'Mum did seem a bit off though, I thought,' said Tom. 'I couldn't put my finger on it, but she seemed, I don't know, maybe sad at times. I hope they aren't having relationship problems; they don't seem as together as they have done in the past.'

'Really? I thought they seemed fine and yesterday was such a lovely day.' Sophie seemed genuinely surprised. 'I didn't see anything to worry about.'

'Maybe you're right, it wasn't much, she just seemed a bit clingy and that's not like her.'

He smiled then, thinking back to the Christmas Day they had all enjoyed.

'It was a lovely day, you are right,' he added. 'And Serena was on good form. Did you notice how many times she mentioned that guy she has had a couple of dates with? I have a feeling we might be hearing a lot more about him in the future!'

'I think it's lovely. Thank goodness she eventually asked him out. It doesn't sound like he would ever have plucked up the courage,' replied Sophie. She was excited that it may only be a short time until they could go on double dates. 'It's a shame he can't make the party though. I would have loved to meet him.'

'Thank goodness my sister is one to take matters into her own hands.' Tom laughed. 'If there's one thing to be said for our Serena, she always goes for what she wants.'

'A girl after my own heart,' replied Sophie.

About twenty minutes later, they parked in front of John's house. Tom got out and wandered towards the back of the car to open the boot. He lifted out a large bag containing homemade mince pies and a present that Sophie had picked out for John.

Movement of the curtain at the front window caught his eye and John's face appeared. He broke into a big grin and waved his hand at them. It looked as if he had been keeping an eye out for them, and by the time they had approached the front door, it had been flung open.

'Hi, guys. It is great to see you. Come on in,' he said.

He moved to one side so Tom and Sophie could pass and shut the door behind them.

'Sophie, it's so good to meet you,' he said and moved forward to give her a quick hug. 'Thank you both for making the time to come and see me,' he added as he hugged Tom. 'Let's go on through.' He gestured towards the lounge and Tom led the way.

It was noticeable how bare it seemed after the abundance of decorations at his parents' house and the lounge looked the same as last time but with the slightly sad addition of a small plastic

Christmas tree. It was about 2ft tall and had been placed on a side table. The fibre optic ends of each branch following a pattern and blinking a multi coloured sequence.

'Take a seat,' said John. 'What can I get you to drink?'

'A tea would be lovely,' said Sophie.

'And a black coffee, no sugar please,' added Tom. They settled themselves on one of the sofas.

Once John had left, Sophie glanced around the room taking everything in.

'He seems happy to have company. I hope he wasn't on his own yesterday.'

'I know. It's sad to think he hasn't really got anyone to talk to,' agreed Tom. He took hold of her hand and gave it a squeeze. John returned and handed them their drinks. He took his own mug in both hands and took a sip before turning to them.

'How was your day yesterday?' he asked.

Sophie replied. 'It was lovely, thanks. Did you see anyone?'

'I did. I have an elderly neighbour whose wife died a few years back. He comes over to me each year, which means we both have some companionship. It's a quiet affair but nice all the same.' He smiled broadly at the pair. 'It's lovely to see some younger faces today though. I really appreciate you taking the time.'

'We wanted to pop in and see you. It's really no bother,' said Tom. Sophie nodded her agreement. 'And Serena sends her best wishes.'

'That is lovely of her. How is she feeling?' John asked.

'Pretty good considering all she has been through. She's still on medication but feeling back to her old self, which is fabulous to see. It was quite a hard period.'

'Well, I am glad she is feeling better. Send my regards when you see her next,' said John.

He reached forward and offered them one of the mince pies they had brought with them.

'Thank you,' Tom said taking one and offering it to Sophie, who shook her head, so he kept it for himself.

'I think I've had enough mince pies to last me a lifetime,' said Sophie. Tom laughed.

'I should probably agree with you but I'm still hungry even after all the food we consumed yesterday.'

John picked a mince pie for himself before placing the plate back on the coffee table. He took a large bite, catching the stray crumbs of the pastry with his other hand. After he swallowed his mouthful, he grinned widely.

'Wow, these are good. I'm not surprised if this is how you are fed.' he said.

'Sophie made a mountain of them, but we are working our way through,' said Tom. He had managed to finish his in-record time. 'It's a hard job but someone's got to do it.' They all laughed, and Sophie blushed as she revelled in their praise.

They stayed for a couple of hours and when Tom made noises about having to get back on the road, John rose quickly from his chair.

'Before you go,' he said, looking nervously at Tom. 'I told you I might have the DNA test back and well, to be honest, it did arrive about a week ago. I've been dying to call you, but I thought it was best to wait until we were face-to-face.'

He walked over to the dresser and from the drawer retrieved a piece of paper. As he handed it over, Tom couldn't help but notice how much the older man's hand was shaking. He glanced at

Sophie, glad she was here with him for this moment and then he concentrated on the words in front of him.

'So, you really are my dad,' said Tom. He could feel tears prickling behind his eyes and he heard a small gasp from Sophie and felt her move closer.

'Yes, it seems that way,' said John. He stood transfixed, anxiously waiting for Tom's reaction. Tom didn't really know what the protocol was for meeting your father later in life. His first instinct was to hug John, but he remained still. It was shocking to read the words in black and white, even if he had believed it for some time. It seemed a much bigger deal when it was confirmed with scientific data. John stood awkwardly, a couple of feet away, no doubt feeling the same way.

'I don't know how this happened or why Katie left, especially knowing she was pregnant, but I am glad, wherever she went, that she had you and that you managed to find me,' rambled John. He looked close to tears and just as over-whelmed as Tom.

Tom found himself reaching out to him. As he held the man who had fathered him, for the first time, he felt a twinge of guilt for the man who had brought him up. He knew deep down that the Mum and Dad he had grown up with would always feel like his real parents, but he was glad he had found this connection with John. It was hard for him to understand the way John must be feeling, finding out he had a son for all these years and not known. It would take time for them both to make sense of it all.

With a last squeeze, John let his son go and they both turned to Sophie. She remained stuck to the spot with a hesitant smile, watching them closely. John was the first to reach over to her and pull her in for a gentle hug.

'It's so lovely to have met you Sophie,' he murmured. 'This has made my Christmas so very special. It's certainly one I won't forget.' As they left the house with the shock still swirling through their minds, they promised to be in touch soon.

Once the door was closed, Sophie put her arm through Tom's.

'Are you OK?' she asked, concern showing clearly across her face.

'I'm fine,' Tom replied. He let out a large sigh. 'It was what we believed. It's just weird having it confirmed. I'm happy to be part of John's life.' He raised his eyebrows. 'Obviously I have a heap of questions for my parents and that will come soon.'

They got back into the car and as they drove away Tom looked thoughtful.

'I'm going to call Serena as soon as I get home and tell her the news. When she comes up at New Year, we can decide how we confront our parents.'

'You both need to remember whatever happened back then, you were loved as their own. And you must always be grateful for how lucky you have both been,' said Sophie.

'Oh, I don't think we would ever feel any differently towards them. Maybe it's just me who was adopted? Serena at least knows her father is the man she was brought up by, even though we don't know about mum. We need to get to the bottom of it all so I can learn to come to terms with it.'

## TWENTY-SEVEN

They were exhausted by the time they got home and as Sophie pushed open the front door, it swept a pile of letters out of the way. She reached down to pick them and carried them towards the kitchen. After plonking her bag down on a breakfast stool, she placed the letters on the worktop and wandered off to fill the kettle. Tom flicked the heating on, his body giving in to a small shudder.

'It doesn't feel any warmer in here than outside,' he said. He picked up the pile of post and started sifting through it. Sophie agreed. It was a bit chilly.

'I'm going to keep my coat on for a while, until I warm up' she decided.

'It's mainly Christmas cards by the look of it,' said Tom. 'There's a couple for you.'

Sophie made the drinks and joined Tom on the sofa. He passed her the remaining envelopes, and she opened the first letter which turned out to be a three-page update from her auntie who lived in Canada.

'How lovely when you get an actual long letter in the post. It's quite a rare thing now,' said Sophie curling her legs up underneath her while reading. 'We will have to go and visit one day,' she said. 'I've always planned to, but not got around to it.'

'Sounds great,' agreed Tom.

As Sophie opened the second envelope a little squeal of delight escaped her lips. Tom jumped and drew his eyes away from an email he was reading on his phone.

'Everything OK?' he said.

'Oh, my goodness, better than OK,' she said. She leapt up and began pacing. 'It's about that last audition I did before the Christmas break. I got the part! I'm going to be a supporting role in a new musical.' She danced from one foot to the other with excitement.

'That's wonderful!' said Tom. He caught hold of her arm and pulled her down onto his lap. She giggled, letting herself be cuddled up in his arms.

'I knew that audition went well but I still wasn't expecting that!' she said, beaming from ear to ear. Tom picked up the letter which Sophie had dropped when she leapt up. His eyes skimmed the contents. Halfway through reading he looked up at her.

'It says here, that if the show is a hit in the West End, you may be required to go on Broadway with the show after its initial run in London. Wow that's massive Sophie.'

Sophie was back on her feet. She just couldn't sit still. It was the best Christmas present she could have wished for, knowing that all her hard work had materialised into her dream job. She wouldn't miss the auditioning process for a while that was for certain. It was relentless and she found it hard not to take the criticism personally. In some auditions she had just got through the door and barely said hello, when she had heard the words "next, thank you for coming".

All her new acting friends said the same though. Sometimes you just didn't look right for a job and not to take it personally, but you had to be thick skinned to not let it affect you a little. At least now she could relax for a while, knowing she had a job and a fantastic opportunity that she would enjoy every minute of.

'I think we have a bottle of champagne in the fridge,' she heard Tom say. He stood up and disappeared into the kitchen. After a minute or two he reappeared with an open bottle in one hand and two champagne flutes in the other. Sophie took a filled glass from him, thanked him, and then went back to staring intently at her mobile phone.

'I'm sending a text to everyone,' she said, looking up at him. 'My goodness, can you imagine if I end up on Broadway!'

Tom couldn't help the flicker of worry that showed across his face. It may have just been for a second, but Sophie picked up on it and her smile faded.

'What's wrong?' she asked.

'Nothing, I was just thinking if you are going to be away for a few months what that means for us?' Tom didn't want to put a dampener on their celebrations but the thought of being separated filled him with dread. Sophie put her phone down and got up, flinging her arms around his neck.

'It's not a definite anyway, so don't look so glum,' she said. She kissed him. 'I mean I do know the show will be a big hit, so it's a possibility but we can work something out. I don't want to be apart from you either.'

As Tom looked deeply into her eyes, he knew he couldn't ever come between her and the job she loved, and he realised he would go to the ends of the earth for this girl.

'We do have an office in Philadelphia, so I could always make enquiries about working there for a while if it comes to it?'

'Is that close to Broadway?' said Sophie a big smile creeping across her face. She was grateful that he would even consider moving for her and it gave her goosebumps that he was prepared to sacrifice his lifestyle for her.

'I don't actually know,' Tom admitted, 'but we could investigate. Let's not get too far ahead of ourselves. You can speak to your agent after the

Christmas break, and we can see how likely it is that the USA is an option.'

'I love you,' Sophie said. She kissed him again, deeper this time. 'I love you for even considering it.'

'It would be an adventure for me to see somewhere else and it would be exciting to work in another country. And once your contract has finished, we could always stay in America for a few weeks and do some travelling before coming home.'

'That sounds perfect!'

Sophie was distracted by the continuous pinging of her phone as congratulations came through from Lana and Jane as well as others. As they sipped their Champagne they skimmed through the countless messages, and it wasn't until about an hour later that they realised they hadn't eaten. Tom's stomach had begun to make loud growling noises and he went into the kitchen to rummage in the freezer.

They had stocked up before Christmas Day, knowing that when they arrived home, they probably wouldn't want to cook elaborate meals. Two ready meals were plucked from the freezer and Tom pierced the film on both before placing one in the microwave. A macaroni cheese for Sophie, which he heated first, and then a Spaghetti Bolognese for himself.

They sat at the breakfast bar silently eating, realising how hungry they were and after polishing off every mouthful Sophie yawned.

'I think all that excitement and Champagne has finished me off,' she said reaching for the dirty plates. Seeing her yawn started Tom off too. He got to his feet and took the plates from her.

'You go up, I'll tidy this and be up in a minute,' he said. She smiled gratefully at him.

'My, you are well trained,' she said with a glint in her eye and wandered towards the door.

'You can thank my mum for that,' he replied.

Sophie turned as she passed through the doorway. 'Oh, I will thank her when I see her,' she said. 'That's just the kind of parenting I agree with!' She dragged her tired body up the stairs towards the sanctuary of their bedroom.

Tom placed the plates and cutlery into the dishwasher and wiped the worktop over, then he filled a couple of glasses with water and switched off the kitchen light. As he entered the bedroom, he could hear Sophie breathing softly and he smiled at how quickly she could drop off to sleep. He placed one of the glasses onto the bedside cabinet on Sophie's side of the bed before putting the other on his side. He crept as quietly as he could towards the bathroom, so not to wake her.

A few minutes later he lifted the bed clothes and crawled under them. He put his arm across Sophie and gently pulled her towards him. She didn't even stir. A thought crossed his mind of how happy he was as he slipped into a deep sleep.

# TWENTY-EIGHT

Jane was the first to arrive at the New Year's Eve party. She had promised to turn up early and help to get the place ready. Armed with an assortment of crisps and snacks she came in like a whirlwind, dumping the bags onto the worktop. There was a distinct clink of glass that gave away how much alcohol was inside. Sophie peered in and started to empty it.

'Blimey, I said bring a bottle Jane, not five!'

'We don't want to run out on New Year's, do we?' replied her friend giving her a big grin. Tom had met the actors from Sophie's last show after the wrap party and he was pleased to see Jane when he wandered in to join them in the kitchen. Serena followed him in, and he made the introductions. They dished out tasks, with Serena hanging a long 'Happy New Year' sign up with Sophie across the hallway so it could be seen as soon as the guests arrived. Tom dug out bowls for Jane to fill with the snacks and he poured a mixture of alcohol and juice into a punch bowl. Around an hour later the doorbell rang again.

"I'll get it,' said Serena and when she returned the rest of Sophie's acting crowd had arrived all together. Lana and Harry came in first. Lana looking fantastic in a sparkly silver dress showing off her incredible figure. She had her arm through Harry's, and she catapulted into the room, dragging him with her. He stood slightly awkwardly at her side, grinning at everyone. Sophie knew that parties weren't really his thing, so she was pleased he had made the effort.

Sophie kissed them both on each cheek before waving her hand towards the drinks table and telling them to help themselves. Jane was pouring goodness knows what else into the large punch bowl and bravely or stupidly – depending how you looked at it – they both took a filled glass from her.

Then came Trent, ambling through the doorway with a girl on each arm. They looked familiar and Sophie realised she recognised them as dancers from the show, but she couldn't recall their names. Trent helped her out as he greeted the group at large, making sure everyone remembered Tina and Paula from the show and they all exchanged kisses. Sophie would rather not have invited Trent, but as the invitation had been extended to the others it was awkward not to. She had introduced Trent and Tom after the show had ended but she had never spoken to Tom about her concerns.

She had managed to corner Trent a few days before, the day after boxing day, when she had gone out with the other actors for a Christmas party. It gave her the opportunity of bringing up the subject while the others were dancing, when they were left alone at the table. With the 'Dutch courage' from the alcohol it had felt like then was as good a time as any.

Still, Sophie had found the chat awkward, and it made her cringe even now. She had told him how serious things had become between her and Tom and that although she was flattered by his interest, it could go no further. He had seemed to take it well enough, although he stared forlornly at her throughout her speech. And when he replied it was only to say, "Ok my lovely, I understand." And she hoped he did.

The fact that he had shown up with a girl on each arm was probably a good sign. She still had the flamingo hanging from her keyring. It would have been awkward to take it off, what with Tom thinking it was a present from her aunt. Trent never even mentioned it so she had convinced herself that it was just a friendly gesture and for all she knew he could have sent the others presents. It was best left as it was. She wanted to remain friendly with them all. They were bound to end up at some point in another play or musical together.

The doorbell continued for the next half an hour or so and Serena took on the task of running to open the door each time. There were friends and colleagues from Tom's office, Simon, Jenna, and finally Carrie. She came in and nodded towards Simon, and Sophie was glad that her friend could be civil with him.

'You look amazing!' said Sophie. They hugged before Sophie held her childhood friend at arm's length, getting a proper view of her. Her skin was bronzed, and her hair had been lightened a few shades by the sun. She looked happy and carefree and before long Carrie launched into a long monologue about the adventures she had been on. When she finished Sophie got a drink for each of them.

'God, I missed you,' said Carrie hugging her friend tightly again. 'How's the lovely Tom?'

'He's wonderful,' said Sophie. 'And he's right behind you,' she finished. Tom embraced her and welcomed her back.

The party was in full swing by 10.30pm and Tom hadn't seen Sophie for a while. He'd been chatting to a guy from work called Paul for the past half an hour, although he'd done his best to shut the conversation down as it kept returning to work related issues. As soon as Paul had mentioned needing the toilet, Tom had pointed him in the right direction and gone off in search of Sophie. He poked his head into the kitchen and said hello to Jane and Carrie who were deep in conversation while guarding the last of the punch.

'I was looking for Sophie,' he said.

'Last time I saw her she was in the lounge,' said Jane, taking the opportunity to top up her glass with the last dregs from the bottom of the bowl.

Tom moved away towards the lounge, dodging the people milling around in the hallway. He glanced around the lounge, but she wasn't there. Just as he was about to look elsewhere, he noticed a couple of figures outside the bay window. He headed for the front door and found it on the latch. The cold air hit him as he went outside, and he spotted Sophie and Simon before they noticed him. They were standing facing each other just to the left of the front door and to Tom it looked like he was interrupting an argument. He approached and his movement caught Simon's eye. His friend dropped the frown and smiled.

'Hi mate,' he said. 'Sophie was feeling a little drunk, so I came outside with her to get some air.' Tom glanced at Sophie, registering how pale she looked. But was it more than that? She had the strangest expression, something between annoyance and tears but as she focused on Tom, she relaxed a little.

'Yeah, I was feeling a little peaky,' she agreed. 'I don't think gin agrees with me. I get a bit emotional. I'm OK now though. I'll come back inside with you.' She moved towards him and linked her arm through his. A little tug on his arm and they both moved away. Before entering the house Tom turned and looked back towards Simon. He was still stood in the same place, staring after them.

They saw the New Year in, and an hour or so later the guests began to thin out considerably. There were only a few of their friends left and they were congregating in the lounge, some sitting on sofas and some dotted around on beanbags.

Carrie was still there and Jane too, both of whom were staying over on blow up mattresses, which were ready to set up in the lounge once everyone had left. Trent and his two dancer friends had left for another party just after the chimes had rung out and Sophie had to admit she felt more comfortable with them gone. Harry didn't even make it until midnight, but they were all glad he had made the effort to show his face. Serena was busy texting the man she had been seeing for months now. He had been obliged to go away for a few days on a family get together, but they were meeting up as soon as they could.

Before leaving earlier Tom had sat in a group with Simon, Jenna and Sophie and everyone had acted normally, so his worry over what happened outside had disappeared. Sophie had been drinking water since she had come back inside, and she was obviously feeling better. Her and Jenna got along amazingly well, and Simon seemed back to his old self.

Tom was feeling quite tired now and he was glad when Lana got to her feet, quickly followed by a work colleague of Tom's, who had been following her around like a lost puppy for most of the evening. They said their goodbyes and left together to share a taxi home.

'I don't think he can believe his luck,' said Tom. He grinned at Sophie. She laughed and agreed.

'I'm seeing Lana on Tuesday so I will fill you in if there is any gossip,' she said. 'We are both at an audition so there will be plenty of time to quiz her.'

'What's the audition for?' Serena asked. She had finished texting and sat back in her beanbag, wriggling around trying to get comfortable.

'It's a comedy play. It was written by a friend of Trent's and it's his first play which is very exciting.'

'Shame I couldn't audition too,' piped up Jane. She had already committed to a small speaking part in a soap opera. 'It would have been lovely to get us all working together again. Mind you, if Trent ends up acting in the play as well as you two, that is most of the gang.'

Serena looked over at Sophie.

'I thought you had the musical coming up?' she asked.

'I do but the rehearsals for that don't start for a couple of months and this play is going to be a few weeks rehearsal, which will start in two weeks' time, and then only a week on stage. So, if I'm lucky enough to get it, I just about have time to fit it in.'

'Sounds fantastic,' said Carrie. She smiled proudly at her friend. She had already become Sophie biggest fan and was happy to tell anyone who would listen about her best friend the West End actress.

Serena was the first to let out a big yawn and the others laughed. She looked momentarily horrified.

'Sorry guys. That sounded like I was bored, but it's just the late hour creeping up on me.'

'Don't apologise,' said Tom. 'I think we could all do with our beds now.' He was glad they could finally bring the party to an end. 'I'll go and drag your beds in,' he said to Carrie and Jane.

'It's a good job we pumped them up earlier, I don't think I'd have the strength now,' said Sophie. She followed Tom to give him a hand.

Once they were all settled in their own rooms Tom turned to Sophie.

'Come here you,' he said. He kissed her deeply. 'Happy New Year Sophie, let's have a great year ahead.'

'Happy New Year,'

'That was a great party. Everyone seemed to enjoy themselves,' said Tom as he started to undress.

'It was lovely to have them all over. I didn't realise we knew so many people. Maybe we should make it a yearly thing?'

'Sounds like a plan,' agreed Tom, 'I'm pretty sure I'm going to have the mother of all hangovers tomorrow though.' He drank a glass of water and placed the empty glass on the nightstand. Within minutes, they were cuddled up in bed together and had drifted off to sleep.

# TWENTY-NINE

When Sophie arrived at the audition, she was pleased to see that Lana was already there. *God, I feel like I'm never going to get used to being subjected to this judgement,* she thought. She excused her way past some other actors to join her friend.

'Hi Sophie, how are you feeling?' Lana asked.

'A bit nervous,' Sophie replied. She sat herself in the chair next to Lana. 'It takes a little bit of the pressure off knowing the director is Trent's friend and that he already introduced us at the wrap party. Hopefully he will remember both of us.'

Just then a lady who was tiny in stature but had the loudest voice Sophie had ever heard shouted some names.

'Hayley Marks, Greta Summers and Lana Rivers, please come with me,' she screeched over the hubbub. Her voice was sharp, and Sophie could see a young girl jump up as she heard her name and scuttle over as fast as she could. She looked petrified. Another girl got up and followed and then Lana rose elegantly, as if in no hurry at all.

'Good luck Sophie, you'll be great,' she said and with a quick smile she turned and followed the others. Sophie took out her phone and started to scroll through her emails glancing up every so often to see what was going on. After about another thirty minutes of waiting, she had seen around twenty more hopefuls follow the tiny woman away and she began to fidget, wishing they would hurry up. The longer she waited, the worse her nerves became.

A sudden murmur of low, whispered voices emanated across the room towards her. She couldn't see what the fuss was until the crowd parted and she spotted Trent confidently striding through. Inwardly she rolled her eyes at the reaction he seemed to have on the females of the species, but she had to admit she was relieved to see another friendly face. As he approached her, she looked up at his chiselled features and smiled.

'Hi Trent,' she said. But he didn't miss a step. He glanced sideways at her as if she was a stranger and moved on. A rush of blood shot to her cheeks and she felt mortified. The girls who were sat next to her probably thought she didn't know him, and they smirked openly at her audacity to speak to this godlike creature. As the minutes moved on even slower now, she kept her head down, not wanting to make eye contact with anyone until she could bring her embarrassment under control.

When the bellowing voice called her name along with some others, she wasn't sure could move her body. Part of her wanted to run away and not go into the room where she would no doubt be scrutinised. But she couldn't let him win. She took a deep breath and pushed herself up from the chair, feeling how wobbly her legs were. *Maybe he was late and just didn't register my greeting?* She thought. *It's probably my nerves making it into a big deal.*

With all the energy she could muster she joined the back of the line heading towards the audition room and forced herself to smile as she entered. By the time she left the building it was 5.30pm and she knew getting across town would be bedlam. As she gulped in the fresh air, she could feel a tear slowly dripping down the side of her cheek. She felt consumed with frustration, the embarrassment had dissipated but it left her feeling angry.

Trent had sat on the panel and blanked her then too. She had tried her hardest to concentrate on the lines she was reading but couldn't help but stumble. She could feel his piercing gaze watching her every move. His director friend had made no mention of briefly meeting her before, although he had politely watched her audition before making notes and thanking her for her time.

There was no chance she was going to be chosen for the part, she could almost see the pity in the director's eyes. And to top it off, she was sure she had seen a sneer from Trent, just for a split second before he covered his underlying feelings with the mask he usually wore. *Damn him,* she thought. *If this was the way he wanted to play it just because she had turned down his advances, he was more dangerous than she first thought.*

A few days later, a letter arrived, and Sophie left it on the side, knowing full well it was from the audition team. She had no interest in reading a rejection letter today. She still had the job coming up that may eventually take her to Broadway but the rehearsals for that had been delayed again and wouldn't start for another couple of months at least. Her plan of finding something to keep her busy until then was fading, which was a shame as Trent's friends play would have been perfect.

Tom wandered in whistling to himself.

'You sound happy,' she said. Still smiling away, he planted a kiss on her lips.

'It's Saturday and I have you to spend the day with, so why wouldn't I be happy?' he asked. He looked closely at her and noticed she didn't seem quite herself. 'Although you look like you've had bad news. What's up?'

'Nothing really, I'm just a bit panicked that I won't get another job soon. Lana heard two days ago that she got the part in Trent's friends play and I'm happy for her, really I am, but I guess I'm still reeling from the way he treated me that day and annoyed at myself for letting him throw me off.'

She had filled Tom in about Trent's rudeness that day and explained about his bruised ego. Tom wasn't overly happy that Trent had moved in on Sophie, but he was glad she had told him. He agreed with her that it was a rotten way to treat your friends, and she could tell he planned to keep an eye on Trent whenever he was around.

'Look,' he said to her now. 'We all have an off day every so often. If the director couldn't see through that and realise your talent, then more fool him.' He picked up the letter and waved it at her.

'Is this from them?' he asked, reading the stamp on the back of the letter.

'It looks like it, but I already know I didn't get the part,' she replied.

Tom lifted his eyebrows, questioning her logic.

'And are you psychic now my love?' he said, raising his eyebrows further. 'Come on Sophie, it's not like you to give up so easily. Would you like me to open it?'

She sighed.

'No, you're right,' she said. 'Throw it over. Let's get it over with.'

He watched as she ripped open the white envelope, quickly scanning the enclosed letter. Tom waited patiently.

'I got the part,' said Sophie, looking a little sheepish. 'Goodness knows how with that performance, but they are offering me the part I wanted.' Her mind was already whirring. *Why on earth did they want her and how was she going to cope with seeing Trent each day?* She looked at Tom and how proud he was and pushed her worries aside. It was a great part, and she would just have to be professional in her interactions with Trent and there was no way a bully like him would get away with upsetting her again. She was glad Lana would be there too though.

'I knew they couldn't resist your talent and your charm,' said Tom. 'Shall we go and get an afternoon tea at that place you like? A little celebration?'

'Sounds lovely,' she agreed. 'I'll have a shower and we can go.'

The little cafe was her favourite. She loved the pretty tablecloths and the delicate China, all mismatched and original and she liked to support the nearby cafe culture. The staff were always friendly and attentive and although it wasn't somewhere Tom would come alone, she appreciated him joining her on the odd occasion. The decor was a bit too feminine for him to feel totally comfortable, but he could put that to one side for the amazing brownies they served alongside his latte.

They picked their usual seat in the window and once the waitress had taken the order, he held Sophie's hand across the table. Even a stranger could see the bond they had between them and an old lady from a nearby table smiled at the image of young love.

'Has it sunk in yet?' asked Tom.

'I suppose. I'm still a little in shock but pleased too. I need to call Lana when we get home. She will be so glad we will be working together again. Rehearsals start next week so it will be all go then as opening night is not that far away. They said it would be an intensive build up. You don't mind, do you?'

'Not at all, don't worry about me. I'm in full support of your career and I know it's not a nine to five job. I've got plenty to keep me busy the next few weeks.'

The coffees and brownies arrived, and they both started to dig in, both silent for a moment.

'Well, it's not long until your birthday so I'll make it up to you then.' Sophie said. She had shaken off her concern and was now feeling quite uplifted. 'What did I do to deserve someone like you?'

# THIRTY

The following weekend Sophie was busy with rehearsals, so Tom decided to pop down and see Serena and his parents. He had persuaded Serena to join him paddle-boarding. Neither of them had tried it before but he had windsurfed a few times in his younger days and thought it looked fun. There was a harbour about ten minutes from the house and Tom had booked them in for an afternoon session.

He arrived at the house and found Serena in her bedroom hunting for her swimsuit.

'I can't remember the last time I needed it,' she said and proceeded to pull the entire contents of a drawer out onto the floor. Fiona poked her head around the door and looked mortified at the mess her daughter was making.

'Serena, I put your swimsuit in the second drawer down in your tall chest if that's what you are hunting for. I could have told you that if you had asked.' She tutted and carried on down the corridor leaving Serena grinning sheepishly.

'Oh well, I'll clear this lot up later,' she announced. She reached into the drawer which her mother had indicated and found her favourite swimsuit right on the top.

'Get it on then and I'll see you downstairs,' Tom said. He went down to the kitchen and found both his parents there. His mum was putting some food shopping into the fridge while his dad was washing up a used chopping board from breakfast.

'You missed a great fry up this morning,' he said to Tom.

'That's a shame, I suppose that'll teach me to have a lie in and not get down here sooner.'

'I'll make you something for when you both get back,' said his mum. She held up some cheese and onion pasties and then placed them on a shelf before shutting the fridge door.

'My favourite, thanks mum,' he said, and he kissed her on top of her head.

'Right,' said Serena appearing in the doorway. 'So, I assume we are hiring the wetsuits as well as the paddleboard?'

'Yes, I thought that was easier. I think I used to have a suit, but goodness knows where it is.'

They left the house and as they got to Tom's car, Mr Trowbridge from next door came around the hedge and walked towards the house.

'The postman posted this through my door instead of yours,' he said as he waved the letter at them. 'Oh, you two look ready for something energetic,' he added.

'Hi, Mr Trowbridge,' Serena said. She could feel his eyes on her, taking in the swimsuit which could be seen through the flimsy cover up she had thrown on to get there. She smiled at him and got into the car. Tom took the letter from him.

'Thanks for bringing it over,' he said. He peered questioningly at Serena through the window. It seemed a bit rude to have got into the car mid-conversation. 'I'll give it to them,' he said to the older man. 'Have a nice day Mr Trowbridge.'

He watched their neighbour walk back up the driveway before he opened his car door and climbed in.

'What was that all about?' he asked Serena.

'Oh God, nothing really, he just gives me the creeps.' Her body did a little involuntary shudder as if to prove her point.

'Eww, you mean in an old pervy kind of way?' He looked shocked.

'Yes, I'm not sure if it's just me but his eyes seem to linger just a little too long and dressed like this, I felt awkward. I was going to ask Sophie if she noticed too.'

'Why would Sophie have noticed?' he asked, surprised. 'She's only met him once.'

'I know but his eyes lingered all over her and I meant to ask her if she was conscious of it too. I'm sure she must have been.'

'Really? But I was there. I didn't notice.' He looked disgusted. He turned the engine over and moved off, heading down the hill towards the water. They remained silent for a minute or two and Serena realised Tom was still thinking about it.

'Stop worrying about it, Tom. He's just a bit creepy that's all. It's not likely that any of us will be on our own with him.'

'That's true I suppose, but I'll ask her when I get home. It's not right for either of you to feel uncomfortable.'

He pulled the car into a parking bay by the side of the road and smiled at her.

'Are you ready for this?' he asked.

'Actually I am. I'm looking forward to a bit of adventure in my life,' she replied. Tom was glad. He had been looking forward to this all week. A whole afternoon of fun stretched out ahead of them.

Later as they entered the house Tom handed the letter to his mum.

'Mr Trowbridge gave it to us,' he explained. 'It had been delivered to his house.' He still felt a bit annoyed by what Serena had told him. It was disgusting, an old fella like that ogling the young girls. He would certainly keep his eyes open next time they saw him. His mum took the letter and placed it on the side.

'Did you have fun?' she asked. She reached into the oven and pulled out a tray of piping hot pasties before placing a plate in front of each of them.

'We did. It was a great afternoon,' he said. 'I'm exhausted now, but it was lovely to get some fresh air. I expect we will have another go sometime and probably bring Sophie.' Serena voiced her agreement.

'It sure works up an appetite,' she said.

Fiona looked happy. Even now that they were grown up, she still enjoyed looking after them.

'Well, you two tuck in. I'm going to go and join your father in the lounge for a while.'

'Thanks mum, you are a lifesaver.' Tom picked up a pasty and took an enormous bite.

# THIRTY-ONE

When Tom arrived home that evening it was quite late, and he found Sophie in the bath surrounded by fragrant bubbles.

'I ache everywhere,' she said. He wandered in and sat down on the toilet lid. 'How are Serena and your Mum and Dad?'

'Everyone's fine thanks. They asked after you too.'

'That's nice.' She yawned and sat up. 'I think I better get out before I fall asleep.'

She stood up and his eyes travelled over her naked body as he handed her a towel. The sight of her skin, soft and wet would usually have aroused him but tonight he realised he was too tired, and she obviously was too. He still watched as she dried herself and then he remembered what Serena had said earlier.

'Sophie,' he said carefully. 'What did you think of Mr Trowbridge who lives next door to Mum and Dad? Serena told me today that she finds him creepy.'

Sophie wrapped the towel around herself and looked at him.

'He seemed OK,' she said. She seemed confused about the questioning. 'I guess I see what she means but I didn't really think much of it. I did pick up on him being a little strange. A little, I don't know, intense maybe?'

'It surprised me. I suppose since his wife died and his son left, I just felt sorry for him. He didn't seem to have much to smile about, but I've not picked up on anything else. If you feel uncomfortable at any time when we are at Mum and Dad's and we see him, please tell me.'

'I will' promised Sophie. 'He's probably completely harmless. Like you said he hasn't got a lot to be thankful for.'

'Anyway,' said Tom changing the subject. 'Have you eaten yet?'

'No, but I think there's some chilli in the freezer from that batch we made a week ago if you fancy it?' Sophie said.

'Sounds good. I'll go and dig it out while you get sorted.' He shut the door behind him and made his way downstairs. First, he went to the fridge and took out an unopened bottle of Chardonnay. He put it on the side while he got two Tupperware pots full of chilli con carne out of a freezer drawer. After loosening the lids, he put them one on top of the other in the microwave and switched it on. Opening a cupboard, he retrieved a glass and filled it to the brim with wine and took a large gulp.

Sophie came into the kitchen, and he held up his glass.

'You want some?'

'I'd love some,' she replied. He reached back into the cupboard and took out another glass, filling it and handing it to her.

'What do you want with the chilli? Rice or Nachos?' he asked.

'I'm happy with Nachos if you are? Whatever's easiest.'

He nodded his agreement and between them they sorted the food into bowls and within ten minutes they were happily sat on the sofa eating. They talked about each of their days and Sophie said she would love to join them the next time they went paddle-boarding.

'I'm glad you had some quality time with Serena though,' she said, and Tom agreed it was the most fun they had had for a long while.

'We need to fit these things in our busy schedules,' he said. 'Otherwise, life just drags you along and you have to remember to make time to enjoy these moments.' Sophie smiled in agreement.

'Well, we have your birthday next week so that'll be fun and when we see Serena, we can book something in for the following week.' She moved forward and kissed him.

'Although saying that,' she carried on, 'next week I have a crazy rehearsal schedule and I need to get your present sorted too, but we will have a nice meal together the night before we go and see your family.'

The morning before Tom's birthday, Sophie woke him up as she placed a cup of coffee on the bedside table.

'What time is it?' he asked sleepily. 'Did I miss the alarm?'

'No, you're fine,' she said. 'I'm off early to the market to get some lovely produce for tonight's meal. You still have at least half an hour before you need to get up.'

'Oh good,' he said. 'See you later then.' He kissed her and watched her leave the room. He plumped up his pillow and lay his head back onto it, smiling to himself. It felt great knowing he had longer in bed. Although he found he couldn't get back to sleep, he lay relaxing until the alarm cut through the silence.

At work they were behind on a project, so he wasn't really looking forward to today if he was honest. It would help him get through knowing Sophie would be cooking a lovely meal for him tonight though. He threw back the covers and stretched his neck from side to side as he made his way into the bathroom. A quick shower later and he was dressed. He grabbed a cereal bar from Sophie's stash of all-sorted ones, for the days when she ran out of time to have a sit-down breakfast.

The earlier he managed to get to the office, the earlier he could leave, he hoped. Armed with the cereal bar and a hastily made coffee in his reusable cup he locked up the house and walked towards the station.

In the end it had made no difference that he had arrived at work early. His day ended up being a long one regardless, but at last, he was finally home. He put his key in the lock looking forward to being greeted with tantalising aromas and a kiss from his girlfriend. But as he entered, he was surprised that the flat appeared to be empty.

There were no signs of Sophie, no cooking smell and no music playing. He was sure Sophie had said she would be home before him tonight and cooking him a birthday feast. Although technically it was his birthday tomorrow, they would be seeing family then and so tonight, a cosy evening in had been planned for just the two of them.

He was sure she had said this morning that she had gotten up extra early to go to the food market. Although he had still been sleepy so maybe he hadn't really listened.

He looked at his watch. It had just gone 6pm now. He guessed she must have popped out for something she had forgotten and was now probably stuck in the rush hour traffic. He could imagine her cursing as she came around the corner, realising that he had beaten her home. That meant dinner was going to be at least a couple of hours away and Tom's stomach was already growling for some sustenance.

He fought the desire to go and rummage for something to eat in the kitchen and instead decided to have a quick shower. By then Sophie should have arrived back and he could help her with the preparations. He grabbed a towel from the airing cupboard and as he entered the bedroom, he threw his jacket onto the bed. He stripped off the rest of his work clothes on route to the bathroom, leaving them strewn across the floor.

As the warmth of the shower hit his body, he realised it was just what he needed to revive his energy levels and he stayed under the strong jets for longer than usual. Once out, he dried himself and pulled on a pair of dark denim jeans and a fresh t-shirt. He paused to collect his discarded clothes and dropped them into the wash bin behind the door.

As he reached the bottom of the stairs, he glanced towards the lounge focusing on the clock on the far wall. 6.45pm. *She should be home by now* he thought. He wandered into the kitchen expecting to hear some music playing and to see her preparing the meal but as before, the kitchen was in its pristine state with no one present. *Strange.* As his eyes took in the empty space, he reached into his pocket for his mobile and dialled her number. It went straight to answerphone.

'Hi honey,' he said. 'Just wondered what time you'll be back. I thought you'd be here before me. If there's anything you want me to start doing as you are held up, let me know. See you soon.' He hit the end call button and perched on a bar stool. He reached over to flick the kettle on, but by the time the kettle had boiled he had changed his mind, and he grabbed an ice-cold beer from the fridge instead.

He hadn't had much for lunch in anticipation of the feast tonight, so he reached into the cupboard for a bag of crisps to take the edge off his hunger. About ten minutes later, his phone, which he had left on the kitchen worktop started to vibrate and he rushed across to answer it. Glancing at the screen he saw that it wasn't Sophie, but Serena.

'Hi Serena,' he said.

'Hey you, how's things? Ready for our meet up tomorrow?' She sounded happy.

'Yes, we're going to come down to you just after lunch. Mum said she had booked the Chinese at 8pm so we can go for a walk and then get ready,' he replied.

'Sounds like a plan. Sophie rang me this morning saying she was sorting a birthday treat for you, but she wouldn't tell me what it was,' said Serena. Tom walked over to the window and looked out at the darkness beyond.

'I'm waiting for her now. I thought she would be home already but maybe she's just running late.'

'Well, she sounded quite excited about it, so let me know when you find out,' said Serena. 'I'll let you go as I'm sure she will arrive any minute. Look forward to seeing you both tomorrow.'

As he hung up, Tom looked at the time again. It was now 7.18pm. He scrolled down to Sophie's number again and pressed call. The answerphone kicked in. He hung up again and decided to send a text instead.

*Call me when you get this. Just checking you're, OK?*

He grabbed another beer and wandered into the lounge. He turned on the television and started absentmindedly watching a game show that was on. And he waited…

# THIRTY-TWO

By 9pm he was beside himself. The extra five calls he had made to Sophie's phone had gone unanswered and she hadn't returned home. He was trying hard not to panic. He realised it was only a few hours after she had been expected. It was plausible that her phone was out of signal so she couldn't call him, and she wasn't receiving his messages. He paced up and down keeping one eye on his phone and the other on any movement outside the window.

The plan tonight had been to celebrate both his birthday and the start of Sophie's new play in just a couple of days' time. Since getting the part in

Trent's friends play, she said she had enjoyed the rehearsal time although she had also told Tom that she was keeping as far away from Trent as she could, whilst remaining professional. Apparently, Trent would always maintain his jovial persona if they were in the company of others and as she was more comfortable with this, Sophie had told him that she had found ways to make sure they were never alone.

She wanted to fully concentrate on making sure she would shine in the show. Tom had read lines with her and thought she was fantastic, but he was always going to be biased. His family were as thrilled as he was for her, so the meal tomorrow was just another excuse to celebrate her new show, alongside his birthday. They were all looking forward to a good night out.

The phone went again, making Tom jump and in his haste to answer it he dropped the handset onto the carpet. As he scrambled to retrieve it, he saw that this time it was his mum calling. He swiped his finger across to answer.

'Hi Mum, I can't talk now, I need to keep the line free. I'm waiting for a call from Sophie. She hasn't come home yet and I'm getting a little worried.' He tried to keep his voice light as he didn't want to worry his mum unnecessarily, but she had always been able to tell exactly how he was really feeling.

'Oh, I'm sorry to hear that son. I thought she was at home today making your birthday meal?'

'That's what I thought too, but she had to go shopping this morning and she may have had other errands to do. I don't know but when I got back from work the house was empty and I've tried calling but her phone goes straight to answerphone.'

He knew his mum would pick up on the distress in his voice. Even to his ear his words were clipped and unnaturally brittle.

'I'm sure she'll be fine,' he could hear her saying, trying to comfort him. 'What time is it?' He could sense her movement into the lounge so she could check the time and then she was back on. 'Oh yes, it is quite late.' There was a slight shuffling about, and he could hear her relaying the situation to someone, no doubt his dad.

'I'm sure she will turn up soon,' said Tom wanting to get his mother off the phone. 'Look, I'll call you later when she turns up, so you don't worry either.'

'OK. We will speak with you soon,' she said. He ended the call. Tom put his head in his hands hoping that Sophie would walk in any minute. He knew his parents would start worrying themselves sick too.

He didn't have the telephone numbers of any of Sophie's acting friends, so he couldn't get hold of any of them easily. He could look up the number of the rehearsal rooms and try to speak to someone there, to ask if there was a meeting today. He did a search on his phone and looked out of the window again before pushing the button to connect the call.

He listened to a continuous ringing tone and then just as he was about to put the phone down, it switched to answerphone. He left a brief message for someone to give him a call as soon as they could. He knew Sophie had social media accounts, but he'd never been into all that stuff and didn't have her passwords otherwise that would be a way he could have contacted her friends. He decided to have a look through any drawers and see if he could find an address book.

He was tempted to drink more alcohol hoping that it may numb his growing feeling of panic, but then thought better of it, just in case he needed to go out in the car and look for her. Almost instantly he dismissed the idea. That wasn't really a viable option as he had no idea of her movements. He knew she was heading to the market but that had closed hours ago, and she could have gone anywhere after that.

He went back into the kitchen to make himself a strong coffee. He sat nursing his drink, restless and trying to control his wild imagination and the worrying thoughts racing through his mind of where she could be.

# THIRTY-THREE

When Tom awoke, he felt disorientated. He squeezed his eyelids shut and opened them again. It hit him immediately. He wasn't in bed but on the sofa because Sophie hadn't come home. He must have fallen asleep while waiting for her. He struggled to his feet rubbing his left arm which had gone numb from sleeping at an awkward angle. Holding on to the banister with the arm that was working, he strode up the stairs, calling out her name. He poked his head into the bedroom but there was still no sign of her.

Tom glared at the made-up bed, his anguish and pent-up frustration directed at the perfectly smooth bedding. *Why couldn't she just be there, tucked up safe?* He could feel his heart beginning to pound, and this combined with the sudden rush up the stairs, left him feeling light-headed. He perched briefly on the bed to gather his thoughts and took a couple of deep breaths, until his vision cleared.

In his haste to check every room he had left his mobile on the table beside the sofa so as soon as he felt able, he descended the stairs to retrieve it. The clock on his phone showed 8.32am. He rubbed at his face, trying to make himself more alert and then he took another look out of the window. Sophie's car was still missing from its spot and the rain from the night before had pooled where her car should have been. Tom unlocked his phone and dialled 999. The operator sounded far too chirpy for this time of the morning.

'Hello. You have reached emergency services, which service do you require?'

'Police,' stated Tom. He found himself nervously tapping his fingers against his thigh.

'Please hold the line,' came the voice.

A split second later another voice.

'Police, what's your emergency?' a female voice asked.

Tom found it hard to speak, his mouth felt so dry. His brain didn't seem to be working either, so seconds ticked by before he could blurt out why he was calling.

'My girlfriend hasn't come home. She should have been home last night and she's not answering her phone.' He moved into the kitchen and with one hand collected a glass from the cupboard and poured himself a water.

'OK Sir,' came the voice on the other end of the phone, calm and precise. 'Could your girlfriend have stayed at a friend's house?'

'She wouldn't have done that without letting me know,' Tom replied. 'And she was meant to be cooking a meal for my birthday last night so she should have been here.'

'When did you last see her?'

Tom positioned himself on a bar stool and tried to concentrate on what he was being asked.

'I last saw her yesterday morning, early before I left for work. She was popping out to get some food from the indoor market and then coming back home. She wasn't here when I got in from work around 6pm. There is no way she would leave it this long without calling me.' He finished his sentence with the panic beginning to creep into his voice.

'Had you argued or had any disagreement?' she asked.

'No, nothing like that. She left home as normal and then no contact.'

The lady at the other end gave him reassurances that most missing people turn up on their own accord and that he should try not to worry. He gave her his details and a brief description of Sophie, and she told him to call any of her friends and family to see if anyone had seen her and that someone would visit his house in the next few days to take a statement.

As soon as the call was disconnected, Tom made himself a strong black coffee before picking up his phone again. It was Serena who answered on his parent's landline. She sounded as if she was out of breath.

'It's Tom,' he said quickly. 'Sophie still hasn't come home. Has she contacted you since yesterday morning?'

'No, I haven't heard from her,' said Serena, breathing heavily. 'Sorry I've been for a walk, and I was rushing as it has just started to rain. I haven't seen Mum or Dad yet this morning but I'm sure they would have called you if they had heard anything.' She paused for a moment, before she continued. 'Are you OK? I can come over. It'll take me at least a couple of hours but I can set off right away?'

Tom sighed.

'I don't know what to think,' he said. He was pacing up and down the kitchen. 'I can't think of any reason she wouldn't come home or for her not to call me. I feel sick to my stomach.' He could feel his hand shaking as it held the phone to his ear. 'I'm so glad I had already taken the day off to come down to Mum and Dad's, so I don't need to call in sick. I don't think I could face work today.'

'Tom, hold on a minute, Mum and Dad have just come downstairs.'

He could hear Serena relaying the latest events to his parents before she replied. 'They haven't heard anything,' she said when she came back on the line. 'Look, I'm going to pack a bag and I'm on my way. You shouldn't be alone dealing with this.'

A flood of relief took over, knowing in a few hours he would have her there by his side. Tom could only manage a subdued response as the emotion threatened to take his voice.

'Thanks Serena,' he managed.

'I'll be as quick as I can.'

After he had hung up, he sat for a few minutes in a trance. Although she had sounded calm, Tom knew Serena wouldn't be rushing up to him unless she was seriously worried too.

He took a few minutes to pull himself together and fired off some text messages to his friends asking if anyone had heard from her. He knew it was unlikely, but it felt good to be doing something. He put a spin on it making it sound like she was due back this morning and only a little late. A couple of replies came back joking that it was still morning and that he should be enjoying the peace for as long as it lasted. Each time his phone beeped he jumped, speedily reading the message, each time hoping someone would let him know she was there.

The peal of the doorbell dragged him from his thoughts, and he raced to answer it. *Maybe it would be Sophie having lost her handbag and with it her phone and keys?*

It was Serena standing on his doorstep looking equally as worried as he felt.

'Goodness, you were quick,' he stuttered.

'It's been three hours since I spoke to you, I said I'd leave straight away,' she said moving past him into the hallway. She dropped a hastily packed bag of belongings onto the floor and gathered him into a hug.

'I didn't realise the time,' he said, still bewildered. It felt like they had just put the phone down and he was surprised at how much time he must have wasted staring into space.

'I'm so happy to have you here,' he said holding her tight for a second hug.

'I tried Sophie's mobile before leaving Mum and Dad's, but it went straight to answerphone. Either there's no signal or it's switched off,' she said as he released her. Serena walked ahead of him into the kitchen and set about making some hot drinks.

'Have you checked the wardrobe and bathroom cabinets to see if any items are missing? I know it's unlikely, but we need to think of anything we can to understand where she could be,' said Serena. Tom slowly shook his head.

'I'm sure there will be nothing missing but I suppose it's worth a look,' he agreed. 'I'm positive though that she left home only to go to the market, and she should have been home at least by the time I arrived last night. It's impossible to think anything but the worst.' Tom put his head in his hands. Serena moved to his side and placed a hand on his shoulder.

'We have to stay positive Tom,' she said to him. He watched her face as something obviously dawned on her. 'Have you called the hospitals?'

He looked shocked.

'No, I hadn't thought about that. Oh God, she could be unconscious somewhere and they haven't been able to identify her.'

'I'll get on to it. What about friends and family?'

'I haven't got numbers for her friends either and I'm also waiting for a call back from the rehearsal rooms now you mention it.'

'Don't worry,' said Serena. She could see how useless he was feeling. She was happy to take charge now that she was here. 'Have you got Carrie's number?'

'There's an address book of Sophie's somewhere but I can't find it. I can't believe I haven't got any of her friend's numbers. It's not something I've ever really thought about before.

Oh, hold on, I suppose Simon may still have it. I'll text him now.' He quickly typed out a text to ask his friend before placing his mobile on the counter.

'I have Jane's number,' said Serena, scrolling through her contacts. 'She gave it to me at the party. I'll call her now and she can check with the others.'

'Thank goodness! I didn't think to ask you,' replied Tom. He looked relieved.

'Then, I'll call the local hospitals,' she added.

'I'd better give her mum a ring soon and let her know what's going on,' he said to Serena. 'It's not really something you should hear over the phone, but I haven't got time to drive over now. I've been putting it off. She will be devastated. I was hoping to find out more before we need to tell her.' He looked at Serena and all she could see was sadness etched across his face. 'I'll go upstairs and check the wardrobes and then I had better call her,' he said.

'Of course. Look Tom, I know how hard this is for you too. Why don't you have a shower before you come back down? That will give me some time and if I haven't found out anything else, you can call her then. Then I will make us something to eat, you need to keep your strength up.'

Tom nodded and gave her a tight smile.

'Thanks, Sis.'

'Oh, and leave me your phone,' she added as he went to turn away. 'I can answer it if it rings.'

'Thanks,' he said, giving her another weary smile.

He placed his phone onto the worktop next to her and she watched him walk up the stairs like a man going to the gallows. Once he had gone Serena found a pad of paper and a pen and began to call.

# THIRTY-FOUR

When Tom came back downstairs, he could read her face, even before she could tell him that she had had no luck.

'It's good in a way,' she said hesitantly. 'At least she hasn't been injured or worse found…' She trailed off not wanting to state the worst-case scenario out loud. Even though he hadn't been expecting a miracle his face dropped and his sadness was plain to see.

'I spoke to Jane, and she promised to call around the others to see if anyone has seen her.'

Just at that second Tom's phone began to ring. Both sets of eyes homed in on the screen. It was John. Tom sighed and picked it up.

'Hi Tom, how are you?' said the voice at the other end of the line. Tom paused for a moment before he could reply.

'John, hi,' he said. He could hear how strained his own voice sounded. 'Something has happened since we last saw each other. Sophie didn't come home, and I don't know where she is,' he continued his voice breaking a little.

'Oh Tom, that's terrible, I am so sorry to hear that. When did you last see her?'

Tom could hear the instant concern in John's voice and somewhere at the back of his mind he was aware that this must bring back horrendous memories for him. If he hadn't called, Tom wouldn't have told him, but it impossible to hide the situation now that they were speaking.

'She should have been home when I got in from work yesterday. There's still no sign and her phone goes straight to answerphone.'

'Are you on your own?' asked John.

'No, Serena has just turned up, so I'm OK. I just don't understand where she could be.'

The conversation felt stilted. Neither of them knew what else to say.

'Look, if I can do anything to help,' said John, 'please let me know.'

'Thanks John. I will let you know if we find her.' Once they had finished the call, Serena looked at him gravely.

'You don't think this could be anything to do with John, do you? I know it sounds farfetched, but in your own words he seemed very taken with Sophie and we only have his word that his girlfriend went missing in the way he told us. He seems like a lovely guy, but you just don't know…'

She was chewing fiercely on the end of a pencil, deep in thought.

'I can't see that,' Tom started to reason automatically. Then he began to consider her point. *How well did they know John? What if he did have more to do with his girlfriend's disappearance all those years ago? Was it just a coincidence that he had called just now, when he had never done so before?*

'I think I've still got that detective's number somewhere,' he said now. 'Maybe I should find it and just run this scenario past him.' He opened the top drawer of the cabinet pushing things aside in hope of finding the card he had picked up while at the detective's office.

*Why didn't I put the number in my phone?* He thought, annoyed with himself. The more he let his mind wander, the more he worried it could have something to do with John.

'I think that is a good idea. He was after all the man who interviewed him at the time,' he was saying to Serena.

'It is a long shot,' replied Serena, 'but what have you got to lose from making one call.'

She wandered over to the fridge. A couple of cards were pinned on top of each other with a watermelon fridge magnet. There were three cards: an out of hours plumber, a local taxi number and underneath that, the card that Tom had been looking for.

Before calling the direct number for Detective Fairbrother, Tom tried Sophie's mobile one last time and took a cursory glance outside to check her car hadn't mysteriously re-appeared. Her phone went straight to answerphone and outside the window her parking spot was still frustratingly vacant.

'While you call him, I am going to try the rehearsal hall again,' said Serena. She took her phone and the piece of paper with the number on and went outside to make the call.

Tom dialled the number on the card and waited.

'Detective Fairbrother,' came the gruff answer.

'Oh hi, I don't know if you remember me, but my name is Tom, Tom Beatty. I contacted you before about the woman that went missing in 1998. Her name was Katie Reed, and she was possibly my birth mother.'

'Yes, I remember,' replied the detective. 'What can I do for you Mr Beatty?'

'Call me Tom please,' he said. He took a deep breath and launched into his predicament.

'Look I know this sounds far-fetched, but I wanted to get some feedback on John Hanson.' He paused trying to make sense of the thoughts whirring around his addled mind. 'The thing is my girlfriend didn't come home yesterday, and I'm worried. I just had a call out of the blue from John, and to be honest it got me thinking; How I don't know him very well, and with what happened to his girlfriend it just didn't sit well with me...' He trailed off.

It seemed like an eternity before the detective answered but could only have been a matter of seconds.

'How long has your girlfriend been missing?' he asked.

'She should have been home yesterday by the time I got in from work. We had a special evening planned and for her not to arrive home or to call is something she just wouldn't do. I've spoken to the local police, and I know it's probably too early to be panicking but this is so unlike her.'

'And had John met your girlfriend?' the detective was asking. Tom forced himself to concentrate.

'Yes, just the once, we went to see him together just after Christmas.'

'And how did that meeting go?'

'Fine,' replied Tom, thinking back. 'He seemed interested to meet Sophie and to be honest, they got on like a house on fire.'

'And is there any reason you would think Mr Hanson could be involved in Sophie's disappearance?'

'Well, no not really. I just started to think that maybe what he told me about Katie going missing was too much of a coincidence and… I'm completely jumping to conclusions, aren't I?' he finished feeling somewhat foolish.

'It's better to be that way than not to think things through,' said the detective gently. 'Although it's also probably best if you don't go around accusing anyone without any proof.'

'Of course,' replied Tom.

'I did pay him a visit after speaking to you last time and I've re-read Katie's file recently,' the detective carried on. 'He's still very cut up about the disappearance but as he was the last person to see Katie, I suppose there will always be doubt in people's minds that he could know more than he let on at the time. There was always the possibility that they had had a disagreement. People never like to say in these instances in case the police think they had something to do with the disappearance. Katie could have found out she was pregnant and didn't want John to know or have anything to do with a baby. He always maintained that they had a perfect relationship, but we can never know that for sure.'

'Do you think he could have had any part in Sophie going missing Detective?' asked Tom. He held his breath waiting for a reply.

'I suppose it is possible but truthfully, no I don't believe he would. For one thing, if he did have anything to do with Katie's disappearance, why would he want to jeopardise getting away with that? And it's unlikely that Sophie would go to his house without you.'

'Yes, it does sound unlikely when you put it like that,' agreed Tom. 'I'm probably clutching at straws.'

'Who are you in contact with at your local police station? I can give them a call and see if I can find out anything if that helps?'

'Thanks,' said Tom feeling a little more relieved to have someone else to help. 'I would appreciate it.' He gave the details.

'No worries,' said the detective. 'Now, if anything else happens in the next few days, let me know, otherwise I will contact you if I find out anything. And try not to worry Tom. Most people who go missing are found safe and well within a few days.'

An hour had passed, and they hadn't heard anything. Tom had been running the last few days through his mind trying to figure out if there were any signs about her disappearance that he had missed. He thought of how Simon and Sophie had seemed at the party and then dismissed it as quickly as he thought of it. He knew deep down that Simon would never intentionally hurt him.

Then his mind flitted to Sophie's actor friend Trent, and he toyed with the idea that he could have had something to do with it. As far as he knew Sophie had told him all about her concerns, but it was possible that she hadn't told him everything. Maybe he should have given his name to the detective just in case. He was beginning to imagine that everyone who had ever met Sophie could be guilty.

For now, he would keep it all to himself, he didn't want Serena worrying more than she already was, but he sensed an urgency. If he didn't find Sophie soon, would he be too late?

# THIRTY-FIVE

Tom woke with a start, his body covered in sweat. He felt achy, as if he might have caught a cold. Closing his eyes, he struggled to repel his dream, but the vivid images stayed with him.

He had been holding Sophie's hand and she was dangling over a cliff edge, the sea lapping angrily on the rocks below. He had held on desperately, trying to use his strength to lift her but just as he pulled her to safety, a hand came out of nowhere and pushed her back over the cliff. He could still hear the blood-curdling scream as her body tumbled towards the sharp rocks below. Tom had turned to look behind him and a familiar face stared back at him as John moved forward, his face full of anger. He forcefully spat his words at Tom.

'Why should you have someone when I lost everything?'

He screamed the words, his face crumpling before he broke into heart-wrenching sobs. As Tom turned back to look for Sophie all he could see was her broken body at the bottom of the cliff. He blinked rapidly, reminding himself that it was just a dream. He remained motionless, his eyes firmly open but still re-living the dream over and over until he could take it no longer.

In his groggy state, Tom crawled off the bed and stumbled towards the shower. As soon as the steaming water began to pummel his body, he was able to gradually shake the images from his mind. He rested his head against the glass door and only realised how long he stayed that way when the water became lukewarm.

He knew he shouldn't go and see John, but something made him anyway. Of course, he wasn't going to accuse him of anything, but just being there in case she was somewhere close, meant he was at least doing something. He didn't know John that well, but he knew he had a much better chance of seeing if he had something to hide when they were face to face.

'Tom! I wasn't expecting anyone. Come in,' said John. He looked shocked to see Tom at his door but that was probably a natural reaction after their conversation yesterday.

'Has Sophie come home?' asked John.

'No, I haven't heard from her,' replied Tom as he followed John into the house. 'I was on my way to my parents when I thought I'd drop by and see you too.' This was a complete fabrication, but it served as a flimsy explanation. The telephone began to ring, and John walked back to the hallway, while Tom made himself comfortable on the sofa.

'Hello,' said John. Tom strained to hear who it was, but all he could make out was that it was a very stilted conversation.

'Yes,'

'OK,'

'Sure, see you then.' He heard John replace the handset and then he reappeared at the door. His expression was pinched.

'Why are you here Tom?' he asked. His teeth were gritted and his expression hard. Tom's palms became sweaty, and he stood up to show the fact that he was taller and bigger built, in case an argument got out of hand.

'Who was that?' Tom said nodding towards the hallway and the telephone beyond. He tried to remain composed.

'That was Detective Fairbrother,' replied John. There was anger on his face but that soon gave way to distress, and his body slumped backwards to lean against the door frame. 'That's why he's ringing and why you happened to pop in, isn't it? You think I had something to do with Sophie's disappearance, don't you?'

He seemed to crumble before Tom's eyes and Tom could barely look at him.

'Actually, I wanted to chat to you as you've been through the same thing,' said Tom, but he knew his face gave him away and John could tell that wasn't the only reason.

'I don't believe you,' said John quietly. 'How could you think I would do anything to hurt anyone? We may not know each other that well but…oh, I see.' It suddenly occurred to him. 'Obviously you think I had something to do with Katie's disappearance too.'

Slowly he slid down the door frame until he was sat like a rag doll at the base of the doorway. Tom moved towards him to try and help the older man up.

John shook his head violently.

'I think you better leave,' said John from his position.

Tom felt ashamed. The devastation on John's face brought out feelings of disgust in himself. He kicked himself for coming here and for making John feel this way without any proof. Underneath he had known it was unlikely John had anything to do with it and now he had brought back all those memories of Katie. He was annoyed with himself.

'John, I'm sorry.' He knelt beside him, but John wouldn't look at him.

'Just go,' he whispered. The disappointment he felt showed across his tired, craggy face and the vision stayed with Tom as he silently left the house.

It had seemed too much of a coincidence for the same thing to happen to John's girlfriend all those years ago, and even as Tom drove away, he was unsure who to believe. And worst of all, he knew how the story ended for Katie. She never returned, so how could he be hopeful that it would be any different for Sophie?

He had no plans to go to his childhood home, but something lured him in that direction. Maybe seeing Serena would calm him down? She had returned home a couple of days before, but they had spoken each day. She had confirmed with the rehearsal rooms that no extra rehearsals had taking place, so that was a dead end. She had also spoken again to Sophie's friend Jane, who in turn had spoken to the other acting friends but nobody knew of her whereabouts. They were all upset to hear the news and had promised that if any of them heard from Sophie, they would call.

As he drove, Tom thought of Trent and how Sophie had felt about his advances. He had to remind himself that he had no proof that Trent was obsessive about her, he only knew that Sophie had felt uncomfortable around him. After what had just gone down though, he could be driving all over town accusing people of all sorts of things. Even his best friend Simon had sounded off when he called Tom with Carrie's number. Tom couldn't really put his finger on it, but it seemed like he wasn't as concerned as he should be. He had said all the right things to reassure Tom but something about his tone didn't ring true. He asked him if Sophie had seemed happy, like he knew that maybe she wasn't but as soon as Tom said this, he backtracked. He didn't say the exact words, but he made it sound as if she could have left Tom, that she wasn't as happy as she had made out. It was all so confusing, and Tom didn't believe that at all. He was the one who knew her best, wasn't he? But why would Simon seem keen on making it sound that way?

He was only a couple of roads away now and he needed more than ever to see Serena, rather than just speaking to her on the phone. She was a calming influence on him, and he craved her support. She had always managed to make him feel better, not that this kind of despair had ever presented itself before.

As he pulled into the driveway, he saw that his dad's car wasn't in its usual spot, and he kicked himself for not calling ahead. He clambered out and slammed the door shut. As he stood looking at the house, he decided he was still glad he had come here. Somehow, being close to his childhood home made him feel secure and that feeling grew when the door opened and he saw Serena, standing barefoot in the doorway. The concern on her face warmed his heart.

'Tom! What's happened? Have they found Sophie?'

'No, she's still missing. I just needed to see you.' He moved towards her and collected her into his arms.

'I've done something I shouldn't have,' he muttered into her hair. He felt her pull away and she looked searchingly into his eyes. They moved inside to the kitchen, and he explained about his disastrous visit to John. Serena perched on one of the breakfast stools and held on to his every word.

'Oh Tom, I know you feel bad for John but at this stage it's natural to jump to conclusions. We barely know him and if he did have anything to do with Sophie's disappearance, he's hardly going to tell you, is he?'

He sighed.

'It's just all so confusing. I can't even think rationally anymore. I can't sleep. I ran all the scenarios over in my mind and in none of them does she just turn up at the door safe and sound.' A sob escaped his throat and he let himself be comforted.

'Look Tom, we need to get to the bottom of what happened when Katie disappeared, and I think the only way is to speak to Mum and Dad and find out once and for all, how this man is your father.'

The sound of someone clearing their throat loudly brought their attention to the doorway and they turned to see their parents waiting for an explanation.

# THIRTY-SIX

As they came through the door into the kitchen Tom reached forward and gathered his mum into his arms.

'Hi Mum, how are you?' he asked. He felt compelled to reassure her that they would always be her children, no matter what. She softened slightly in his embrace and then in turn wrapped her arms around Serena.

'I'm fine,' she said stepping back to look at them both. Her voice was a little tentative and she looked at them questioningly.

'What was it that you wanted to talk to us about?' she enquired. David had set about making a drink and generally keeping himself busy, but he turned now to hear what they had to say. Serena glanced over at Tom, and he saw her take a deep calming breath, before she started speaking.

'Look, this is difficult to say but while we were getting tested for my bone marrow transplant, we were told that Tom and I are not related.'

There was a loud crash, as the keys Fiona had in her hand dropped to the tiled floor. Tom leant down to retrieve them and placed them carefully onto the worktop. His mum resembled a deer in headlights, and she kept opening her mouth as if to speak but no sound was coming out.

'Sit down mum,' he said gently and guided her to the nearest chair. David had arrived at her side with another chair in tow and sat next to her, taking her hand as he did so.

'We always meant to tell you.' His mum let the tears fall down her cheeks.

'Your mother's right,' added David. 'We tried over the years but then we felt we had left it too long and didn't know how to bring it up. We could see how close you two are and I suppose we didn't want to ruin that for you.'

Serena moved behind her mum's chair and wrapped her arms around her.

'We understand. Honestly, we aren't here to blame anyone. Obviously finding that out was a shock but we have had time to mull it over. All we want to know really is about our biological parents. Nothing would make Tom and I feel differently about you guys or each other.'

David glanced at his wife before beginning.

'Your mother couldn't conceive, so we used a surrogate with my sperm and donated eggs. But your mother always wanted you both and that was the only way for us to have a family.' He squeezed Fiona's hand as her sobs continued.

It was Tom and Serena's turn for a questioning look before Tom broached the next delicate subject.

'I'm not sure you are my biological father though,' he said watching both his parents closely. 'Neither of our tests had a match for a mother and Serena's test came back with you as her father but mine didn't. Mine came back with a completely different name and saying I was not related to any of you.'

'That's impossible,' his mum blurted out. She sat up straight. 'The only explanation is that there was a mistake in the test.' She looked franticly at her husband for reassurance.

'Your mother is right; it must be a mistake. That just doesn't make any sense.'

'But it's been checked, the man in question got a test too and it shows the same result,' said Tom gently. He knew that pushing this point was upsetting but he needed to know what had gone on. His mum was still sobbing, and Serena moved from behind the chair to face her mother, bending down so that they were face to face.

'Mum, it's OK. We don't blame either of you, we just want to know the truth.'

As her mother looked into her eyes a sharp noise came out of her mouth as if gasping for air. It shocked Serena and she backed away a little. The sound grew louder very quickly.

'Move out of the way,' said her dad. He lifted Serena to her feet and gently pushed her to one side. He took her place in front of Fiona's chair. 'She's hyperventilating.' He started to make soothing sounds and rubbing Fiona's hands. 'Honey, please calm down and listen to me.

Everything's going to be fine.' He kept repeating the same line, over and over.

Tom and Serena stood back watching. They were taken aback at how their usually confident mother had descended into such a state so quickly. Tom felt guilty for upsetting her and he wanted to remove himself from the situation. Giving them a bit of space seemed like the best idea.

'Dad, we will go into the garden and give you and mum a minute. If you need us just shout,' he said. He steered a shocked Serena outside, gently shutting the door behind them.

Serena stood to one side of the window so she could still see them inside and she watched distractedly while her dad continued to try and calm their mother down.

'Flipping hell, I feel awful now. I didn't expect such a reaction,' stated Tom. He looked crestfallen. 'The last thing I wanted was to upset mum so much. Doesn't she understand that we don't feel any differently towards her?'

'It was bound to be a shock when they realised that we knew. Maybe it's because they've bottled it up for so long. She'll be fine in a while and we can talk it through rationally,' replied Serena. At least she hoped that would be the case.

Serena kept one eye on Fiona, who was still crying but she seemed to be calming down. She watched as her dad stood up and moved out of sight. They both heard the click of the door and turned to him as he came out to join them.

'She's OK. It was just the shock of having to face it. She has years of guilt from not telling you before. I do too. I'm so sorry.' He took hold of them one by one and hugged with such a force that Tom felt even worse.

'We didn't want to upset either of you. It was such a hard thing to bring up and now we wish we hadn't. Once we found out about it, there was just no going back. There would have always been this part of us that needed to know,' said Tom.

'You know how much we love you both,' added Serena giving her dad's arm a squeeze.

'We know,' said David. 'I think your mum will need time to come to terms with the fact that you know she didn't give birth to you. It would be nice if you could both be here for a couple of days, so that will give her time to chat to you properly?' He looked so forlorn that Tom and Serena both agreed. It would be difficult with work for Tom, but he still had some holiday time he could take, and he promised to go and call his boss. The three of them went back into the house feeling the trepidation of the conversations that they knew were ahead.

# THIRTY-SEVEN

Tom opened his eyes the next morning to sunlight streaming through the thin curtains and for a second, he forgot where he was. As he rubbed each eye the misery quickly set back in, weighing heavily on his shoulders. The last time he had slept in his old bedroom Sophie had been with him.

Even though Serena and Tom had stayed over last night, there had been no more discussion about their parentage. Fiona had calmed down but by then she had a raging migraine and had gone to bed early. The others felt it wasn't right to discuss everything without her and David had gone up to bed to join her earlier than he would have on a normal night. Tom and Serena had shared a bottle of wine and chatted, but they had kept to the subject matter of Sophie and how Tom was coping. That was probably why Sophie was all that he could think of now.

It had been nearly two weeks and although the police had set up a campaign asking if anyone knew of her whereabouts, nobody had come forward. The CCTV close to the indoor market had been checked on the day she went missing, and the days after, but there had not been a single sighting of her. As Tom didn't know where else she could have been heading for that day, they had no idea where else to look. And now as the weeks went by, he was as helpless as ever. Not a minute of the day passed without thinking of her and worrying if she was hurt or in danger.

Tom climbed out of bed and slowly pulled his clothes on. He unplugged his phone which had been charging on the nightstand and scrolled down to Sophie's number. He hit the dial button. It went straight to answerphone. Every time she recorded herself speaking, she would want to laugh, and he could pick up on the amusement behind her words asking the caller to leave a message. The sound of her voice made his eyes fill up with tears.

He knew he wasn't the only one missing her and he could understand the pain that Sophie's mum and grandad must be feeling too. Tom had spoken to Sophie's mum almost every other day since she had been missing, and the raw emotion he heard in her voice was heart-breaking. The poor woman had already lost her husband to Cancer and now her only child had disappeared. He couldn't begin to know how that felt for a mother. He found it torture to speak to her so often, but he felt it was his duty, and what Sophie would have wanted him to do. There was nothing he wanted more than to go out and find her daughter, for her as much as for himself and it tore him up inside not to be able to do anything.

As he entered the dining room, he could hear an array of voices and knew that the others were already around the table. He had decided to try and leave by lunchtime but that meant a conversation would have to be had as soon as they had eaten their breakfast. He hoped he could steer the conversation that way and he knew they would understand his need to get home.

They were all smiles as he walked in, as if it was a normal day in the Beatty household. There were no signs of the upset from the day before.

'Morning,' he said as he took his seat next to Serena. As he looked across the table at his mother, he realised on closer inspection that there were signs after all. It was obvious that she hadn't slept well. She had made a valiant attempt to cover her tiredness with full make-up, but the tension underneath still showed through. Tom dragged his eyes away and helped himself to the bacon and eggs that were on a hot plate in the centre of the table.

'Thanks Mum, you really shouldn't have gone to so much trouble.'

He was glad she had though as his stomach felt nauseous with hunger. He added some toast to his plate and began to lather some butter on it, watching as it melted in.

'You're welcome,' said his mum, looking pleased. 'I thought we could all do with a decent breakfast today.'

'I'm full already,' said Serena, pushing her own bowl away. It looked to Tom like she had only managed half of the bowl of cereal she had in front of her. As he lifted his eyes to meet his fathers, he realised he was thinking the same thing.

'Your mum and I are finished too, so we will make some extra coffee. When you have finished Tom, we will see you in the lounge.'

'OK Dad, I do need to get home later so I thought I would head off after lunch,' said Tom between mouthfuls. He was sure he saw the veins in his mum's neck tense as she quietly followed her husband. As soon as they had left Serena started on him.

'Could you not stay another night? Please, for me? I feel so on edge, and I've got to stay here ready for work on Monday.'

'I would like to, but what if Sophie turns up? I just feel I need to be home. Once we've had a chat, I'm sure mum will be feeling less het up.' He did feel guilty leaving Serena to deal with the aftermath but the pull from home was strong enough to ignore those feelings.

She sighed.

'Fine, I do understand,' said Serena. She looked glum but resigned to the fact that even if he stayed one more day he would have to head back then. 'It's not the best time to be doing this, with all that is going on, but now it's started there really is no going back. Let's just make this talk a good one, so we all feel better. I half wish we hadn't bothered bringing it up now!'

Tom swallowed his last mouthful and before it had even settled in his stomach, he stood.

'Come on then, let's get this over with.'

## THIRTY-EIGHT

Detective Fairbrother just couldn't shake the conversation from his mind. How could Tom's girlfriend now be missing? It didn't make any sense. Yes, lots of people went missing every year but this was all too closely entwined. He had just put the phone down after speaking to John Hanson and there was something that man wasn't telling him.

He had sounded cagey and although he had agreed that the detective could visit again, Alan realised that John hadn't asked what the visit was for. Now that was strange. It was almost as if he knew there would be contact and what Detective

Fairbrother was looking into. He sat back in his chair replaying the conversation word for word.

'I wondered if I could pop over to ask you a few more questions?' Alan had asked.

'OK,' came the reply. There was a slight hesitation. 'I'm rarely ever out, so anytime you are passing.'

'Maybe later today then?'

'Sure, see you then.' And that was it. No mention of why or what type of questions. None of that was asked. *Yes, strange,* he thought.

He muttered under his breath as he stood and collected his coat from the hook behind the door. *There goes lunch again,* he thought. It would take his whole lunch hour to get over to the Hanson house, but he couldn't let it go. He had a bad feeling about this. Traffic was quiet and he made the journey in less time than usual. He had been running the notion through his mind of finding Tom's girlfriend at the remote place John lived. *Is that what happened to Katie? Was it John all along and as he had not been stopped, was this him doing it again? Jesus it's been over twenty years. What if he had done this again and again?*

The house looked exactly as it had on his last visit. The dirty, beat-up old car was still out front. Possibly it didn't run, so had been left there all this time slowly rusting.

Detective Fairbrother lifted his body from the driving seat. His belly scraped passed the steering wheel and he made a mental note to cut down a little on what he consumed. If he carried on eating the way he was, it would become a struggle to manoeuvre himself in and out of the car at all. Once up the steps he pounded on the front door and waited.

'Come in,' said John, as he opened the door. He looked upset and as the detective moved past him into the house, his eyes quickly took in everything around him. He was poised, ready if something happened, glancing behind him at short intervals just in case. John followed him meekly with no sign of anything sinister at play. He walked into the now familiar lounge and again everything looked the same.

'Why did you want to see me?' John said. There was no note of curiosity in his voice. He looked like a man who knew exactly how this was going to be played out.

'The girlfriend of your son Tom has gone missing...' he started.

'And you're here to pin that on me!' interrupted John. An almost animal sound of rage filled the room, and the detective was taken aback. 'What is it with you all? Why can't you just leave me alone?'

'I'm not accusing you of anything,' reasoned the detective. He put his hands out in front of him to gesticulate remaining calm. 'I just want to know if you have heard from her?'

'You know he's been here, accusing me too. Said he was on his way to his parents' house and just happened to have time to pop in!' John's whole body was shaking with rage. 'Haven't I been through enough? I didn't ask for him to come here and bring it all up again about Katie and I know nothing about his girlfriend. He should just stay with his perfect parents in their perfect house in Greenbay and leave me alone!'

The frown on the detective's face made him stop. John sensed that something he had said had struck a chord with the detective.

'What?' He asked.

'Tom's parents' live in Greenbay?'

'So what? They live a few miles from here, I don't know exactly where but it made it easier for Tom to visit when he was nearby,' replied John. It was his turn to frown, the rest of his anger dissolving.

'Doesn't that strike you as a coincidence?' asked the detective. 'Tom's parents living near to where Katie was last seen. Were they living in that area at the time?'

John put his head in his hands. He tried to concentrate on what the detective was saying.

'So, you now think they could have known Katie or taken on her child? That doesn't make any sense.'

'Maybe,' said the detective thoughtfully. 'Have you got Tom's number? I might just give him a call. I can at least tell him to stop bothering you for now.'

John wandered back into the kitchen to retrieve his phone and wrote Tom's number on a scrap of paper before passing it over. Then both men walked towards the front door.

'Look John, I just came to see what you knew about Sophie disappearing. You tell me you had nothing to do with it and that's fine, but I had to come and check things out. And as far as things go, I don't think Tom is really focusing at the minute. He's just worried about her and I'm sure you can relate to that. If you just let me have a look around now that I'm here and then I'll get out of your hair.'

John stood aside with a dejected look on his face. He shrugged.

'Go ahead. I have nothing to hide. But I want you to promise me you will get to the bottom of it all. I need to know what happened to Katie and I pray you find Sophie too, for Tom's sake. I would never wish that on him.'

Detective Fairbrother took a swift look around the house, from top to bottom. There was nothing out of the ordinary and he felt somewhat sorry for John as he left. Before getting back into his car, he wandered down the pathway to the side of the property and poked his head into the two small outbuildings at the rear. They were dilapidated and in need of a good amount of repair, but he looked carefully into every nook and cranny and found nothing untoward.

As he got back into his car his mind turned to the new information about Tom's parents living in Greenbay. He decided to check in with Tom and find out exactly where they lived. Digging around in his pocket, he located his mobile. He dialled and when it went straight to answerphone, he left a short message for Tom to return his call.

He was reluctant to go back to the office and as Greenbay was in the other direction, it made him already halfway there. He mulled it over for a minute or two before he picked up his phone again and connected to the internet to search the local electoral roll. He paused, trying to remember Tom's surname and as soon as it came to him, he typed it into the search box. Several people showed up with the name Beatty and he scrolled down the list trying to match the area. Tom didn't live at home anymore, so his name was unlikely to show up and he had no idea of either of his parents' names.

He was just thinking this was like finding a needle in a haystack when an address caught his eye. He was sure it was one of the roads in the report that backed onto the fields where Katie had jogged. *Too much of a coincidence to ignore.* He reversed his car, did a three-point turn and as he left the driveway, he took a left towards Greenbay.

# THIRTY-NINE

The atmosphere in the Beatty household was electric. The normally tranquil lounge area where they enjoyed many a good memory, seemed uninviting as Tom walked in. Serena obviously picked up on it too. Tom noticed her stiffen as she moved towards the window. She came to a stop and lowered herself slowly onto the edge of the window seat. In the past, this had always been where you would find her, often engrossed in a book. Tom felt protective towards her now as she settled in the place he knew was like a comfort blanket to her.

He wasn't feeling too emotional. Obviously, it's a big deal to find out your parents hadn't given birth to you, but he had lovely memories, and personally he wouldn't have changed any of his childhood. Maybe with the added pressure of not knowing where Sophie was, he was not so concerned about something that wouldn't really change anything. All he wanted was to make his parents realise that both he and Serena wouldn't hold on to any anger because they hadn't been told before.

Tom sat directly in front of his parents. They were holding hands and sitting closely together on the large three-seater sofa that dominated the room. His dad was glancing from Tom to Serena and back again while his mother had her head downward and appeared to be studying the pattern on the rug in front of her.

'Can I start, Tom?' asked his dad.

'Of course, go ahead.'

'OK,' He cleared his throat. 'Well, we wanted to know what you meant about me not being your father the other day. And how it came about, that you think this other man could be your father?' He was looking directly at Tom with the hurt etched across his face.

'Well,' said Tom gently. 'I told you that we both had a DNA test done around the time Serena needed treatment,' he continued. 'Serena's test came back with you as her father but mine came back with the name of a John Hanson. Neither of us had a mother's name on our reports.'

David frowned and shook his head from side to side.

'But that just doesn't make any sense,' he said. 'Neither of us have ever heard of this person and as I said before, I supplied the sperm, and we had a donor for the egg.'

'I know it doesn't make a lot of sense, but it seems to be correct. We went and found this man and he had a test which came back the same as mine. He lives not that far from here and he used to live even closer.' He focused on his mum. Could he really accuse her of knowing this man or even having an affair? He thought about it for a second and then made up his mind. They had come this far. The truth had to come out eventually.

'Do you know that name Mum? John Hanson?'

His mum shook her head, but she didn't lift her head to look at him. Serena remained still, with her eyes transfixed on the scene in front of her.

'He used to be known as Lucas back then, which I think he said was his middle name.'

He saw it that time. Or at least he sensed his mum stiffen.

'Did you know someone called Lucas?' he said again.

At first, she didn't respond and then there was sudden jerk as she lifted her head. The look she gave him was tormented but there was also something else. He couldn't define it immediately but as he looked her in the eye, he also registered a hint of disgust. He glanced over at Serena who had been watching them. She looked shocked as she stared back at him. Slowly she turned her head so she could see her mother's face and her blood ran cold.

# FORTY

'Why couldn't you just leave it alone!' The words that flew from her mouth were high pitched, and so sharp that Serena winced. She had never heard her mother's voice this way.

'We brought you up with everything a child could need.' She spat the words towards them. Her angry stare looked from one to the other.

Tom was so taken aback that he pushed his body backwards against the soft cushions behind him and away from her. He watched as his dad tried to hold on to her hand, and then his eyes widened further as she flung his father's touch away from her and leapt to her feet.

'I'm sorry Mum…' Tom started to rise to his feet, automatically reaching for her. She resembled a mad woman and the only thing he could think to do in order to calm her down, was to wrap his arms around her.

'Come on Mum, we are not accusing you of anything. We just wanted to understand that's all.'

Serena stayed rooted to the spot and David sat motionless watching his wife, as if too scared to try to touch her again. Fiona avoided an embrace from her son and visibly agitated, she paced up and down. Her breath was coming fast, and Tom was worried she would have another panic attack, like the one she had yesterday. He tried to sooth her with his voice while staying where he was, holding out his hands in front of him trying to mollify her. He watched her closely, ready to dart forward to catch her if she were to collapse.

'Your mum's just getting worked up over nothing,' said his dad and patted the sofa next to him. 'Come on love, come and sit back down.'

'How can you say that?' shrieked Fiona, sucking in enough breath to spit the words out. She looked from Tom to Serena. 'They are my babies, MY BABIES!' This outburst seemed to focus her mind and she straightened up and span around to face her husband, her words now coming fast and hard.

'You useless idiot, why couldn't you just get that one thing right. You promised me they would never know the truth.' The anger behind her words was breath-taking. David sat with his head in his hands, looking miserable and almost cowering in his seat.

'What is happening?' cried Serena. She moved around the back of the sofa. 'Mum please stop this.'

Fiona hadn't been aware of any movement until her daughter was by her side and as Serena reached out to her Fiona lashed out, her fist striking Serena cleanly in the face. It was so shocking that both David and Tom gasped. Time seemed to slow as they watched Serena's delicate frame fly backwards, hitting the wall hard and crumpling into a heap on the far side of the room.

'Jesus!' shouted Tom pushing his way past her, towards his sister. 'What have you done?'

There was a trickle of blood from Serena's temple as she lay motionless. 'We need to get her some help.'

Stunned by the image of his sister's broken body, he turned to face his parents. David reached for his mobile phone and then stopped as if transfixed, staring intently at the screen.

'What are you waiting for?' Tom screamed. He looked at his dad, willing him to function.

'Dad!' Tom shouted again, louder this time. He looked over to where his mum had been standing but there was just an empty space.

A weak cough and the slightest movement at his side, brought his attention back to Serena. He stroked her hair.

'You're going to be fine, Dad's going to call an ambulance,' he said. Her eyes opened and closed. The blood coming from the side of her head was slowing but she was still dropping in and out of consciousness. Tom turned his attention back to his dad and found that his mum had reappeared and was standing next to her husband. It took a moment to realise that she had taken the mobile away from him and was looking at Tom with sorrow.

'We can't call for an ambulance Tom,' she said. 'You must realise that.'

Her voice was stronger now. It was as if she had turned into someone else, someone who was in complete control. His dad walked towards him, and Tom saw the glint of a knife in his mother's hand, edging him forward. David sat heavily onto the sofa, in the same spot he had previously vacated. Fiona moved away from him towards where Tom stood, and where Serena lay.

'Come away from your sister,' she said. Her eyes were set and there was a hardness Tom had never seen before. Tom held his ground.

'I'm not leaving her,' he said, shaking his head. Fiona was holding the knife out in front of her, but she stopped before she got too close.

'She won't be on her own. I am the one to look after her,' she continued. She waved the knife and waited.

'Don't you hurt her,' he said, backing off a little.

'I won't hurt her. She is my baby. All I have ever done is for you two.'

As Fiona inched closer, Tom slowly backed away. He moved to the window seat where Serena had recently been sitting, and lowered himself without taking his eyes away from the scene in front of him.

He watched as his mother knelt next to Serena. She placed the knife on the carpet nearby and lifted her daughter's head gently onto her lap. He didn't understand what was happening. *Was his mother completely mad?*

Fiona stroked Serena's hair and in a sing song voice, she began to repeat the same words over and over.

'Mama's going to look after you honey. No one is going to take you away.'

Tom took the opportunity to steal a glance at his dad, whose head was down, his chin resting on his chest. It was the body language of a defeated man. Tom tried to stretch his leg out and connect with his dad's foot, but he couldn't quite reach. With his eyes trained on his mum, he shuffled quietly down a little way praying that his legs were long enough to nudge his dad and make him take notice. A slight brush against his foot must have made enough contact, as his dad looked slowly towards him. His face was crumpled with despair.

'I'm so sorry,' he mouthed silently.

Tom shook his head. It was meant as a warning that he was not just going to let his dad sit there. His eyes pleaded with his father's. A second or two passed as David sat staring at his son and then finally something from inside seemed to kickstart. He turned now to look at his wife and daughter.

'Fiona,' he said. It came as no more than a whisper.

'Fiona,' he said it louder this time.

She didn't move but she must have heard him because the incessant rambling stopped.

'Fiona, please,' he said again. 'This has to stop.'

By now he had dragged himself to his feet and turned towards her, his eyes focused on the knife's blade glistening where it lay.

'Fiona, we can't hide this any longer. They're going to have to know the truth. Please my love, leave Serena now and come over to me.'

He edged a few steps closer, trying to coax his wife towards him and away from Serena. She stayed knelt where she was. Tears began to fall from his eyes as he pleaded with her.

'I tried to make things right,' he said. 'We can't undo what we did Fiona. You know that. Please don't make this any worse.'

Tom watched intently, trying to figure out what was going through his mother's mind. He was relieved to see Serena's chest gently rising and falling, so although her eyes were firmly closed, he knew she was still breathing. He was glad that she wasn't aware of the danger she was in and that she hadn't seen the knife held in her own mother's hand.

Tom longed to run over and snatch the knife away, but he knew he wouldn't make it before Fiona could react, so he stayed where he was, watching the scene unfold between his mother and father. Fiona seemed to have forgotten that there was a weapon nearby. Instead, she was staring almost comatose towards her husband.

'I just wanted children. That's all I ever wanted,' she was saying.

'I know, but we can't hide the truth from them any longer. You must understand that?' replied David.

'Mum, we are still your children,' stated Tom from the window seat. 'I know you didn't mean to hurt Serena, but we need to help her.'

Fiona glanced over to him.

'It won't be the same, nothing will be the same again' she said sadly. She looked so small, kneeling in the corner of the room, her daughter beside her.

'Yes, Mum it can be. We are not going to change our feelings for you over someone we have barely met.'

'I love you so much Tom,' she said. Her eyes softened as she looked at him and tears were beginning to well up. 'This was all to have the family I needed, but you won't understand.'

David had now moved within reach of his wife, and he leant down to place a hand on her shoulder.

'Fiona,' he said. 'They need to know what happened.'

She pulled away from him and surveyed the scene in front of her.

# FORTY-ONE

A silence descended and Tom could feel his heart beating, stronger, faster. He waited and watched as his dad placed his hand for a second time on his wife's shoulder and this time, she allowed it to stay.

'Honey,' he said softly, 'I'm going to tell Tom what we did and then we are going to get help for Serena.' There was no movement from Fiona, she just stared out in front of her, and Tom concentrated on his dad.

'Dad, please,' he said, 'I need to know what is going on.'

His dad took a deep breath and then with his voice shaking, he started to speak.

'Your mother wanted children so badly and we tried to conceive for many years. Tests told us that she couldn't naturally have children and so we came up with the idea that I would supply the sperm and we would find a surrogate mother to carry the baby. Then at least any child would be my flesh and blood and we could both cope with that.'

He squeezed his wife's shoulder again, as if to take the sting out of his words. She remained silent but let her head drop forward so she was looking down towards Serena. His father carried on.

'As time went on, your mothers' health began to deteriorate. We couldn't find a surrogate and it was then that she started hallucinating. She talked of finding someone fit and healthy and befriending them with the purpose of persuading them to help us. Someone that would want to help a childless couple have the joy of a family. We didn't mean it to go the way it went, honest to God. She planned for me only to get the girl to come to the house so she could befriend her, not to…'

A sharp sudden movement caught Tom's attention. At the same time David realised what was happening. Neither of them spotted the knife, but a shocking gasp from David stopped him mid-sentence. Fiona had sprung to her feet, far faster than either of them thought possible and the fierce anger behind the knife shocked Tom to the core.

As he saw his father collapse to the floor, Tom unconsciously darted towards her and with a sweep of his arms knocked the knife from her hands. They both watched as it came to rest in the far corner of the room.

Fiona was knocked off balance and fell back towards the window. She steadied herself. The look on her face was what scared Tom the most. She was devoid of emotion. She had not even a backward glance for the man she was supposed to love.

'It wasn't my fault Tom, it was his idea,' she blurted out. The distain for her husband was clearly shown across her face but she knew she wasn't fooling anyone. Tom could only stand open-mouthed at the unrecognisable figure in front of him.

'He was so spineless,' she went on. 'He was such a mess after I made him go in and impregnate her. Couldn't live with himself. He wanted to change things then when it was too late. There was no way I was letting this family fall apart.' Her eyes were wild, and Tom could see madness had taken over.

'I have to get help,' he said in a voice that sounded far too controlled to be his own. She wasn't listening. Instead, her eyes focused on her husband, lying a couple of feet away from them.

'I couldn't let him tell you. I had to stop him.'

'But he's hurt Mum, please, I need to get an ambulance.'

She ignored his plea.

'Tom, you must listen to me. I need you to love me. I am the one who is your mother, not that girl. I'm the one who gave you love for all these years.'

He could feel the anger brewing inside him.

'You didn't give her a choice,' he said in disgust. 'How could you have done that? And now you've hurt Dad and Serena. When is this going to stop?' He stared into her eyes. 'I'm calling for an ambulance and the police unless you are going to try and stab me too?'

An audible gasp escaped her.

'I would never hurt you or your sister. Not intentionally. All I have ever wanted is for you both to be happy. It was me who saved you from any mistakes. You wouldn't have liked to be away from us in America and I couldn't let that girl take you away.'

Time stopped. *Was she talking about Sophie?*

'What are you talking about?' he shouted. He moved with lightning speed and pushed her body against the wall.

'Did you hurt Sophie? Tell me.' He spat the words at her. All his pent-up fear rushing to the surface. As he held her there, the sickly scent of her perfume overwhelmed his senses. A smell that was once so comforting now made him want to gag. 'Please you have to tell me.' He begged. 'What did you do?'

Her voice sounded whiny as she tried to convince him that she was the victim.

'She was going to take you away from me. I wasn't going to let that happen. Your dad didn't know until he returned home and found her here. He was so angry with me, but once I had drugged her and put her in the room, we couldn't just let her go.'

Tom was shaking her now.

'What room? Where is she?' He was screaming the words into his mother's face.

He felt a sharp bang to his head and his hands let her go as he stumbled backwards. He couldn't focus, but he felt a whoosh of air as she rushed past him and by the time he had righted himself, she was nowhere to be seen. He held his hand to his head and stared in disbelief at the sticky blood left on his fingers. Looking down, he could see the fragments of the heavy China ornament she had hit him with, splayed across the carpet. A sinking dread coursed through his body. He'd let her get away.

He knew now that she had done something to Sophie, and he had no clue what that was or where she was now. His head was woozy, and he knew he wasn't stable enough to run after her. The sound of a bang as the front door shut with such force alerted him that he was too late, and he could just make out her figure running down the driveway in a bid to escape. He fumbled in his pocket trying to locate his phone and once he found it, he dialed the emergency services.

# FORTY-TWO

Tom told the operator the address and was advised that an ambulance and police car had been dispatched. He glanced over at Serena and noted her breathing hadn't altered. Then he moved his attention back to his dad. He raced to the kitchen drawer and grabbed a clean tea towel which he pressed tightly to the wound once he returned to the lounge. He knelt beside his dad's body praying the emergency services would arrive soon.

'Dad, please stay with me.' He realised he was holding his breath as he listened closely for any sound that his dad was still fighting for his life. He kept one hand firmly holding the cloth and with his other hand he reached out to feel for a pulse. As he touched his father's skin, the older man's eyes slowly opened.

'Dad, the ambulance is on its way. Please, hang in there.'

David let out a little cough and tried to speak. Tom could feel the blood pump faster from his wound as he tried to force the words.

'You need to stay quiet,' he said. He pressed the cloth harder against his dad's chest, where the knife had entered. His dad tried to shake his head and he motioned for Tom to bend down lower. He could feel the fine breath against his ear as he strained to listen.

'She killed them, and I had to bury them,' he whispered.

'Them?' Tom repeated, his heart racing faster. 'Who? You mean Sophie too? Dad, please I need to know.' He was frantic. David's eyelids fluttered shut and it was all Tom could do not to shake him awake again.

'Dad, is she dead? Where are they?' His voice was urgent, his pain plain to see.

'In the…garden,' groaned his dad. He coughed and specks of blood spurted from his mouth. Tom turned his head away quickly, but he felt a tiny amount splatter against the side of his cheek. He lifted his head enough to see through the window towards the driveway willing the ambulance to appear. When his dad's eyes opened again, Tom could see how much effort it took to force the words from his lips.

'She killed them. I'm sorry… so very sorry.'

Tears began flowing freely down Tom's cheeks blurring his vision, making the sight of his dying father swim before him. His fingers reached forward and touched his father's wrist, feeling again for a pulse. There was still one, but it was weaker than before, almost undetectable. He spent a couple of long minutes observing the rise and fall of his chest, only just visible.

A screech of tyres announced the arrival of the paramedics. Tom knew he must go and open the door for them, and he placed his dad's head gently onto a cushion that he pulled hastily from the sofa.

'Are they buried in the garden here?' he asked quickly, lingering despite the continued chime of the doorbell. It seemed like an eternity before his dad answered.

'Both of them…' he gasped for another breath, 'in the garden…'

Tom backed away and forced himself to move towards the door. When he opened it, he found he couldn't speak and so he just pointed his finger towards the lounge. The paramedics rushed past him, and he slowly followed them. As he entered the room, he saw the younger of the two paramedics kneeling, tending to his father. The other paramedic had located Serena, who was still lying unconscious in the corner of the room.

The police would be arriving soon, and Tom knew they would have plenty of questions, but for now he closed his eyes and lowered himself on to the sofa trying to blot out any thoughts. The sound of a bell ringing drew Tom back into the room and as he slowly opened his eyes, he focused on the young paramedic who made a gesture towards the door. Tom rose tentatively, and as if in slow motion, he moved into the hallway. The silhouette of a man could be seen through the glass panels of the front door and as he opened it, he recognised the bulky frame of Detective Fairbrother.

Tom felt like he was in a dream, and he found it hard to focus on what was going on around him. He was aware that the detective was talking to him but however hard he tried he couldn't hold onto the words. Something about John?

As Alan Fairbrother had seen the ambulance, he knew something was happening and that Tom was in deep shock. He closed the door behind him and gently helped Tom towards the lounge. He surveyed the scene from the doorway. A young paramedic looked up as they entered. He was sitting alongside an older man's body, and he shook his head sadly.

'I'm sorry Sir,' he said, looking directly at Tom. 'There was nothing we could do.'

Tom found his knees buckling beneath him and he sank to the carpet in despair. His sobs were loud and heart-breaking. Tom felt the detective's strong arms lift him up and reposition him against the familiar soft cushions of the sofa. He watched glassy eyed, as the detective walked over to where the other paramedic was attending to Serena, and a few seconds later he was back by Tom's side.

'Your sister is going to be fine Tom,' he said. 'Where is your mother?'

His words pulled Tom back to the present and he stiffened at the thought that she was still out there.

'She ran,' he said. 'She stabbed him,' he added, gesturing to his dad, 'then she ran.'

'She killed my real mum… and Sophie. My dad told me they were buried in the garden.' Once the information had spilled out of him, he put his head in his hands and wept.

'I'm so sorry Tom.' The detective placed a reassuring hand on Tom's shoulder. 'A couple of officers will come to speak with you later and take a statement. I need to go now and join a team to look for your mother. Is there anywhere you can think of that she may have gone?'

Tom lifted his head before shaking it from side to side.

'There isn't anywhere I can think of, I'm sorry,' he said.

'No problem, if you think of anywhere, tell the officers. I will let you know if we find her and, in the meantime, look after that sister of yours.'

Tom turned to see the paramedics lifting Serena onto a stretcher and he watched as they started to wheel her towards the waiting ambulance. He stood up shakily and followed along behind and at the doorway he spotted two police officers making their way down the driveway. They stopped when they saw Detective Fairbrother and he spoke to them for a minute or two. Tom switched his attention back to the paramedics and watched as Serena's lifeless body was loaded into the back of the ambulance. They had placed an oxygen mask over her face, and she looked pale and fragile. He wanted to get this over with so he could go to the hospital and be by her side.

He was glad to see the officers approaching the house and he nodded towards Detective Fairbrother, who with a brief wave, got into his car and drove away. The ambulance followed shortly after. Tom listened vaguely as the officers introduced themselves and he allowed himself to be taken back inside.

# FORTY-THREE

A few hours had passed by the time Tom entered the hospital room where his sister lay. She had regained consciousness and although she still looked deathly pale, she managed a weak smile. He moved to her side and took her small hand in his.

'You look awful,' she said. With his free hand, Tom moved a grey plastic chair closer to the bed and sat down.

'You're not looking your best either,' he replied. He grinned at her. He was relieved that the doctors had assured him she just needed a little time to recover.

'Do you remember what happened?' he asked her. She shook her head slowly, her eyes wide. 'I remember it was mum who shoved me into the wall and then nothing until I woke up here. Nobody will tell me anything.'

Tom tried in vain to keep his expression even, but Serena knew him too well.

'She's crazy, Serena. She must be, the things she has done,' he said, not quite able to look her in the eye.

'I was afraid you were going to say that. You need to tell me everything Tom,' she said. Her forehead crinkled into a frown, and she spread her hands out on the bed sheet as if steeling herself for what he was about to say.

Tom started with the little amount of the truth that he knew. He told her how their parents had abducted a young girl and that their father had forced himself on her, thinking that the baby she eventually had, was his.

'I think they must have always believed that he was my father, up until we confronted them with the information about John. The police said that

Katie Reed must have already been pregnant when she was taken, and maybe even she hadn't known.'

Serena shed tears for the poor girl who had been abducted all those years before. Her face was grim and even paler than when he arrived and he paused, wondering if this was the right time to tell her.

'I can't believe the people we thought were so kind and loving could be capable of this,' she began. Anger was beginning to show across her delicate features. 'Where are they now?' She looked desperately behind him. 'I don't want to see either of them at the moment.' The expression on Tom's face, stopped her in her tracks and she looked up at him questioningly.

'I don't know where Mum is, the police are still out searching for her,' he said, 'and Dad, he got hurt and I'm sorry Serena, but he's gone.'

He watched as Serena wrestled with her emotions. The anger turning to despair, realising she would not see her father again. He understood those feelings. He wanted to hate them both for what they had done and the lives they had taken, but it was hard to eject all the love they had felt for their parents their entire lives.

Serena dozed off soon after. She had wept for a long time and Tom waited until he was sure she was asleep before he got to his feet. He would stretch his legs and grab a coffee from the vending machine at the end of the hall. There was no way he was going to leave her for long in case she woke again.

He hadn't even had the chance to tell her about Sophie and he didn't know whether she could handle that just yet. There was time for all of that as they rebuilt their lives, and he was more grateful than ever that he and Serena had each other to lean on.

Tom passed the police officer guarding her room as he left. It was a precaution, to keep her safe, until their mother was located. He didn't really believe she would come after them or hurt them in any physical way. In her mind at least, she had always wanted to protect them and now the secret was out, she surely wasn't stupid enough to try and make contact?

He though back to earlier in the day and the expression on the faces of the police officers who took his statement. As much as they tried to stay poker faced, neither of them quite pulled it off. He wasn't sure if it was pity or disbelief, but they obviously found it hard to comprehend the events of 1998 and how it had remained secret for so long.

When he returned to her room Serena was breathing gently, her face relaxed for the first time since she had been injured. A long sleep would do her good. He moved to an armchair in the corner of the room and despite the caffeine he had just consumed he let his eyelids fall and neither of them awoke until the following morning.

It was 7.30am when he got in his car the next morning and he drove towards his parents' house. Every part of him resisted as he turned the car into the driveway and parked next to his dad's pride and joy. Reluctantly he got out of his car, listening to the familiar crunch of the gravel beneath his trainers. He gazed sorrowfully at the family home he had always loved. Already it appeared in a different light, tainted by the events so raw in his mind.

Yesterday the police had told him that he wouldn't be able to go back in until they had collected all their evidence. He wasn't sure he wanted to, but he had promised Serena that he would collect her phone and some other belongings for her, if he could. From where he stood, he could just make out one of the forensic team moving around inside as they gathered what they needed. It shocked him how vividly he could remember the scene inside; the blood on the carpet where his father had died only yesterday, and the ceramic ornament that had been broken against his own head.

A crunch of gravel caught his attention, and he swung around to see the detective's car turning into the driveway, with a squad car following closely behind.

'Hi Tom, how are you holding up?' asked the detective, through his open window. Tom managed a weak smile.

'I'm OK. I've just left the hospital and Serena is going to be fine. I need to pick up a few things for her if that's possible. I can wait around. Any news?'

'We haven't found your mother, but the stations and airports are being checked as we speak. You haven't thought of anywhere that she may have headed for?'

Tom shook his head.

'Nothing comes to mind.'

The detective got out of his car and walked behind it to stand next to Tom. The officers from the squad car jumped out with a bit more speed and one guy opened the boot of the car. Tom watched as he reached in and grabbed a spade. He handed it to another officer before picking out one for himself. He slammed the boot shut and nodded towards Tom and the detective as they walked past and disappeared through the side gate. The detective faced Tom with a grave look.

'I was hoping we would be finished before you returned,' he said. 'We need to dig up the garden and see if what your father said to you is the truth. I'm sorry. It would have been better if you had stayed away. Maybe you should go inside while they start. I think forensics are nearly finished. Give me a second to check out the state of play and then you can wait in there or in your car if you prefer?'

They both looked towards the house and could see that men and women in white suits were just beginning to come out and walk towards their cars.

'Bear with me a minute,' the detective said. He left Tom and moved to where a heavy-set man was loading his van. Tom watched them for a minute and then the detective re-joined him.

'He said to give them five minutes and then they will be leaving.'

Tom swallowed the lump in his throat.

'Of course,' he muttered.

'I'll just go and see what's happening in the garden and then I'll join you inside,' said the detective. He gave Tom a subdued smile and left him to stand alone once more.

Tom thought of the pretty garden on the other side of the fence, once the pride and joy of his mother, now about to be dug up to reveal some of the horrors that had happened in this house. He waited until the last of the forensic team had left and a police officer gestured to him that it was OK to step inside when he wanted to.

He walked slowly to the open door and moved through it. He made a beeline for the kitchen, avoiding a look into the lounge area as he passed. His eyes were drawn to the garden, and he couldn't help but look curiously at the activity out there. Someone behind him cleared their throat and he turned to see the detective had returned.

'I turned up yesterday because I'd spoken to John and he mentioned where your parents lived,' he was saying. 'I'm sorry I didn't realise earlier, maybe we could have saved you from some of what happened.' He looked upset at the thought. 'As soon as John mentioned Greenbay I looked up where your parents lived and when I saw how close they were to the field, my heart sank. I realised that maybe they had something to do with Katie's disappearance, and I came over straight away. I am so sorry Tom. I wish I had realised sooner.'

Tom could see how sincere he was, and he shook his head.

'Nobody could have guessed what happened here back then or the recent events either. I just can't believe the people I thought I knew and loved could do something like this and that we lived here for all those years not knowing. That's going to be the hardest thing to come to terms with. That and burying the only girl I've ever loved.'

He had shed so many tears, that they would no longer come. Instead, there was an overwhelming sadness and an all over body ache that made everything he did an effort. Tom distracted himself by making some tea and he handed a mug to the detective before carrying his own to the nearby table. A soft knock against the glass of the patio doors interrupted them and he nearly dropped his mug as he placed it on the coaster. One of the officers he had seen earlier was stood on the outside and he twitched his head as an indication that something may have been found.

'Stay here,' the detective said. He put his mug alongside Tom's and strode towards where the officer waited. He unlocked the sliding patio doors and pushed it across. He stepped carefully through and closed the door firmly behind him. Tom could feel his heart starting to pound and he wished he had stayed longer at the hospital with Serena.

He observed the silent conversation through the glass, watching their body language intently to see if he could pick up on what was being said. He hadn't bothered to sit down at the table, and he moved back towards the worktop, leaning his elbows on the granite surface. A minute or two past and he witnessed a frown developing on the detective's face. As the door re-opened, he braced himself for the news he was about to receive.

The large man stepped back inside, again carefully sliding it closed before he spoke.

'They've found two bodies.'

Even though Tom knew it was coming it felt like a sledgehammer had hit him in the chest. He doubled over the worktop and closed his eyes.

'Tom,'

He could hear the detective saying his name, but the room was spinning, and his words sounded as if he was underwater.

'Tom,' he heard him say again, louder this time. 'It's not what you think. You need to listen to me.' He had reached where Tom was standing, and he gently touched his arm. 'It's not Sophie.'

Tom's eyes flew open, and a sound escaped his lips. A strangled groan. His whole body was shaking. He stared at the detective confused.

'There are two bodies,' the detective continued, 'but both have been buried for many years. I'm guessing one of the bodies is your real mother and right now we have no idea who the other one is. But it isn't Sophie. We are sure of that.'

Tom reached for the back of a chair to hold himself up, relief across his face. He swallowed hard and eventually found his voice.

'Then what happened to Sophie?'

# FORTY-FOUR

As Tom came to terms with the fact that Sophie could still be alive, the detective went to check on the progress outside. When he returned to the kitchen, Tom was facing away from him at the sink. He was mid-way through washing a mug, when something occurred to him, and he whirled around.

'Oh my God,' spluttered Tom.

'What?' The detective was watching his every move.

'I've just remembered what my mum said to me yesterday. Something about when she put Sophie in the room... It didn't register until now, but she mentioned a room. Do you think it's a room in this house?'

The detective stared at him for a split second before he moved towards the door again. He pulled it open sharply and shouted into the garden.

'Leave what you are doing and come into the house. Now!'

Once they were all congregated inside, the detective relayed the information and within minutes officers were dispersed to various areas all over the house. Tom couldn't think of a single place in the house where there could be a room he knew nothing about. He watched the progress of the officers and tried to keep out of their way as they combed the house from top to bottom.

The detective had stayed on the ground floor and was just outside the kitchen in the utility area when he called to Tom.

'Hey Tom, is this door a cupboard?'

Tom tried to imagine which door he was talking about and in that instant he knew. He raced through the doorway nearly knocking over the detective who was coming the other way.

'Careful fella,' said the detective, putting out a hand to steady himself.

'That isn't a cupboard, it's a wine cellar,' blurted out Tom. 'Why didn't I think of it? Dad used to keep his precious wine and whisky collection down there. We were never allowed to go in there from an early age so we couldn't accidentally damage any of his collection. They were adamant about that and when we did get caught once down there in our teens, trying to sneak a bottle for a party, we got in a massive amount of trouble. After that my father even put a padlock on it so we couldn't get down there again. There's a key somewhere to unlock it, but I don't know where it is.'

'We don't need a key, I'll get a couple of the guys to break it down,' said the detective. He bellowed down the hallway again and an officer appeared almost instantly. He listened for a second before disappearing and returning almost immediately with another much sturdier officer in tow.

'Let's go into the hallway while they get in,' suggested the detective.

They positioned themselves just outside the utility room so the men could get to business. Tom listened to the banging and then a second or two later the sound of the door breaking apart. He felt relieved that they had broken through so quickly. Now that he realised the cellar was the only place, they could have kept someone, he couldn't wait to search it. He feared what they may find in the darkness, but he couldn't dwell on that now.

Tom and Alan poked their heads around the doorway into the utility room. Tom saw one of the officers flick the light switch before him and the other officer slowly disappeared down the wooden stairway. Tom held his breath and waited. He moved forward until he stood at the doorway and peered downwards. He could feel the detective's breath on his neck as he leaned in too.

'Sir, there's nobody down here,' came the voice from within.

The detective gestured for Tom to move aside.

'Follow me down,' he said. Tom followed and they squeezed into the space at the bottom. There was not enough room for them all in the small space, so the two police officers went back upstairs to wait. It was immediately obvious that there was no-one down there. The room was far too small. A vast array of bottles were displayed along each wall and that left only a small space in the middle for the two of them to stand quite close together. It seemed more compact than Tom remembered it, but maybe that was because he hadn't been down here since he was much younger. He was filled with disappointment that this wasn't the conclusion he had hoped for, and he wracked his brain for any other place she could have been held against her will. It was more than likely that they had some other place, other than this house but where could that be?

'Wow, this is quite a stash,' said the detective, bringing Tom's thoughts back to the here and now. 'I must admit I love my whisky,' he added.

'You're welcome to it all,' said Tom. 'I can't stand the stuff.' He looked around once more, his hope ebbing away and then took a step towards the stairs.

'You know, some of this lot is worth quite a bit of money,' said the detective. He bent down to pick up an especially pricey bottle but found that it wouldn't budge. He pulled on the one next to it and found that one didn't move either.

'Hold on a minute,' he said. Tom stopped and turned towards him. 'This is a fake collection,' he said. He struggled to get his fingers behind the wooden casing which held the bottles against the walls and he did his best to prise it forward. It moved ever so slightly.

'Give me a hand with this Tom,' he instructed.

They went around the room pulling at each wooden casing. Along two of the walls it felt solid and so they moved back to opposite the stairway where the detective had first noticed the bottles were not real. Between them they wriggled the wood from side to side until it slid forward enough to see that there was something behind. They glanced at each other and then with one last pull the casing came away from the wall and they stood gasping, their eyes focused on a large metal door.

'Well, I'll be…,' said the detective. Tom pounded on the door.

'Sophie,' he shouted. 'Are you in there?' There was silence on the other side.

'We need to find a key,' he said franticly. It would take too long to get through such a door but that would have to be their next plan if a key couldn't be found. He started by unfastening the heavy bolts across the top and the bottom of the metal door. As he did this, he looked around for anywhere you could hide a key. There was nothing.

Exasperated he swung round towards the detective and that's when he saw a large key dangling from a hook on the inside of the casing they had just moved. Tom grabbed it and it fitted smoothly into the lock.

'Oh my God,' he said to himself as he turned the key. He couldn't worry about what he might find behind the door. He pushed the handle down and pulled hard and the door flew open. The two men burst inside one behind the other, and there on a bed in the middle of the sparse room was Sophie.

# FORTY-FIVE

Tom raced forward and swept her up in his arms. She had lost a lot of weight and felt as light as a feather.

'Sophie,' he said softly. Then more urgently, 'Sophie, please be OK.'

Her eyelids fluttered open and when she saw Tom staring back at her, she knew that her ordeal was finally over. Tears poured down her cheeks, but she couldn't manage to speak because her lips were too dry.

'Get her upstairs, to my car. We can take her straight to hospital,' came the voice behind him. The detective moved aside to let them pass. Tom carried Sophie out of the room and carefully up the stairs. At the top he walked past a wide-eyed police officer who looked relieved to see that she had been found alive. The detective gave the officer instructions to return to the garden and to carry on with the uncovering of the bones found earlier.

'I'll take these two to the hospital and radio in the latest findings. I'll be back a bit later,' he said. The officer nodded.

He walked towards the front door with them and opened it for Tom and Sophie to go through, followed by the detective and then he shut the door behind them. Tom gently placed Sophie onto the back seat of the car and got in beside her. The detective got in and then waited a moment while the squad car parked behind him was moved and then he reversed his car out of the driveway. He switched on the blue lights, and they flew though the traffic towards the centre of town.

An hour later Sophie was sedated in a hospital bed with Tom holding her hand. He had asked a nurse to get a message to Serena who was in the same hospital, a few floors above. The police had been in contact with Sophie's family to tell them that she had been found and Tom was sure they would be on their way to the hospital, as quickly as they could.

The doctor said that Sophie seemed fine physically, but she was dehydrated and underweight and would need a little time to feel like her old self. Tom hadn't been able to communicate with her yet as she had slept since arriving at the hospital, but he hadn't left her side.

He heard a gentle tap on the door and realised someone was entering the room. He lifted his head wearily and saw a tall man in a police uniform standing just inside the door. He recognised him as one of the officers who had been at the house to take his statement. Tom reluctantly got to his feet, gently placing Sophie's hand onto the bed and followed the officer outside the room.

'Mr Beatty, they've found your mother,' said the officer. 'She was found it a remote part of the wood, out the back of the house. It was like a children's hideaway. She's not making much sense, but we've taken her into custody, and she will be assessed.'

*The hideaway in the woods?* Somewhere they had only showed her once, a long time ago. He wouldn't have even remembered that she knew of it, but he supposed it made sense for her to flee somewhere where she could feel close to them.

'A neighbour of yours saw her running towards the woods earlier. He tried to talk to her, but she pushed him aside and ran further into the forest. He called us straight away after noticing some blood on her clothes and he could tell she was agitated. He was worried she had hurt herself. We had hoped she hadn't gone too far as we managed to cordon off the area quickly, but it still took some time to locate her.'

The relief showed across Tom's face as he took the news in. He could relax now knowing she couldn't hurt anyone else and that her mental state would be assessed. He couldn't feel sorry for her though after what she had done to Sophie and that was even before he cast his mind back to what his birth mother must have endured.

'Detective Fairbrother said he would check on you later but he's going to interview her, as it was his case originally,' the officer finished.

Tom thanked him for the news and turned to go back into the room.

'Oh yes, just one other thing,' he said, before Tom had opened the door. 'I forgot to say the bones recovered from the garden went off to the lab and the results are due soon.' Tom couldn't help but grimace. He guessed John must have heard by now that a body had been found and soon, they would have confirmation if it was Katie.

It was obvious to Tom from what his father said that it was her, but all of this would still come as a shock to John. Finding out after all this time what had happened to her would bring the pain of her disappearance back and he knew John would need someone to look out for him. Seeing where Katie would have been kept, and knowing she had then been killed, broke Tom's heart.

He hoped John would let him be the person to help him, and he would do his utmost to straighten out the mess he had created last time they had met. At least he could be sure that the crimes his parents committed could never happen again. It was finally over.

# FORTY-SIX

The days moved by slowly, with Tom refusing to leave Sophie's side for any longer than a toilet break or to check on Serena. He was lucky that they were both in the same hospital and that he could visit Serena knowing he was only five minutes away from Sophie if she needed him. He lost track of time and focused only on the small stretches when Sophie was awake.

Tom's work had been fantastic and told him to take all the time he needed, and he was grateful for that. It was one thing less to worry about. Another girl had been cast in Sophie's place and so her chance at Broadway was on hold for now, but he knew there would be other chances when she had fully recovered.

Tom hadn't told her much of what had happened before she was rescued. He had managed to reassure her that she was safe now and that no one would ever hurt her again.

'Why would they do that to me?' she had asked him.

'My mother seemed to think you were trying to take me away from her. That you were intent on us moving away to another country to live. I can't imagine how she thought she would get away with it or how she could do that to either of us. I had been in the house when you must have been locked in that room. What if I hadn't found you quick enough?' He put his head in his hands. It couldn't bear thinking about.

'I'm sorry I went there without telling you, but I had no idea of what would happen. How could I?'

She told him how his mother had invited her over to prepare for his birthday party on the day she went missing. She had been excited to give him a surprise and the next thing she knew she was in the room he found her in. One minute she had been drinking tea and then she woke up groggy and stiff, realising instantly what danger she was in. She was convinced she would die in that room and when no food arrived for the last few days of captivity, she thought she had been forgotten about. It was going to take her a long time to heal from her ordeal, but he knew with his help, both her and Serena would be themselves again.

Tom had managed to coordinate Serena and Sophie's discharge from hospital on the same day and there was only one more evening to wait. Tom wanted to take them back up to London and let them recuperate there. He couldn't bear the thought of either of them having to go back to that house. The garden still held a sharp reminder of what had happened there. The house itself could be dealt with later. Sometime in the future, the house could be cleared and sold or even maybe knocked down. Who on earth would want to live there after the horrors that had played out in their seemingly perfect family home?

A deliberate cough from the corridor outside caught his attention, and he turned to see Detective Fairbrother, who lifted one hand and motioned for Tom to join him. Tom wandered out slowly, giving himself time to compose himself for the news he may hear.

'How's Sophie?' the detective asked as soon as Tom had shut the door.

'She's getting better day by day, thanks to you and your team,' said Tom. He shook his head as the memory of her inside the tiny room fought to take hold. 'I still can't believe I didn't know of that room in the cellar, all this time.'

'And are you OK Tom? I guess you know that we found Fiona?'

'Yes, I heard.' It was painful to even think about her. 'What did she say in the interview?'

'Nothing of much consequence unfortunately, she was mainly rambling. She will be assessed by the psychiatrists today.'

Tom nodded. He wasn't really surprised.

'She can't be in her right mind to do those things. Neither was my dad, although he did show some remorse.' He sighed. 'How can I trust people again after knowing they lied to us for all those years?'

The detective looked squarely at Tom. He chose his words carefully.

'It'll be tough I'm sure, but you have some good people around you Tom,' he said. 'You will get through this. I spoke to John this morning and told him about Katie and what had happened to Sophie too. He doesn't blame you for the argument you had. He understands you were just frightened, and he knows exactly how that feels. Maybe one day he can tell you all about your real mother.'

Tom hoped so. He would get in touch soon and hopefully they could move past the argument. He longed to forge a new relationship with John and although it would be hard to find out more about his birth mother, he knew he wanted to know everything about her. Hopefully in the future he may even meet some of her family too.

'There are a few more things I wanted to talk to you about if you can spare the time?' said the detective. Tom stole a quick glance over his shoulder towards Sophie. He could see that she was still sleeping soundly, so after telling a passing nurse that he was going to get a coffee, he followed the detective into the lift.

Once they were settled in a quiet corner of the cafeteria with steaming hot drinks in front of them, the detective began to tell Tom the results of the tests on the bones they had recovered.

'So, as we believed, the bones of one on the bodies tested were Katie Reed's.' He paused giving Tom a moment to take in the information. 'The other body we haven't been able to identify. The bones are from a girl not far off Katie's age, but that's all we know. The lab has extracted DNA so in time we should be able to uncover who this girl is. My guess is that it could be Serena's real mum, whoever she may be, but we should know for sure in a few days.'

Tom closed his eyes, silently praying that they would be able to find out details of the other girl and who may still be out there looking for her. The detective explained that he already had a team wading through any unsolved missing person files from all over the country. So far nothing had come to light.

'Thank you for everything.' Tom said to the detective as he pushed his chair back and stood ready to leave. 'I just hope we can all eventually make peace with all that's happened. Serena and I are slowly coming to terms with the sadness of how we were brought into this world and the lives that were lost.'

'Before you go, there is one other thing Tom,' said the detective, reaching into his pocket and producing what looked like an envelope. He pushed it across the table towards Tom who could only stare at it. 'We found it taped to one of the Whisky bottles in the Cellar,' he finished. 'We nearly missed it as it was so well hidden.'

It was a discoloured white envelope with two names scrawled across the front in red pen. Tom felt himself recoil from it. He could read the names upside down. His own name, and Serena's. Still, he didn't pick it up.

'I had to read it to see if it shed any light on the investigation,' said the detective, gently. 'It may help you both understand a little more about your father and I think you and Serena should maybe read it together.'

Tom remained silent but he picked up the envelope, pressing it deep into his pocket. He nodded again and left the cafeteria. He would check on Sophie and then he would visit Serena. If she felt strong enough to hear what the letter may say, then they would open it together.

# FORTY-SEVEN

Serena was back to feeling more like herself. She had regained some colour in her cheeks and was beginning to clear her plate when food was brought to her.

Tom started by relaying the information about her birth mother and she took the news as well as could be expected. Tears flowed for the poor unnamed girl who was undoubtably used for the same purpose that Katie had been before her. Anger boiled up in them both and that was the hardest part to deal with. Tom had seen the room first-hand, the place where they would have been held captive throughout their pregnancies, and he just couldn't displace the grim vision from his mind.

They spoke of Sophie, and Serena was as relieved as he was that her life had been spared. Later they talked of their mother and the fact that she was now being held for her despicable crimes. A hatred was building within each of them, but this was all mixed up with the feelings of love that they had felt towards her throughout their childhood. Tom had an inkling that a lot of therapy would be needed to help them come to terms with it all in the coming months and years.

'It's emotionally draining all this' Tom said, 'so if you don't feel up to hearing whatever is in this letter Serena, I can come back another day.' He squeezed her hand.

'No, I'm fine and I think I'll probably feel better once we've heard it all. Then we can begin to put it all behind us and maybe there will be some other news about the woman who was my mother in there?' She looked hopeful and Tom felt a twinge of doubt. He guessed that there couldn't be anything much in the letter that they didn't already know or surely Detective Fairbrother would have warned him?

He reached into his pocket and wriggled the envelope out. He took his time to unfold the letter and smoothed it out with his hand. Serena watched every movement, her face filled with concern. When Tom saw his father's writing, his throat became dry. He glanced at Serena, sitting expectantly on the bed, and noticed that she had unconsciously pulled the covers up around her, as if to protect herself from what they were about to learn. Tom slowly lowered himself onto the bed beside her and they began to read.

*Dear Tom and Serena,*

*If you are reading this, I am no longer of this world and no longer part of the cruelty it can bring. You have probably found out about our actions, and how we made those girls suffer. You will no doubt think of us as monsters, which is basically what we are.*

*Whatever I say now may not make you feel any differently towards me or your mother but after I buried the second body, I felt compelled to write this, so at least you will know the facts. Your mother doesn't know I wrote this letter and believe me I would have been punished if she had found out. I know I am not blameless in this, but I wanted to make sure you understood how much I loved you both and although you may not believe it, I'm sure, in her own way, your mother did too. Maybe that was her downfall? She was prepared to go to any lengths to have you in her life and any lengths to keep you close.*

*Back in the early nineties we had been trying to get pregnant, I think for around three years, and it just wouldn't happen for us. When we were eventually tested, we found that it was your mother who couldn't conceive, and this hit her hard. At first, she turned against me, telling me to go off and have a family with someone else. But I truly loved her, at least at that time.*

*We tried IVF too, until the money ran out and throughout this time Fiona's mental state deteriorated. She became sullen and argumentative, and I wanted her back as the woman I fell in love with. It started with her idea that we would look for a surrogate but as time went on, we couldn't find anyone willing.*

*Around this time Fiona began to have dreams where she believed she had a friend who would help her and become a surrogate for us. Unfortunately, she had no friends to speak* of. We hadn't lived in the area for long and she had been all consumed by the desire to get pregnant and hadn't spent any time getting to know anyone. If I'm honest, I think by then her mental state had declined so far that she believed that the dreams were reality.

She had watched the girl running past each day for nearly a month and would sit at the window fixated by her. To me the girl looked like a happier version of Fiona herself. Their facial features were similar, their height almost identical and it saddened me that she seemed to wish that she was this girl.

On the day before the girl came up to the house, we had an awful evening where Fiona talked of killing herself and I sat up all night with her trying to talk her out of those kinds of thoughts. She kept saying all she wanted was to find a few friends and if that came to anything later, she would be happy with that.

By morning she had convinced me that was the only reason she wanted to meet the girl. To orchestrate a chance meeting and then they could become friends. As we couldn't just invite her in as she ran past, Fiona came up with this crazy plan where I would I go to the park and act suspiciously, hoping that the girl would panic, and I could steer her towards our *house and to safety. Looking back, I can't believe I was so naive, but she had a way to coerce me into things without me realising her true intentions and honestly at that point I saw no harm in it.*

*So, that morning I went out and followed the girl up the hill towards our house. I could see how disconcerted she was with me following her, especially as there was no one else in sight. So, at a certain point I quickened my pace, in the hope that she would feel cornered and rush to our house for help. And this is exactly what happened. She had followed Fiona's plan by the letter, although she had no idea.*

*I waited for a little while and then I went around the back of the house and let myself in through the kitchen door. I was going to stay out of the way in the kitchen while they chatted in the hallway. I could hear Fiona talking although I couldn't make out what she was saying. I felt good for a moment. I had played a small part in helping my wife and although it was cruel to worry the girl, I thought it would all be OK. I knew she hadn't seen my face so once they became friends over the weeks I could be introduced at some point. I was sure they would hit it off immediately. I can honestly say that I didn't realise what was about to happen.*

When Fiona came into the kitchen pretending to get the girl a glass of water, she turned on me. She kept her voice low, but the words were forceful. She stood so close to me that I could feel the pent-up emotion running through her. Her words spilled out venomously as she told me how I'd messed it all up and that the girl was going to call the police and have me arrested. She told me that the plan had changed and that we now had no choice but to make her stay. I was shocked and I panicked. I couldn't believe she could even say such a thing. Looking into her eyes I could tell that she meant exactly what she said, and I knew I had to help the girl escape. I pushed past Fiona and went into the hallway to warn the girl and let her out of the house but as soon as she saw me the girl started screaming. A second later and Fiona was behind her putting a cloth over the girl's mouth.

As soon as she had crumpled to the floor, I knew that our lives would never be the same again. There could be no explaining this away. When I saw the glint in Fiona's eyes, I realised this had been her plan all along and I had stupidly, unwittingly let myself be dragged into it.

If I had realised what would come to pass over the next few years, I swear I would have called the police myself, but Fiona was so convincing, and I became trapped. She forced *me into taking part which fills me with great shame, and I wish I had been stronger. In the early days I voiced my distress and pleaded with her to let the girl go, but I could tell she was never going to listen to me. She threatened to call the police herself and tell them that it was all my doing and that she was an innocent party. She knew that the girl had only seen me and that although she may guess that it was Fiona who put the rag over her mouth, she wouldn't have seen her. She threatened to paint me as a depraved monster who had abducted this young girl, and she was so convincing. I was afraid that I would be taken to prison and at that time this is what I feared most.*

*I'm not guilt free in this, far from it. I bowed down to her and committed despicable crimes, something I could never forget. I knew what I was doing when I forced myself on that poor girl, but I couldn't see any way out and I was weak. Pathetic and weak.*

*Many years after, I realised that I had picked the exact person to marry that I wanted to get away from, and in doing so I let Fiona control my whole life. My upbringing was controlled by my mother, to such an extent that I can't bear to even put into words. I was so desperate to get away from her, I fell into the same pattern with Fiona. She knew of my* upbringing and maybe that's why she chose me. Someone easy to manipulate. I will never know.

The only good thing I ever did was help Serena through her illness and at least I could do that for her. I loved you kids so much. That at least is the truth. The leverage Fiona used the second time it happened was what destroyed me. She knew I couldn't leave you with her. I couldn't go to jail and so I followed her plan a second time, to my own torment.

This time the victim was a homeless girl that she had managed to befriend and coax to the house. Someone that Fiona believed had no family and was unlikely to be missed. She had learnt that lesson from the first time. She didn't want the police at the door this time asking awkward questions. Not that it had been hard the first time really, just a few questions of "Had we seen the girl?", and of course, we denied that we had. I was terrified for a while afterwards, but nobody ever came back.

The homeless girl had just followed her home, trusting that Fiona had a spare room for her to stay and that this clean, upper-class woman was a good Samaritan. The first I heard of it was when I returned home to find Fiona in a great mood. She told me she wanted another child and of course I *said that it wasn't possible. But the girl was already unconscious in the spare room and before long she had suffered the same fate. I'm even more ashamed that I didn't even know the second girl's name. The first was Katie Reed. I read that in the newspaper a few weeks after she went missing. But the police had no leads and apart from coming that one time, they never came back. I closed my mind to whatever Fiona did to them when she no longer needed them.*

*I knew she killed them though in that disgusting little room, and I was summoned to take their lifeless bodies to the garden in the dead of night and bury them. On those occasions I drank as much alcohol as I could, to dull the pain and then in a comatose state, I did whatever she ordered. From the moment the hole was filled in for the second time, I knew I would never let her do that again, even if I was the one sent to jail.*

*From that moment on though, she too was a different person. Engrossed in your lives, she became a good mother and if I didn't bring up the past, we could convince others that we were still in love. By then though, deep down I really hated her, but I kept my feelings to myself. I knew what she was capable of, and I'm ashamed to say that I was terrified of her. I continued to block out the past as best I could, and instead I concentrated on how to bring you up as the lovely people you have both turned out to be. Now that I am gone, I hope you have a few good memories of me, and I can only tell you again how sorry I am.*

*David*

Serena wiped at the tears that were streaming down her face. She looked over at Tom, whose face was grim.

'Jesus,' he said. He looked totally bewildered. 'How could something like that happen? How could we not know?'

# FORTY-EIGHT

The following Wednesday Tom parked his car in the hospital car park for the last time. Today he would collect Sophie and Serena and they would begin to rebuild their lives.

This weekend coming, he had invited John to join them in London for lunch at the flat. Tom had spoken to him on the phone, and although the conversation was stilted, they agreed that they would like to try to develop a bond. Tom truly believed they would in time.

Sophie had received cards and messages from all her acting friends and whenever she felt up to it, they promised to arrange a get together. She wasn't quite ready to get back into the limelight yet but seeing all her friends would be something she could look forward to.

Carrie had visited the hospital and hugged her friend tightly while they both cried. When Sophie's mother had arrived to see her daughter laying in the bed, there had been tears then too and her mum hadn't wanted to let Sophie out of her sight. Only when Tom convinced her that he would take care of her girl, did she reluctantly go home, but she phoned each day to check in. They would go and visit both her and Sophie's grandad as soon as they could.

Tom walked through the automatic doors. He stood to one side to let a man in a wheelchair pass and then carried on towards the lifts. As he traced the familiar steps, he listened to the squeak of his trainers against the pristine, shiny tiles. He pushed the button for the lift and waited as the glass rectangle descended slowly and as soon as the doors opened, he stepped inside. He was alone with his thoughts as it glided smoothly to the 3rd floor.

When he stepped out, he could already see Sophie, sat in a plastic chair in the doorway, watching out for him. She got to her feet as he walked towards her and a smile lit up her face.

'I've been counting the minutes,' she said, lifting herself on to her tiptoes to kiss him.

'You look better,' he said in place of a greeting. 'Do you have enough energy to come up to get Serena, or shall I go and collect you on my way down?'

'No, I'm fine. I've been sitting here for far too long. I need to get some strength back into my legs at some point. We can take the lift though.'

Tom followed her back to the lift and once more he pushed the button. He found it still waiting on the same level. He ushered Sophie in ahead of him and they travelled the couple of floors to where Serena had been staying. Her room was empty, but they found her close by in the day room deep in conversation with a man in his eighties. He was laughing at whatever she had been saying as they walked in.

'Tom! Sophie!' she said as she saw them. She said her goodbyes and the man nodded his head towards them, looking slightly disappointed to have had his companion taken away.

'I'll just grab my bag,' she said heading back to her room. When Tom got to the doorway, he took the bag from her and together they made their way out of the hospital.

As they got into the car Serena surprised Tom with her announcement.

'Before we go back to London, Sophie and I have decided we would both like to go to the house one last time,' said Serena from the back seat.

'Why?' stuttered Tom. 'Surely that would be painful?' He frowned as he faced Sophie. 'I thought neither of you would ever want to see that place again.'

'Yes, we know it will be hard, but we have discussed it in the last few days and we both feel we need closure.' Sophie turned to look at Serena for support.

'I need to see the garden where my mum was buried, and I want to see the room too. It will help me understand more of what happened to them both,' said Serena. Her voice was firm, and Tom knew it would be hard to dissuade her.

'But once you see those things, you may never get rid of that image.' Tom sounded unsure. He wished he hadn't ever seen the dungeon his parents had held those girls in, and his first instinct was to protect Serena from that.

'Sophie? Are you in agreement?' he asked. She nodded.

'I think it needs to be done. One last time and then none of us ever need to step foot in that house again.' She stared sadly back at him.

'If that's what you both want, we can go there now. Are you sure?' He moved his head from one to the other and watched as they both solemnly nodded.

As Tom pulled the car into the driveway, a silence descended. Serena was the first to open her door and clamber out and the others followed. Tom glanced sideways at Sophie.

'Are you ready?' Sophie took a deep breath.

'Ready as I'll ever be,' she replied with a slight grimace.

'Serena?' said Tom.

'I'm ready.' She said it strongly, determined, although he could see the fear in her eyes.

Tom took the keys from his pocket and opened the front door. As they moved through the doorway Tom could see the remains of a 'Do Not Enter' forensic tape which lay discarded to one side.

An involuntary shiver passed through his body, and he wasn't sure if it was from the cold air or a feeling of dread.

'Let's go into the lounge first,' said Serena, taking control of the situation. She led the way. As soon as they entered, a replay came flooding back through Tom's mind. His father laying in a pool of blood in front of the familiar furniture and Serena's crumpled body in the corner. He forced the thoughts away. Sophie sensed his discomfort, and she reached out to touch his arm.

Each pair of eyes focused on every detail around the room.

'Is this where Dad…?' Serena was kneeling where there was still a dark stain on the carpet. She couldn't bring herself to finish the question.

Tom nodded and moved to her side.

'I feel sad for him and so angry too. My emotions are so conflicted,' she said. Tom could understand. That was exactly how he was feeling too.

'It's completely understandable and it will get better with time Serena, I am sure of it. We just need to be there for each other.' He said the words, but they sounded hollow even to his own ears.

'Tom's right,' said Sophie. 'I'm sure once we start with some counselling it will become easier to let some of it go.' There were tears in her eyes. 'I'm not sure we are ever going to understand completely but we must try to move past it. We all deserve to be happy.'

Tom hugged her and motioned for Serena to get up from the floor.

'Come on, let's get this over with and then we can go.' He was bracing himself for how much worse they may find it downstairs.

'Hold on a second,' said Serena and she moved over to the window seat. 'I just want to see the garden from here.' She stood for a long couple of minutes, and the others waited. Then as she turned towards them, her face mirrored the pain inside of her. Tom watched her shake her head from side to side as if she just couldn't understand how any of this had ever happened.

'OK,' she said, 'let's go and see this room.'

Tom pushed the debris from the demolished door out of the way and he reached in and flicked the light switch. As the light came on revealing the wooden stairway, he saw Sophie shudder. He caught her eye and gave what he hoped was a comforting smile.

'Nothing can hurt you now,' he said, and she nodded. He stepped through and started to slowly descend. He could hear the heavy clomp of the girls' shoes behind him as they all made their way downwards.

The thick metal door to the room was still wide open and at the bottom of the stairs it was possible to walk straight in. Serena gasped as she entered. Sophie stayed nearest the door just poking her head in and keeping her body pressed flat against the inside of the door. Tom stayed close to Sophie holding her hand tight, while his eyes took in the grim reality for a second time.

'I need to go outside,' said Sophie in a whisper.

'I'm with you. I've seen enough,' said Serena already beginning to back away. Tom let them both start climbing the stairs as he took one last look around. He then walked out of the room firmly closing the door behind him. He knew none of them would ever come back here again. He couldn't imagine anyone wanting to live in this house, once they had heard what had happened here. Maybe the best idea was to sell it as land and then someone could rip the house down and build something new and fresh. Something that would bury the sins of the past.

Once outside, Sophie steadied herself, leaning her body against the car. She took long, deep breaths. She was proud of herself for facing her demons and as she inhaled the fresh air, she managed to let go of any fear that she would ever be trapped again. It proved to her that she could start to let it go, and with Tom by her side she knew in time they would be happy again.

Serena looked dazed. She had taken everything in, and it was all imprinted in her mind. She was sad that she had never met her birth mother and one day when she felt stronger, she would hunt out any relatives and find out more about her.

But for now, she was content to be with Tom and Sophie and then she would get a job in London maybe and find a small flat of her own. The man she had been seeing was staying nearby so they would remain friends and see how things went. She had given him an open invitation to come and visit her in the big city once she had found her feet and she hoped he would.

Tom turned the car around and took one last look in the overhead mirror. He still had the most important people in his life right here next to him and he would savour that. He would keep them close and do everything in his power to make them happy. As he turned out of the driveway and pointed the car in the direction of home, he felt like a weight had lifted. The lies were behind them now and that's where he would make them stay.

# ACKNOWLEDGEMENTS

Firstly, I would like to thank Deanna for reading my very first draft and giving me the encouragement to keep going. To Marylin for her advice, to Rosemary and Alan for their feedback, and to my lovely friend Hayley for her helpful suggestions and never wavering support.

To Robyn for helping me realise I can achieve anything I set my mind to. To Joe and Jenna for their help with the back cover. How long did that take?!

To Luke for listening to my endless chatter about this book and for being my technical genius. And lastly, to my patient mum, who read draft upon draft. Thank goodness you are a fast reader! I will be forever grateful.

## About The Author

## Carol Gulliford

Carol's love affair with thrillers started as soon as she read her first Sidney Sheldon book and hasn't waned since. She loves nothing more than an edge of your seat movie or a satisfyingly, twisty novel.

She lives on the South Coast of England with her partner and son. Behind the Lies is her debut novel.

Printed in Great Britain
by Amazon

58831918R00239